The Resistance

Invasion of the Elements

By Ilsa Nightingale

Identifiers: ISBN 979-8-218-71979-1
(paperback), ISBN 979-8-218-75729-8
(hardcover), ISBN 979-8-218-76513-2
(eBook)

LCCN: 2025917498

Instagram: @the_resistance_official

Dedicated to Larry Dingee, Kathy Seifert,
Adah Hackworth, Ron and Judy Roberts,
Kayleigh Allery, and the rest of my friends
and family who supported me through this
journey. I couldn't have done it without you.

Chapter 1 (Ley, 2017)

"I saw her again last night," I said, "in that same, weird dream."

Jaime froze in the middle of the school parking lot. She tucked a strand of her curly, blonde hair out of her face and crossed her arms. "Don't go on about *her* again, Ley," she said as she rolled her eyes. "That's all you ever talk about these days, the girl with the dark hair who claims to be looking for you."

"I know that you think I'm going crazy," I sighed.

"You're not *going* crazy, you *are* crazy."

"But I swear it's more than just a dream. It feels familiar, almost real."

Every night, I saw this mysterious girl in my dreams. I could only see from her nose to her chin, and the picture was fuzzy. A strand or two of black hair would occasionally flow in front of her face. Even though I couldn't hear what she was saying and the picture wasn't the clearest, I could still barely read her lips as she said: "I will find you. I promise I will find you." What bothered me the most about the dream was how familiar it felt. It was like the girl was an old friend, but I could never place her.

"I think your dream is an old memory coming back, probably from you watching a movie or something," Jaime said, bringing me back to reality. "After all, you can't remember anything before your ninth birthday. Or have you forgotten that, too?"

"You have a point," I admitted, "but I still can't shake this feeling that—"

"Ley, please just drop it," Jaime interrupted.

"But I—"

"We've been through this about a hundred times already."

"I know that, but I think—"

"I said drop it! I don't want to hear about your stupid dream anymore. You won't get any answers from speculating."

"You just don't get it," I mumbled under my breath.

I'd already considered the possibility that the dream was a memory like Jaime had suggested, though I didn't think it was something from a movie. But that answer wasn't satisfying enough for me. I wanted to know who that girl was and why I forgot about her. I wanted to know what happened in those nine missing years that could've caused me to forget it all.

Jaime and I continued walking towards the car. On the outside, the car looked like a new convertible with a fresh coat of red paint. On the inside, however, it resembled a garbage dump. The leather seats were torn and patched up with duct tape. Old newspapers and magazines were crumpled up on the floor. Crumbs, straw paper, and melted candy filled the cupholders. The passenger seat was the worst part of the car. It was permanently stuck in its position, which happened to be way too close to the glove compartment for anyone over four feet tall. Because of that, I sat in the back seat while Jaime sat at the wheel.

When I first came to school without my memories, Jaime helped me adapt, which gave her a bit of a popularity boost. After I started talking about the dream and speculating about my past, she became annoyed with me. She accused me once of making it all up to get attention. That's when I realized that Jaime wasn't much of a friend after all; she was only helping me out to make herself look better. Our friendship became strained after that. Jaime became the friend who knew how to push my buttons, which she did frequently. She would tug at my hair, make fun of the TV shows I liked because they were "too nerdy," and she would start calling me "Laylay." I hated that last one most of all. My name is pronounced *Lee*, but it's spelled in an unusual way. Because of how it's spelled, most teachers would misread my name as "Lay," which became aggravating, to say the least. Jaime caught onto that and then made the nickname, which spread around the school. I tried to ignore it, but it still bothered me. Most people would probably consider Jaime a bully, but I could never bring myself to go that far. I kept telling myself that she cared about me, even if it was for the wrong reason. Still, I was desperate to find a new friend so I could slowly start to leave her, which I knew she wouldn't mind.

The trip home was completely silent, partly because I was tired, and also because I was mad at Jaime. I needed someone willing to listen to me, but I didn't have any other friends to talk to, not for lack of trying.

Jaime's car hit a bump, causing me to become distracted from my thoughts. I stared up at the evening sky until my red, two-story house came into view. The ride home had felt like an eternity.

"Thanks for giving me a ride," I said politely as I got out of the car and closed the door.

The car slowly pulled out as I entered the empty house. The first thing that greeted me when I turned on the lights was the old, broken couch sitting across from the TV. The adjoining kitchen had dishes piled up in the sink, waiting for me to clean them. I sat my backpack down on the counter before picking up a sponge and a plate. I hated washing dishes, not just because it was annoying, but because I would always end up reflecting on my life. It's like my brain would find any mistake I've ever made and replay it over and over again. Sometimes I'd end up thinking about something that hits harder than my mistakes, my family…or lack thereof.

I was in foster care, but the couple that had taken me in was always too busy to even have a proper conversation with me. I barely knew them. They were gone on a business trip for the next couple weeks, leaving me all alone for the time being. This wasn't unusual for me, and it wasn't that big of a deal as I was fourteen years old and able to take care of myself. They'd leave money for me, budgeting out what was meant for bills, what was meant for food, and what counted as my allowance for doing all the chores. Then they'd leave. I guess neglectful parents are better than no parents, which is why I always acted happy whenever a social worker came to check on me. It was taking a toll on my mental health, though, being so lonely.

As I grabbed another plate to clean, I started to think about who my bio parents could be and why they gave me up, something that I thought about often. Maybe they were too poor to take care of me. Maybe they were looking for me. Or maybe they didn't want me at all. Maybe they didn't love me. Maybe I couldn't remember anything before the age of nine because of some traumatic event from my home life. Maybe whatever it was was my fault. I tried to think back and remember something, anything, from my childhood. A sharp pain filled my head, causing the plate to slip from my hands and shatter on the hardwood floor.

"Dang it!" I exclaimed as I began to carefully pick up the glass.

When I finished cleaning up my mess, I grabbed my backpack off the counter and went upstairs to my room, dumping my stuff on the floor at the end of my bed. I looked into the large mirror attached to my dresser. There I was, dorky as ever. My dark brown hair was down to my waist, tangled. A shorter piece, not enough to be considered bangs, fell in front of my incredibly pale face. My brown eyes seemed darker than usual in the dim lighting. I was wearing the same blue jacket I wore every day along with a pair of jeans that I had been using for the past three days. I was thin and had a few curves "worth showing off," according to Jaime, but the jacket covered some of that up. I was never comfortable in my own skin.

"Maybe one day I'll actually look semi-decent," I sighed. "Then people will want to be friends with me, even if I am *weird*."

I decided to sit down and clear my head for a while. The stress of school had only been feeding off of my thoughts and anxiety, bringing me to tears every night. Not that anyone noticed or knew about it. I kept my anxiety and depression hidden around my foster parents. I didn't feel that it was right for them to have to bear my stress as well as their own.

I looked over at my phone and realized that it was almost time for dinner. I didn't have much of an appetite, so I decided to curl up in my warm bed, not even bothering to change into my pajamas or take my socks off. As soon as I closed my eyes, I began humming a lullaby; I'd known it for as long as I could remember, but nobody else seemed to recognize it.

The girl appeared in my dream again, but something was different. I could hear her, though her voice was muffled. I could also see more of her than before. She had big, brown eyes, and she was desperately holding onto my hands.

"Ley, you can't fight it anymore," the girl's voice echoed. "You have to let go! I will find you. I promise I will find you."

"What do you want from me!?" I screamed as I sat up from a pool of sweat.

The only thing I could hear in the darkness of my room was my fan. After I managed to calm myself down a little, I turned on my bedside lamp and looked around the room. I used my phone to check the time and realized that I hadn't been asleep for very long. I needed to talk to someone, anyone, but I couldn't. I had nobody to talk to besides myself, and I was desperate for answers.

"Who are you?" I asked quietly, fully knowing that I wouldn't get a response.

I heard a loud crack from downstairs. Still rattled from the dream, I stepped out of my bed, my jeans sticking to my legs. I grabbed my phone, got a baseball bat from my parents' closet, and carefully maneuvered downstairs, listening and looking for any signs of an intruder. I peeked around the corner, preparing to dial 911 and expecting to see someone taking all the valuables. To my surprise, all that greeted me was a tall, round beam of green light that made a faint humming sound as I approached it. It was vertical, almost like a doorway. I looked around for the source of the light but found nothing that could have possibly been emitting or reflecting it. It just stood there, bright as can be. Although I hadn't seen anything like it before, something about that light felt familiar. I recognized it as though it were from a childhood dream long forgotten. I dropped the bat and reached out, as I found myself almost hypnotized by the light, and stepped through.

* * *

It felt like the floor gave out from under me as I began to fall. Instead of seeing the kitchen, I saw nothing but a black void. I couldn't hear the normal creaks and squeals of the house anymore. All I could hear was a loud rumble like a storm was approaching. I felt a strong wind on my face as the noises got louder. I could feel myself falling farther and farther. I looked down and saw a white light. It was rapidly getting closer and brighter as I fell towards it. I shut my eyes as tightly as I could, expecting a rough impact and possibly death. When nothing happened, I cautiously opened my eyes.

I was sitting on a cold, metal floor. The walls of the room were made of the same white metal. The wall to my left had one large door that matched the walls and didn't appear to have a handle. The rest of the wall was mainly taken up by a long, translucent panel. It looked like something out of a science fiction movie, like a hologram computer. On my right, there were four smaller doors, evenly spaced from each other. The wall behind me was blank. There was only one other door, which was in front of me. Each door in the room had a small panel next to it with a handprint in the center.

I pressed my hands against my throbbing head. Besides my head hurting, I felt confused and a little nauseous. I tried to stand up, but I lost my balance and fell back down.

The door to my left opened, and a tall girl with pitch-black hair, pale skin, and bright red lipstick stepped into the room. She had lightly toned arms and wore a black tank top with leggings and combat boots. She could've been my exact copy if it weren't for the hair color and clothing, but there was something else about her that I just couldn't place. It was as if I'd met her somewhere before. Then it hit me, she looked like the girl from my dream. I began to wonder if she recognized me or if she was the one who had caused that green light to appear in my house.

"Who are you? And how did you get here?" she asked me.

"It's you," I gasped as I stood up, trying not to fall back down. "Who are you?"

"I asked *you* first."

"I'm Ley," I said nervously, "and I have no idea where I am or who you are."

"You think I haven't heard that one before?" she asked with a grin. "This is a top-secret base; there's no way you just wandered in here accidentally. Tell me right now who you are, or things are going to get messy."

She pulled out a gun and pointed it right at my head. At first, I thought she was just trying to scare me, but then I heard the gun click. I could feel sweat pouring down my face. I still couldn't let go of the idea that maybe she was behind whatever the heck caused me to leave the safety of my kitchen. *Maybe she was testing me.* No matter what, I knew I had to be careful.

"You were in my dream," I explained. "You said that you would find me. I want to know why you brought me here. What's so important about me? Do you know something about my past?"

"I don't know who exactly you think I am," the girl said, her voice becoming bitter, "but I can assure you we've never met before, and I wasn't trying to find you. I want to know who you are and why you brought yourself here."

"I swear I have no idea what you're talking about. This is all just a misunderstanding. So, please, put the gun down, and then we can sort this all out."

The girl's grip on her gun tightened. She wasn't backing down. It became painfully obvious to me that she couldn't have been the one in my dream, and she was serious about shooting me if I didn't comply.

"I promise you I'm telling the truth," I pleaded. "Please don't kill me, I haven't done anything wrong."

"You mean to tell me that you, an unauthorized person, just happened to appear in the middle of a top-secret government base?"

"Well," I mumbled, "y-yes. I'm sorry, but I don't know how else to explain it. One moment I'm in my house and the next moment I'm here. How would you explain it?"

"I see," she said.

The girl put her gun back in her holster, giving me a false sense of relief before she pulled out a Taser instead. As I fell to the ground, I felt a horrible, burning sensation. It was like a hoard of bees had covered my body. I couldn't move. While this was happening, the girl looked down at her watch. The front had opened up, revealing a screen and a speaker.

"Savannah, come upstairs to section one immediately," the girl said into her watch. "We have an uncooperative intruder, and we may need to do a DNA test."

The tasing stopped, but I was left feeling too sore to move. I watched as the girl pulled out a tiny needle with some sort of blue liquid at the end of it. I was too weak to fight as she stuck me. The moment the needle pierced my skin, I became dizzy. My body still ached as everything around me melted into darkness.

***

I opened my eyes, expecting to find myself in my bed, only to see that I was in an interrogation room, and my hands were individually cuffed to the arms of the chair I was sitting in. I looked around, hoping to find a clue as to where I was or at least a way to escape. It was like I was stuck in a nightmare. I tried to calm myself down, but each second only made me more anxious.

"Is someone going to come in here?" I called out. "I swear I have nothing to hide! Please, just let me go already." Silence was the only reply, only adding to the tension. "H-hey, where's the crazy chick with the black hair?" I asked, shouting a little louder in a desperate attempt to sound brave. "Look, I want to get this all over with sooner than later. I don't know how I got here, and I just want to go home." There was still nothing. Either someone was listening outside of the room, waiting for me to break, or I was just talking to myself like the pathetic loser I always saw myself as. I sat around in silence, trying not to think of what was going to happen to me.

After about ten minutes of silence and suspense had passed, the silver door in the left corner of the room flew open, giving a loud bang as the handle slammed into the wall. The girl from earlier came in. Her

9

eyes were piercing through me, and her crimson lips were curled into an unsettling smile. She stepped forward, and her face slowly came closer to mine until she was about an inch away. She didn't even need to speak to strike me with fear; her gaze alone was enough to make my eyes water. I could feel her breath on my face, causing me to squirm in my chair.

"If you want to leave this place with only minimal damage," she spoke quietly, "you'll tell me right now who you are and how you got here." Even though she looked to be about my age, she scared me, and her calm voice somehow made it worse.

"I already t-told you who I-I am," I stuttered. "My name is Ley, and I'm f-fourteen years old."

"Look, usually I take my time when breaking someone during an interrogation, but I'm currently on a time limit," she said. "So, tell me who it is you're working for, *Ley*, and how you got here. I don't want to hurt you."

"I don't have an official job or anything," I said. "I'm too young." The girl grinned and held back a laugh. "I'm so sorry I bothered you by coming here. I'm not even sure how I got here in the first place. I just want to get back home. Please, don't hurt me, I'm begging you."

"What a very convincing act, Ley," the girl said as she gave a slight chuckle. "Unfortunately for you, I'm not falling for it."

She proceeded to throw her fist into my face without hesitation, sending me flying into the back wall. My eyes began to water, and I felt incredibly dizzy. I had never seen or felt strength like that in my life. It wasn't normal. *Who was she? What was she?* Before I could question anything else about her, she pounced. She jumped onto me and put one hand around my throat. The chair was too small to hold the weight of both of us, causing it to break and my hands to become free. I reached up and tried to fight, but I was too weak. I could feel my breath becoming shallow as I began to black out. Before I could lose consciousness, a girl with long black hair came in. Her green eyes were covered by her bright blue glasses. She wore a black suit and tie.

"Linda, you need to release that girl right now!" she shouted upon seeing my current state.

"Why should I do that? Can't you see she's about to talk?" Linda asked, her grip on my neck loosening a little.

"Listen to the glasses girl, please!" I gasped.

"Oh, shut up," Linda said as she began to tighten her grip again.

"You don't understand," the girl with the glasses said, "that girl is your sister."

"That isn't possible. I'm an only child."

"You lost a few *years'* worth of your memories, remember? That means that this is unlikely but very much possible. Numbers don't lie, and neither do blood tests. I took a sample from her when she was unconscious. The results just came back."

Linda lifted her hand from my neck and stood up, leaving me on the ground, gasping for air. She grabbed a clipboard from the other girl as if determined to find proof that it was all just a hoax.

"Did you do a quick scan or a full test?" she asked.

"I did a full test," the girl said.

As Linda continued reading the test results, I started rerunning the events of my arrival in my head. There was no way it could've been real, but it *felt* real. I tried to come up with anything that could explain my situation, no matter how ridiculous it sounded. Maybe I was hallucinating. Maybe I accidentally wandered into the wrong place… from my kitchen. Maybe I was just plain crazy. No. None of those options made sense. I needed a somewhat logical explanation as to why I was where I was. That's when I realized that it had to be staged (sure, the idea sounds far-fetched, but there was nothing else that made sense to me at the time).

"Bravo," I said as I stood up and started clapping, the two pairs of handcuffs still dangling from my wrists. "You guys got me. So, how did you do it? How did you get me here? And who put you up to this? It was Jaime, wasn't it? She even got someone to look like the girl from… from my… oh, what am I even saying? That doesn't even make sense." Linda and the other girl looked at me like I had three eyes, which I understood. To rationalize the situation, I was starting to sound like a raving lunatic. "Great, I sound like a crazy person, don't I?" I sighed. They continued to stare at me in silence. "But this can't be real. I don't know how I got here or h-how I… just please tell me this isn't real."

The girl with the glasses shook her head as she removed the handcuffs from my wrists. "I'm sorry, Ley. This is real."

Linda waited a moment before speaking again. It was like she didn't know what to say. She was just as shocked as I was, though, unlike me, she didn't attempt to rationalize it. "Savannah, take Ley up to my room," she said as she started to leave. "I'll be there in a bit. I have something to take care of first."

"Follow me, please," Savannah said as she gestured towards the door. "You have a lot of adjusting to do."

She led me into a hallway and then into a large room filled with office cubicles. The walls were a pale shade of indigo. White metal doors were all around the room. A couple were larger than the rest, but the others were the same, and none of them had signs or labels. Each of the workers looked like they were teenagers, which came as a shock to me since the base was supposedly government-run.

"Welcome to the Resistance," Savannah said.

"Why are there so many teenagers here?" I asked.

"Ah, so you noticed," she said. "Yes, most of our agents are recruited at the age of twelve or thirteen. That's because younger agents last longer, have better covers, and are more open-minded."

"Why is having an open mind so important when working in a place like this?"

"We deal with some pretty odd threats; threats that most adults wouldn't believe even if they saw them with their own eyes."

"What about these kids' families? Do they know about any of this?"

"No," Savannah explained. "Most of our agents abandon their families. To keep things quiet, we've changed the identities of some of our agents and transferred others to different locations across the country." I wasn't even sure how to react to that. All I wanted to do was find my family while all of those teens willingly abandoned theirs. "I do hope you can forgive your sister for what happened earlier," Savannah continued. "She was just trying to keep our location safe. Only our agents and the highest government officials have access to this base or even know of its existence. So, tell me, Ley, how did you find yourself here?"

"I don't know, to be honest," I said. "I was standing in my kitchen and there was this greenish light."

"A portal then?"

"You've dealt with this kind of thing before?"

"Of course not, but the only other explanation is spontaneous teleportation, and I don't see that as a likely possibility," Savannah said with a chuckle.

"But you can send me back, right?" I asked desperately.

"I could probably find a way to get the portal open again, but I need to know where and when you're from."

"I can write my address down for you. The date was December 5th, 2017. What day is it now?"

"That doesn't matter, what matters is you'll be going back in time, which explains your DNA results being linked to a missing person's case. You were officially presumed dead by 2024."

"Wait, did you say *back in time*? And I've been presumed dead? How—"

"That makes this trickier," Savannah continued, ignoring my confusion, "but I should still be able to do it. It will probably take a while, though, so you'll be stuck here with your sister for a bit."

"I can buy the whole time-travel-portal-thingy," I said as Savannah led me up the grated stairs, "but a long-lost sister in the future? That seems impossible. I know you're probably some top-notch scientist or something, but are you really, *really* sure that girl is my sister?"

"I only work with the science team part-time," she responded, "but I am *very* sure that Linda is your sister. I've never made a mistake on a blood test before, and I certainly don't intend on starting now."

"So, what exactly *is* your job here if you're not a scientist?"

"I work as a field agent, and I gather intel."

"You're a gun-wielding hacker?"

"I guess that's one way of saying it." The door in front of us opened as Savannah placed her hand on the scanner next to it. We were back in the room I was in when I first arrived. "This is section one. The floor below is section two and so on. The only exception is section three, our vehicle department, which is on the same floor as section two. If you ever get lost, feel free to ask anyone here for help. Everyone is very friendly, for the most part, to newcomers."

The wall in front of me had the four metal doors I remembered from earlier. I was led through the second door. As the light flickered on, I gazed into the room, Linda's room. It was quite small and surprisingly empty for a teenage girl. Her room consisted of a queen-sized bed, a dresser with a mirror, and an incredibly small bedside table with a lamp. Almost all of her possessions sat on her dresser. Everything that couldn't fit remained under her bed. She didn't have any posters, shelves, or even a picture frame in her room.

"Wow!" I gasped. "Her room is so bland. She doesn't have any decorations?"

"Nope," I heard Linda say. I spun around to find her less than a foot away from me. "Humans don't need too much to survive. I just have my basic necessities as well as a couple of sources of entertainment. Well, I guess a bed isn't technically a necessity, but you get the point."

"Why do you live like this?" I asked. "Why are you working here? Why aren't you living with your family? I'm sure they miss you."

"Well," she started, "my job is really important, and it gets hard to keep secrets from families. Most people who work here have either abandoned their families or lied to them and destroyed their trust if not their entire relationship. I know that it wasn't easy for any of them, it certainly wasn't for me to leave my foster parents, but it was what needed to be done to keep the public ignorant and safe from what goes on around here."

"I have a foster family, too," I told her. "I understand that your work here must be important, but isn't it hard knowing that your foster parents can't be there for you?"

Linda began to open her mouth again, as if she meant to say something else but stopped. She looked down for a moment before speaking. When she spoke again, her voice turned cold, and her eyes became empty and unreadable as the hard truth came out.

"No, it's not hard at all. Not anymore," she said, "because I've learned that depending on or even caring about someone will only get you or them hurt. I had to adapt. That's why I'm not torn up over my foster parents, and it's why I only have a few friends. Avoiding dependency and emotional attachment keeps me and those around me from getting hurt. In this world, it's kill or be killed. I'm sure things were all happy and perfect before you came here, but the future will swallow you whole unless you learn to adapt. I'll do what I can to help you, Ley, but I can only protect you from so much. Do you understand?"

"You're wrong," I said. "Emotional detachment won't help you; it will only tear you apart and fill you with regret when something happens to the people you *do* care about or the people you chose not to know better. I doubt this place is any worse than where I just came from. Even if I am wrong and this world is just as bad as you say, there's still hope. There's *always* hope. When society hits rock bottom, it can only go up."

"I wish I were still optimistic like you," Linda said. "Sadly, mankind learned that if you dig down hard enough, you can keep going further below rock bottom until you reach the very pits of—"

"Boss," Savannah interrupted, looking down at her watch, "sorry to interrupt, but things have escalated. You need to go now!"

"What escalated?" I asked.

Linda glanced over at Savannah and nodded. "Remember what I just said about this world being kill or be killed?" she asked as she looked back at me.

"Yeah, my memory isn't *that* bad."

"Well, I have to go kill something before it kills all of humanity. But don't worry, I'll be back. Your life is in my hands, after all."

"Should I be concerned about that?"

"Yes, you should be *very* concerned," she said sarcastically. "Speaking of which, don't touch my stuff or I'll have to kill you."

"Can I at least borrow a pair of shoes?" I asked, looking down at my lavender socks.

"Oh, I didn't realize you weren't wearing any," Linda said. "I have a pair of gray tennis shoes under my bed. Try not to ruin them."

"Thank you."

After Linda left, Savannah approached me. "What Linda just said to you about how emotionally detached she is, is complete bull crap," she said. "She does miss her foster parents sometimes, and she gets very attached to her teammates. She just likes to act like she's a lone wolf."

"Why?" I asked.

"Because she hopes that if she keeps telling that lie, she'll eventually believe it."

"And why would she *want* to believe it?"

"She thinks that emotional detachment will prevent her from feeling pain the next time she watches one of her teammates die right in front of her," Savannah said, "the next time she has to step over bodies to complete her mission. I predict she'll warm up to you, though. She's always wanted to find her biological family."

"I've been wanting to find mine, too," I said. "If I'm going to be stuck here, I hope Linda and I can become friends."

I watched Savannah go out the door before stepping back into Linda's room, putting on her shoes, and sitting on her bed. I began to close my eyes when a familiar noise got my attention. It was the same noise I'd heard back at the house, the noise that I originally believed was caused by an intruder. I dashed out of the room just in time to find the green light. Finally, my ticket home. I was about to step through when I found myself hesitating. *What about Linda?* I couldn't leave without saying goodbye, and I was still wearing her shoes. *But what about my chores? What about school?* There were things I needed to take care of back home.

"I can't decide," I mumbled to myself.

The irony wasn't lost on me. I said I wanted to go home, and just moments prior, I would've left in a heartbeat. But there I was, standing in front of my ticket home, wishing I could stay where I was a little longer. Before I could decide what to do, a girl came tumbling out, pinning me to the floor. The light faded from behind her.

"Uh, who are you?" I asked.

Chapter 2 (Elizabeth, 1840)

"Why did you turn him down?" Marina asked me as we walked through town.

"I'm just not interested," I sighed. "We've been over this."

"There's no boy in this whole town that you fancy?"

"No."

"Wait, do you…?" Marina started, her voice barely audible. "Do you fancy women?"

"No."

"…oh," she sighed. "So, *nobody* then?"

"Now you're getting it."

Marina and I had grown up in the town's orphanage. I was found at the age of nine with no memory of where I came from. All I knew was my name, age, and birthday. Marina came around the same time, and we've been best friends ever since. We, like all the other orphan girls, were taught that the only hope for us to be successful was to marry when we got older. Unfortunately for me, I had no interest in that, and nobody seemed to understand why. The very thought of romance and dating disgusted me. Just imagining kissing someone made me squirm.

Marina sat down on a wooden bench in front of the bakery. "You're okay with growing old and lonely?" she asked me. "No husband? No kids? No grandkids?"

"I don't want romance," I said, sitting next to her.

"Then who's going to please you?"

"I can please myself," I said before realizing what Marina had meant. The look of embarrassment on my face caused the both of us to laugh so loud that we drew the attention of Hilda, the one in charge of the orphanage. She was the very definition of an "old hag." Her wrinkled forehead, graying hair, and mean spirit were enough to make a child cry.

"There you are!" she yelled from down the street. "What did I say about running off by yourselves?"

"Don't?" Marina mumbled to me.

"You're going to get us into more trouble," I sighed.

"I didn't force you to join me out here."

"I know, but—"

Hilda grabbed our hands and began dragging us back to the orphanage were I knew we would be punished. It was worth it, though, as it was the only opportunity to talk privately with my friend.

The orphanage was a large, run-down wooden home with olive green wallpaper, which was peeling, and creaky wooden floors. The boys all wore suits, and the girls were each required to wear a long-sleeved dress with a white apron. My dress was a deep red while Marina's was blue.

Sure enough, Marina and I were punished with extra chores and no supper. But since the food wasn't all that great anyway, I wasn't too upset. Marina's dark hair started to fall out of its bun and into her deep blue eyes as we scrubbed the dark, wooden floors. I'd always wished for eyes like hers. Unfortunately, mine were brown and boring, matching my short, wavy head of hair. Marina always told me I had a cute "button nose," so there was at least that feature that I liked.

I began humming a melody that nobody in town seemed to know. I always believed it had something to do with my past, my family. It was my only link to the life I couldn't remember. That and the strange dreams I'd sometimes have. I usually didn't remember much by the time I woke up, but I'd spend the rest of the morning feeling unsettled.

"Elizabeth," Marina said, interrupting my humming, "there's something I need to tell you."

"Can't it wait?" I asked. "If Hilda hears us talking, we'll get an even worse punishment. Cleaning is supposed to be silent."

"I know, but this is important."

I felt a gust of wind blow against my face. It nearly blew away a loose piece of the wallpaper. The orphanage could be drafty, but not like that. The wind was followed by a loud crack, drawing my attention to the broom closet behind me.

"Are you even paying attention to what I'm saying?" Marina asked, nearly tipping the water bucket onto her dress.

"Didn't you hear that sound?" I walked towards the closet and opened the door. A strange green light greeted me. Something about it felt familiar, though I didn't understand why. I was drawn to it, but also afraid even though I'd never seen anything like that before.

"Elizabeth!" Marina exclaimed. "Step away from that portal!"

"The what?" I asked, only half paying attention. With the light's hold growing on me, I almost didn't notice the frost forming on the floor. A wall of ice started to form from the ground, trying to block me. Without thinking, I jumped over the ice and went through the light.

I was falling, and I wasn't in the orphanage anymore. Darkness surrounded me. I couldn't quite make out what I was hearing. Various sounds were all loudly jumbled in my ears. I looked down and saw a bright light. I didn't expect death to be so complicated.

***

"Uh, who are you?"

I looked down and saw that I had fallen on top of a girl. She appeared to be my age and, besides the much longer hair, looked exactly like me. The room I was in was all white, much to my relief.

"Are you an angel?" I asked as we stood up.

"Unfortunately, no." She laughed. "I'm just a regular, human girl."

"Aren't I dead?"

"No, though I totally get where you're coming from. I thought I was gonna die when I fell through the portal, too. Really scary, huh?"

"I'm sorry, what?"

"Where are you from?"

"I'm from the orphanage. I—"

"I should've said 'when,' not 'where,'" the girl said. "What year do you think it is?"

"1840."

"I'm so sorry."

"For what?"

"The current year is 2145. You're in a secret government base."

I didn't fully understand what the girl had just told me, but I understood enough to realize I wasn't anywhere near my home anymore. I didn't know how to react. I felt scared and confused, but also excited. If I truly was in the future, I could learn so much. But how would I get home? Could I even get home?

"My name's Ley," the girl said, "Ley Smith."

"I'm Elizabeth Smith."

"Hey, we're both Smiths. Funny coincidence."

"Y-yeah."

"I figure you have a *lot* of questions. I can try to answer them, but I just got here myself."

"So, you aren't from here either?"

"Nope. I'm from 2017."

"How did you get here?"

"Same way you did. A portal opened, and I went through."

"Portal? You mean that green light?"

"Yeah," Ley said.

I broke down crying. I wasn't sure if it was from being overwhelmed or from fear of being so far away from home. Sure, the orphanage wasn't great. In fact, it was awful. But it was familiar, and Marina was there.

"It's going to be okay," Ley said, wiping away my tears. "This is scary for me, too, but now I know I'm not alone. We'll make it through this together."

"Thanks, Ley."

I couldn't quite explain it, but I began to get the feeling I had met Ley before. Her name felt like it was at the tip of my tongue long before she introduced herself. But there was no way we could've met. Since she came from 2017, I knew I had to be long dead before she was even born. That was a strange thing to wrap my head around.

The largest door in the room opened, allowing a girl with black hair and blue glasses to enter. I wasn't sure how to take her. Her facial expression seemed stern and intimidating, but Ley seemed relieved to see her, leading me to believe she was someone that could help.

"Savannah, I am so glad you're here!" Ley exclaimed as we both stood up. "This is Elizabeth. She just fell through a portal of her own from 1840."

"Fascinating," Savannah said. "You're a long way from home, Elizabeth. Even farther than Ley. Would you mind giving me a blood sample?"

"Blood sample?" I asked. "What do you need my blood for?"

"With today's technology, even a small amount of blood can tell me a lot about you."

"No need. I can tell you anything you need to know about me."

"Oh really? Okay. Let's start simple: Who are your parents?"

"…I can tell you anything but that."

"You have a gap in your memory, don't you?" Savannah asked me.

"Yes," I sighed. "I can't remember anything before I turned nine."

"And, Ley, you're the same way?"

"Yeah," Ley said, leaning back against the wall. "How'd you know?"

"Simple," Savannah said. "Linda has a gap in her memory, too."

I was informed that Linda was both Ley's sister and the leader of the "Resistance," the organization which I was currently in. The reason Savannah wanted a blood test was to see if I was related to the sisters. I didn't fully understand how it would be possible, but considering I knew nothing of my past, I let the test be done. Savannah pulled out a small, blue device with a button. After the button was pressed, a small blade came out and was used to slice the tip of my finger. As soon as blood touched the blade, it retracted. A panel made of light was projected from the device, displaying the results.

"According to the quick test, you're Ley's identical sister," Savannah said. "Though I could've guessed that just by looking at you."

"How is that even possible?" I asked. "Are you sure it's right?"

"Well, I could run a full scan, which would take more time, but I can guarantee you it will yield the same results."

"Wow," Ley said, "two sisters. And here I was thinking this couldn't get any more complicated."

I was once again met with a mix of conflicting emotions. On one hand, I was discovering things that could lead me to figuring out my past. But on the other hand, I was so upset I wanted to vomit. Three of us. Sisters. But somehow in three different time periods? I didn't understand how that could happen, but I knew one thing: the technology needed to make that happen couldn't have come from 1840. That meant that either Ley's time or Linda's time was my real home.

Another girl entered the room, briefly distracting me from my racing mind. Before she could say a word, Savannah pulled her aside and began whispering. I presumed she must've been Linda, my other sister, but I didn't know for sure until she walked over to me and introduced herself.

"It's nice to meet you, Elizabeth," she said, shaking my hand. "I'm Linda. I see you've already met Ley and Savannah."

"I… I have," I said, my mind racing once again. I was trying to keep myself from breaking, and I think Linda could tell because she quickly changed the subject.

"Are you girls hungry?" she asked. "I think the cafeteria is still serving dinner."

"I'm starved," Ley said, "but shouldn't we get Elizabeth some different clothing?"

"What's wrong with what I'm wearing?" I asked.

"Your dress is old-fashioned, to say the least," Linda told me, tugging at my apron. "One could argue Ley's outfit is, too, but jeans have never gone out of style, so she should be fine."

"I don't have any other clothes on me, so—"

"Don't worry about it. We look like we're about the same size. Ley, take Elizabeth into my room and find her some clothes. I'll go downstairs and make sure the cafeteria keeps dinner available until you're able to eat."

"But what about the, um, undergarments?" Ley asked. "I figure Elizabeth doesn't want those to be hand-me-downs."

"Well, luckily for her, I bought some new ones yesterday. Check my top left dresser drawer."

"Okay. Elizabeth, follow me."

Ley led me into a small, bare room. She began searching in Linda's dresser for clothing that she thought would suit me. In no time, she had found a blue shirt and a pair of pants that she called "jeans." She then handed me the undergarments, which were shockingly small compared to what I was used to wearing.

"Could you turn around while I get dressed?" I asked.

"Of course," Ley said. "Let me know if you need help getting anything on."

The modern clothing I was given was incredibly comfortable, more so than I was expecting. When I went up to the mirror, I was surprised to see how well the outfit suited me. Ley seemed to like it, too. It wasn't until I saw her reflection in the mirror that I noticed part of her jaw was swollen.

"Are you alright?" I asked. "Who did that to you?"

"Oh," Ley said. "You mean my jaw? Linda did that."

"What? Why would she do that?"

"It was just a misunderstanding. She thought I had broken into the base for information."

"But—"

"Please don't hold it against her. She was just doing her job."

I couldn't believe someone would see Ley as a threat. She seemed so innocent. Even if she were up to something, I thought physically hurting her (at least that soon) was a step too far. As much as I wanted to question Ley further about her injury, I could tell the subject bothered her, so I moved on to something else.

"So, what's your life like?" I asked.

"To be brutally honest, it's kinda boring."

"Mine is, too."

"Oh, really? I figured you'd have a lot of excitement going on."

"I live in a run-down orphanage, so there isn't much 'excitement' for me."

"I live with my foster parents, who are almost never home."

"Foster parents?"

"People who take care of you but haven't officially adopted you."

"And you said they're not home a lot?"

"They're too busy for me," Ley said. "But that's okay. I wouldn't want to be a burden to them. I'm just lucky to have a place to live."

"Oh, Ley, I—"

"Let's go find the cafeteria," she interrupted. "Linda's waiting on us."

Chapter 3 (Ley)

I stood behind Linda in the line at the cafeteria, which was in section two. Long gray tables filled the center of the room and smaller, square tables stood against the walls. Agents were sitting everywhere, chatting about work while eating their dinner. Elizabeth, who stood behind me, was carefully reading through all the choices on the menu with a puzzled look on her face.

"Is she gonna need help?" Linda asked, gesturing towards Elizabeth.

"I think she'll be fine," I said. "Ordering food isn't all that complicated."

"Excuse me, Ley," Elizabeth said as she tapped on my shoulder, "but what exactly is a cheeseburger?"

"Second thought," I said to Linda, "she may need some help." Linda chuckled, causing Elizabeth to give her a deadly glare. "Sorry, Elizabeth." I laughed as I pulled out my phone. "Just let me look up a picture of a cheeseburger so I can show you."

"What's that?" Elizabeth asked upon seeing my phone. "Why is it glowing?"

"Here we go," Linda groaned as she stepped up to order. "Good luck with her, Ley."

"Never mind," Elizabeth sighed. "There's no point in explaining it to me now. We're about to order anyway."

"Hello, ladies," the guy at the cash register said after Linda finished her order. He had bright red hair and stunning green eyes. "I don't think I've seen you two around before. Are you new here?"

"Yeah. I'm Ley, and this is Elizabeth," I told him. "We're Linda's sisters."

"Really?" he asked. "I didn't know she had any siblings."

"Neither did she before today." I laughed. "We didn't know either. We just met a little bit ago."

"Well, I hope you enjoy your time here with her," the guy said. "I'm Dillan, by the way, Dillan Rollins. So, Ley, what can I get for you?"

"I'll take a cheeseburger, fries, and a bottle of water."

"Okay," he said. "Your food will be set out on the counter when it's done. And what can I get for you, Elizabeth?"

"Uh, I'll take what Ley is having, I guess," Elizabeth said, sounding a little nervous.

"Oh, crap!" I panicked. "I just realized that I don't have any money with me. I left my wallet in my purse at home. Do you have something, Elizabeth?"

"No, I don't have any money on me either," Elizabeth said. "Even if I did, I doubt it would be acceptable here."

"Don't worry about it," Dillan said. "We only charge money for special items, like extra sides or energy drinks."

"Well, thank Heaven for that," I said as I let out a sigh of relief.

Elizabeth and I stood around, waiting for our food to be ready. I noticed that, while she was definitely hungry, Elizabeth looked nervous as she kept looking at the pictures on the menu. I understood that trying new things could be uncomfortable, though I always believed in trying (almost) anything at least once. I looked towards the cash register and caught Dillan staring at me. As soon as he realized I had spotted him, he gestured for me to come closer.

"Hey, are you alright?" he asked.

"Well, this whole experience is a bit strange, but—"

"I meant your jaw; it's looking a bit swollen."

"Oh, uh, rough interrogation," I said. I'll be fine."

"Does it hurt?"

"A little bit, but it's nothing I can't manage."

"Take a couple of these," Dillan said, placing a small bottle of pills on the counter. "You'll be feeling better by tomorrow."

"Um, alright," I said as I started to pour the pills over into my hand.

"Just keep the bottle. It's easier for you that way, and I can always get more."

"You sure?"

"Yeah. There wasn't much left in there anyway."

"Thanks."

After we got our food, Elizabeth and I searched the vast sea of tables until we found Linda, who was talking with a blond guy in a lab coat and glasses. He looked to be about sixteen, though his youthful, cleanshaven face could've been throwing me off. Something about his pale blue eyes and his chiseled jaw seemed familiar. I glanced over at Elizabeth, who appeared to be thinking the same thing as we sat down across from them.

"I guess I should introduce you guys," Linda said. "Ley and Elizabeth, this is my friend, Jonathan Davis, but everyone calls him John. He's the head of our science department."

"It's nice to meet you," John said as he extended his hand for me and Elizabeth to shake.

"I… I know you, don't I?" Elizabeth asked. I couldn't tell if John's expression was one of shock, confusion, or fear. "We were… we…" She went quiet as she reached for her head.

"Are you alright?" Linda asked.

Elizabeth stood up. She looked pained and concerned. "I feel like I'm about to explode," she whimpered. "My head…" As soon as those words left her mouth, her eyes, hands, and part of the floor burst into flames. Everyone but Linda jumped down to the floor to avoid possibly being blasted. Some of the agents drew their weapons.

"Stand down!" Linda ordered before standing to face Elizabeth. "I guess you really are my sister. How long have you been able to do that?"

"What are you talking about?" Elizabeth asked.

"You really don't know? You can't even feel it?"

"Feel what?"

"Look at your hands, Elizabeth," Linda said gently. "Don't freak out."

Elizabeth obeyed and held her hands up to her face. Her eyes, which had already gone back to normal, widened. She looked as if she were about to be sick. "What's happening!? Someone, help me!" she yelled.

"You're going to be alright, I promise," Linda replied without raising her voice. "Look, I'm different, too." She lifted the table over her head using only one hand. "See? You and I are special."

"How do I make it stop?" Elizabeth asked as Linda put the table down. "I just want it to go away."

"Just calm down, alright? Try to relax yourself," she suggested. "Take a nice, deep breath, and focus on the flames disappearing from your hands."

Elizabeth's hands slowly went back to normal. She froze for a moment as if she feared moving would bring the flames back. Everybody else appeared to be thinking the same thing, as nobody dared to move from the floor. After a minute or two had passed, Elizabeth looked over at me and extended her hand to help me up. I reached up cautiously before taking her hand and getting back on my feet.

"So, what can you do, Ley?" she asked.

"Oh, me? I can't do anything," I replied. "I'm not that special."

"I highly doubt that," John said as he got up. "I'm sure you can do something, but before we find out what, there's something we need to take care of. Linda, can I speak with you for a moment?"

"Sure," she said. "Ley, Elizabeth, stay here and eat. I'll be right back."

Elizabeth and I ate in silence for a bit, unlike everybody else who started talking like nothing had happened (though I caught the occasional glance in our direction). I was trying to figure out what secret powers John thought I had, and poor Elizabeth kept looking down at her hands to make sure they weren't on fire again.

After a moment, I glanced over and noticed Elizabeth carefully biting into her burger in an attempt to prevent sauce from getting on her face. If even a drop of ketchup stained the corner of her lips, she grabbed a napkin and tried to wipe it away as quickly as possible, causing me to laugh.

"What?" Elizabeth asked.

"Everyone gets food on their face, Elizabeth. There's no need to scrub it all off until after you're finished."

"I get in trouble if I make a mess when eating. All the girls do. It's not 'ladylike.'"

"Screw being 'ladylike.' You're human; humans make messes. Enjoy the freedom, and be as messy as you want. Just remember to clean said mess when you're done."

Elizabeth smiled before scarfing down a large portion of her burger and trying a few of her fries, which she quickly became addicted to. It was nice to see her happy after… whatever it was that had just happened.

"Thanks for helping me up earlier," I said after we finished our meal.

"It's the least I could do," Elizabeth said. "You've been so kind to me this whole time. You treat me as if I'm your dearest friend even though we just met."

"Well of course," I said. "I mean, you are my sister… apparently. Besides, you need some help adjusting. I may not be from this time either, but at least I know what a smartphone is."

"I don't think I've met anyone like you before, Ley."

"You mean a nerd from the future? Yeah, I doubt it."

"That's not what I meant."

"Then what do you mean?"

"You treat strangers with kindness, and you're brave."

"Let me stop you right there," I laughed. "I am *not* brave. I'm afraid of the weirdest things. I'm surprised my own shadow doesn't scare me."

"You weren't afraid of me," Elizabeth said. "Everybody freaked out when the flames appeared, but you—"

"I was on the floor just like everybody else," I interrupted. "Linda was the brave one."

"Well, sure, she was brave too, but you still took my hand even though you saw what I can do," Elizabeth said. "I could've easily burnt you, yet you took the risk." She went silent for a moment as she fought to hold back tears. "I didn't even know I could do that. How will I control it? I don't want to hurt anyone." She buried her face in her hands. "I'm a monster now, aren't I?"

"You are not a monster, Elizabeth," I said. "I'm sure you'll figure it all out. We'll just have to find somewhere for you to safely practice using your powers. Once you're able to control it, you won't have to worry about accidentally hurting people."

"Thank you, Ley," Elizabeth said.

Linda returned with John, Savannah, and Dillan. "Elizabeth, we'd like to run another blood test, if you don't mind," she said calmly.

"I'd rather not," Elizabeth sighed. "My fingertip is still sore from the first one."

"Boss," Dillan said, "As I tried to tell you before, a blood test isn't necessary."

Linda rolled her eyes. "Well, if you would've paid attention, you'd know that you're right; it isn't necessary, but John and I are concerned that the other agents will think she's an Element. To prevent any conflict, it doesn't hurt to test again."

"Wait, what do you guys mean by *Element*?" I asked. "Do you mean the four elements: fire, water, earth, and air?"

"Sort of, but it's a bit more complicated than that," John explained. "The Elements are a species. Their home planet is Elahntra, and each one of them controls one of the four elements: fire, water, *wind*, and earth. They're also very dangerous."

"You mean, they're aliens?" I asked. "*Real* aliens? From space?"

"There's life on other planets?" Elizabeth gasped. "That's amazing!"

"Yes, it is amazing," Linda said, "but some of these aliens, like the Elements, are incredibly hostile. The reason we want to run another blood test is because—"

"Because I can apparently wield fire?" Elizabeth asked, interrupting Linda. "I understand where you're coming from, but it just doesn't make sense. If you're not an Element, then neither am I. We're sisters. So how could I be an Element if you aren't?"

"She's right," I said. "She may have powers, but she's one hundred percent human just like everybody else in this room. None of the agents here should have any reason to think otherwise."

"Okay, fine. If any of the other agents are nervous, I'll just tell them to deal with it," Linda caved. "Savannah, keep working on a way to get my sisters home. John, take Elizabeth back to my room. Dillan, take Ley outside. I'll join you in a moment."

***

I followed Dillan back to section one and out the front door. After we'd walked a few yards away from the base, he stopped. I turned around to see nothing but the side of a hill. The door to the base was nowhere to be found.

"You didn't expect our base to be out in the open, did you?" Dillan asked upon seeing the look of confusion on my face.

"I don't know what I was expecting," I said. "I've never been around a secret base before, at least not that I know of. It's not like it's something common, like a library or a grocery store. Hence the term *secret*."

"Well, duh, but surely you've seen a secret base in movies."

"Yeah, but they're nothing like this."

As the conversation grew into an awkward silence, I started focusing on my surroundings. Because it was almost winter, there was a thin layer of frost on the grass, and the sun was already down, though the sky still had a hint of light. There was a clear view of the stars, which I loved; I'd enjoyed stargazing for as long as I could remember. I looked at the base once more. It fit in perfectly with its surroundings. There were even trees and flowers growing on and around it.

"So," I said, still in awe, "was the base built inside the hill, or was the hill built around the base?"

"A bit of both, actually," Dillan answered. "The base was built inside the hill, but the hill was one of many man-made landscape additions from about fifty years ago. That's why it's so easy to climb to the top if you go around the back."

"That's so cool! And *nobody* knows about the base?"

"Nope, not unless they work here. Technically, a few people in the government are aware of it, since they're the ones funding our work, but most people don't know a thing about it. I don't even think the president is allowed to know about it."

"Wow."

"It's a clever disguise, isn't it?" Linda asked as she walked over to us. "I'm still impressed with it myself."

"May I leave now, boss?" Dillan asked. "I need to get back to the cafeteria to finish helping with the dinner and dessert rush."

"Yeah, you can go," she said. "Ley and I will be fine here alone."

"Why did you have him bring me out here? Do you think I have powers, too?" I asked as Dillan walked off.

"I wouldn't waste my time if I didn't," she said. "I can't explain why, but I have a hunch that you and I have something specific in common." As she spoke, a pair of large black wings grew out of her back.

"You have wings!?" I gasped.

"Yes, and I think you do too," she said.

"How do I find out? Would my wings be black, too? How do you—?"

"Try to relax yourself," Linda interrupted. "Oh, and you may wanna take your jacket off."

I took off my jacket and tied it around my waist. I took a deep breath and relaxed my muscles as best as I could. I felt the muscles in my back shift around. I started to panic and tense up. Linda put her hand on my shoulder and told me to take another deep breath.

"There's nothing to be afraid of, Ley," she said. "Just let it happen. Don't fight it."

I began to relax again. As I focused on my breathing, two big, beautiful wings appeared from my back. They were white as snow and they looked incredibly soft.

"Wow!" I exclaimed as I looked behind me. "This is amazing!"

"They're beautiful, Ley," Linda said.

"Thanks," I said. Though, as new as it all was, something about my wings felt right. It's like part of me knew they were there all along.

"Careful, Ley! You'll crash into the chandelier!" A child's voice called out in my head. A sharp pain followed, causing me to stumble forward.

"Are you alright!?" Linda exclaimed as she caught me.

"I'm fine," I said as the pain faded. "I just... I think I remember having wings, but I swear I've never seen them before."

"Maybe you're starting to remember your past," she said. "I sometimes get random blurs or even voices that kind of hit me, but it almost always causes a headache, and I forget what I started to remember soon after. It's like forgetting a dream."

"Do you think we knew each other like Savannah implied? Or were we separated at birth?"

"I don't know, but if we were together, then I'm sure you and I got along just fine. You're a good kid, Ley."

"You're a good kid, too."

"Kid isn't quite accurate. My file may say I'm fourteen years old, but mentally, I think I'm closer to twenty-five. My training kind of screwed me up; my way of thinking changed a lot."

"I can see that, but underneath the whole *secret government agent* thing, there's something else. I just can't tell what."

"Well, if you figure it out, let me know so I can bury that part of me, too." Linda laughed.

Things grew quiet for a moment, allowing both of us to collect our thoughts. Linda's wings looked gorgeous in the moonlight. I'd like to think mine looked just as good, though it was kind of hard to look.

"Can you fly?" I asked.

"Yeah," Linda said. "Do you wanna try flying?"

"I do, but I have a feeling it won't end well."

"If you fall, I promise I'll catch you. Just trust me," she said as she held out her hands.

"Okay."

I took Linda's hands and she began to fly. Even as she was pulling me off the ground, my wings were still. I focused and tried to move them. I closed my eyes as I continued to concentrate. I was getting higher and higher off the ground. I could feel the wind against my face.

"Good job, Ley," Linda said, sounding farther from me. I opened my eyes and realized that she had let go of my hands. I was flying all on my own.

"I can't believe it, I'm flying!"

"It's easy, isn't it?"

"Yeah, it is," I said, trying to maintain my balance. "But how do I get back down?"

"Slowly fly back towards the ground until your feet are touching. You may need to walk forward a couple of steps to keep your balance. Once you're balanced, clear your mind, and focus on the wings going away. Otherwise, you'll have to try to tuck them into your clothes."

I did what Linda instructed me to do and began flying towards the ground. Once my feet touched, I started to walk forward, but tripped, causing me to end up sprawled on the frosted grass.

"My first landing was bad, too. I ended up face-planting into a mud puddle."

"You're joking."

"Sadly, I'm not." Linda laughed. "You'll get better the more you practice. Just make sure you don't push yourself too hard right away. I don't think your wings are strong enough for long-distance travel yet. It wouldn't be *impossible*, but your body would be weak and tired after. Oh, and one other thing, I recommend cutting small slits in all your clothing unless they're lower cut around the back. That way your wings won't rip through anything. It won't be too noticeable with your long hair to cover it." Once my wings were gone, Linda helped me up and began walking me back to the base.

"Do you think Elizabeth has wings, too?" I asked.

"That's what we're about to find out," Linda said, "but I honestly don't think so; I would've brought her out here otherwise. Even if she's not an Element, she still has elemental powers, and no Element has ever had wings. In case I'm wrong and she does have wings, I left her with John, who knows how to walk her through it."

"Does he have—"

"No, John isn't like us, but he knows how to handle people like us because of all the time he spends around me."

"Are you two dating or something?"

"Oh heck no," Linda said, blushing. "John and I are nothing more than friends."

"How come? He's really cute."

"Ley—"

"Actually, cute is an understatement; he's *hot*. Like, all caps, HOT," I insisted, quickly wishing I hadn't said that out loud.

"I haven't noticed."

"Oh, come on! There's no way you haven't noticed that."

"We're just friends, okay? Nothing more than that, and we never will be."

"Is he gay?"

"No, he is not gay," Linda said. "He asked me out once, and I turned him down."

"Why would you do that?" I asked. "He's gorgeous, and you two are already friends. What could go wrong?"

"A relationship turned sour that also ruins our friendship. John and Savannah are my only real friends around here because—"

"You don't want to get too attached to anyone else? Yeah, I figured."

"I used to be more like you, so full of love and hope, but then the longer I worked here… I, well, let's just say my job did a number on me. I'm used to it now, and I find myself almost craving missions, but if I could go back in time, I'd give myself a normal life."

"Normal life has its own set of issues," I said. "I wish I had your confidence and leadership qualities. Maybe I'd be happier."

"Maybe if we'd had a sibling to talk to over the past few years, both our lives would be better," Linda said. She had let her guard down around me, which made me feel special and also made me feel like she truly was my sister. "Hey, I'm sorry about almost killing you earlier," she said. "I—"

"I was an intruder at a top-secret government base," I said. "You were just doing your job. We're good."

"How's your face doing after that punch?"

"It's alright. You missed my nose. My jaw is swollen on the left side, though."

"I have some medicine that will help with the swelling."

"Dillan already gave me some," I said, pulling out the bottle.

"Oh he did, huh?" Linda snatched the bottle. "…yeah, that's the stuff, but if you ever need any more, I got some in my dresser. I deal with swelling way too often."

"I'm sensing some tension between you and Dillan," I said as she handed the bottle back.

"He's a great agent."

"But?"

"But he was a horrible boyfriend."

"You two dated?"

"Unfortunately, yes. We used to be friends beforehand, now we're just coworkers."

"Which is why you won't date John?"

"Exactly."

"Uh, well, if you aren't looking to go out with John, could I ask him out on a date?"

"Knock yourself out, Ley."

As Linda approached the base of the hill, a beam of light came out of a hidden panel and began scanning her eyes. Once her eyes had been scanned, part of the hill lifted, revealing the door to the base, which opened after Linda's hand was scanned on another panel to the right of the door. Linda led me back to her room where Elizabeth and John were talking.

"So, John, how did it go?" Linda asked. "Is Elizabeth like me or not?"

"Elizabeth doesn't have wings," he said. "It seems like she can only wield fire just like we suspected. What about Ley? Does she have wings?"

"She has wings just like mine but white," Linda said.

"Wait, you have wings *and* enhanced strength?" Elizabeth asked her.

"Yes, which is why I thought Ley, and possibly you, might have wings as well," she said.

"So, since she seems to be more like you," John started, "do you think Ley can do something else?"

"Maybe," Linda sighed, "but I think we should stop for today. These girls have gone through a lot. They need to rest."

"Alright," John said as he left the room.

"How long have you had these abilities?" Elizabeth asked Linda.

"I've had them for as long as I can remember," Linda said. "Not that that means much considering that I have a huge honkin' gap in my memory, just like the two of you."

"Do you really think it's possible that I can do something else?" I asked, my mind still stuck on my wings.

My wings were wonderful, but part of me wanted more. I wanted something that could be even more helpful than wings, something that would make me like the superheroes I read about in comics and watched in movies.

"Yes, I do think it's possible," Linda said, "but we'll have to find out what your other ability is, if you do have one, on another day. Right now, we should be focusing on sleeping arrangements since it looks like you and Elizabeth will be staying here for a bit."

"Oh, wow, I hadn't even thought about that," I said. "Honestly, none of this seems real. I'm still in shock."

"I completely understand," Elizabeth said. "I, too, am still trying to wrap my head around this whole situation."

"Well, Linda, what kind of sleeping arrangement did you have in mind?" I asked. "Will we get our own rooms here in the base?"

"No," she said. "At the moment, we don't have any spare rooms, so I'm afraid you'll have to stay in here with me. The two of you can share the bed, and I'll sleep on the floor."

"It's *your* bed. I'll sleep on the floor," I insisted.

"Ley, you don't have to do that," Linda sighed

"I know, but I want to."

"I can't let you—"

"I'm gonna sleep on the floor no matter what you do, so you might as well take the bed."

"…thanks. Now that the sleeping arrangements are settled, do you girls want to go back down to the cafeteria and get some dessert? I think they're serving cake and ice cream tonight."

"I'd love to," Elizabeth replied.

"What about you, Ley?" Linda asked. "Do you want dessert? They normally have cookies available, too, if you don't want cake."

"I'm good," I said. "I'm just feeling pretty worn out."

"Okay," Linda said. "I'll send Savannah in here with a toiletry kit and a nightgown. I'll also have her add you to the computer system so you can use the hand scanners in the base. Elizabeth, I'll do the same for you after we eat."

"Are you sure you don't want anything, Ley?" Elizabeth asked.

"Yeah, I'm sure," I sighed. "I normally don't turn down dessert, but right now, I just want to go to sleep."

"Are you feeling homesick?" Linda asked as she gave me a hug.

It wasn't until she was that close that I realized her hair smelled like strawberries. She had obviously tried to mask the scent with something more earthy, but she couldn't hide it completely. I could tell by how gentle she was with me that what Savannah had told me before was true. Linda had a soft side, she just tried to hide it.

"No, I'm not homesick," I said as she let go. "I think I prefer it here over my home in 2017, but this is a lot to take in in one day. First, I find out that I have two long-lost sisters from different centuries, and then I find out that I'm some superhuman with wings. Like I said before, it just doesn't seem real. I guess I'm a little overwhelmed by all of this."

"This day has been overwhelming for all three of us, but we'll adjust," Elizabeth said. "Well, since you're not coming down for dessert, goodnight."

"Goodnight."

Chapter 4 (Linda)

I woke up to the loud, startling screeches of my alarm clock. Ley, who was used to this kind of thing, was unfazed. Elizabeth, however, jumped at the sound.

"What's that noise?" she asked. "Is it the Elements? Are we being attacked? What do we do?"

"Relax, Elizabeth, it's just an alarm clock," I said. "There's nothing to worry about. Well, nothing to worry about besides your lack of smarts when it comes to modern tech. If a clock scares you this much, I bet most of the other stuff around here will give you nightmares."

"Patronize me all you want, Linda," Elizabeth said, "but I won't let anything you say get to me. I know what a clock looks like, I know what a clock sounds like, and I don't see or hear a clock anywhere in this room."

Ley put the alarm clock on snooze before lifting it from my nightstand and handing it to Elizabeth. "The time is displayed here on the screen," she explained. "When people need to wake up at a certain time, they set it to make noise at that time. That way, they don't sleep in too late."

"That's amazing," Elizabeth said as she stared at the clock, mesmerized by the screen. "This is so much easier to read than a normal clock."

"I'm surprised alarm clocks like this still exist," Ley said. "I was expecting a hologram alarm clock, or a hovering alarm clock, or maybe an implanted microchip that wakes you up."

"I take it your only ideas of the future come from sci-fi movies," I said.

"…maybe."

"Well, I'll tell you right now, most of those old movies turned out to be completely inaccurate," I laughed. "They're called science *fiction* for a reason. Flying cars are still a no-go, laptops are still widely used even though hologram computers exist, and there are no sentient robots trying to take over the world."

"That's disappointing," Ley said.

"I'd love to take this device with me when I go home," Elizabeth said, still staring at the alarm clock.

"Alright," I said, "as much as I would love to have more conversations about alarm clocks or the future Ley was expecting versus the disappointing reality, we need to get going."

"Where exactly do we need to go, Linda?" Ley asked.

"School, obviously," I said. "Surely you didn't expect all the agents here to just drop out of school. Do you realize how suspicious that would look?"

"Wait, why do I have to go to school? Why can't I just skip today?" she groaned. "I don't even know what schools here teach. It's not like I'm transferring to a school in a different *town*; I'm transferring to a school in a different *time*. People here don't even know I exist!"

"Ley, I—" I stopped myself as I thought about how bad things could be if Ley or Elizabeth accidentally exposed the Resistance, or worse, their powers. "I do want you to be able to get out of the base and have as close to a normal life as possible," I said, "but it probably *is* best if you stay here for now. Maybe I can see if Savannah is willing to stay here for the next few days to give you two a crash course on the city, the school system, and everything else you'd need to understand to make it around here."

"Uh, I don't think we can learn everything we need to know in a few days," Ley said.

"True, but you can at least learn enough to blend in."

"So, just to make sure we're on the same page, Elizabeth and I are staying here with Savannah, and you're going to school today?"

"Yes."

"What about the Elements?"

"I'll be in a public place. They'd be stupid to come after me."

"Just be careful, alright?"

I could tell Ley looked genuinely concerned about me, even though we'd only just met. I wanted to say something witty, but instead, all that came out was, "I'll come back, I promise."

"When you come back, if you're okay with it, I was hoping maybe you could show us around the base?" Ley asked.

"Yeah, I'd be glad to," I said.

After throwing on my school uniform and getting Savannah to stay with my sisters, I took off.

***

I spent the entire day feeling anxious, though I had no reason to. Ley and Elizabeth were safe, yet I almost felt guilty for leaving them. By the time the bell rang at the end of the day, I was more than ready to leave.

When I got back to the base, Savannah let me know that she had explained modern lingo, transportation, and debunked quite a few sci-fi ideas that came from Ley.

"Elizabeth seemed pretty confused until I mentioned trains being the second most used form of transportation in today's world," Savannah said. "Since she's familiar with a significantly early design, she took interest in how they've evolved."

"Okay, I'm making a mental note that Elizabeth likes trains," I said.

"Ley likes them, too, but she was slightly less impressed since the Japanese bullet train already existed in her time."

"I get that, but modern trains go a bit faster, and they can be found worldwide."

"As I said, she was *slightly* less impressed than Elizabeth."

"So, where are the girls now?" I asked.

"They're in your room. I think Ley is trying to show off her phone to Elizabeth."

"Speaking of phones, will Ley's work with ours?"

"Surprisingly, yes," Savannah said, "though I had to work my magic to connect her phone to our service plan. Sadly, the time it takes her to receive messages is a lot slower, and also the picture quality is awful compared to ours."

"At least we don't have to worry about getting her a new phone, though," I said.

"If she gets stuck here long term, we will have to worry about it."

"But, as of now, we're fine?"

"Yes."

"That's all that matters."

When I entered my room, Ley and Elizabeth were both sitting on my bed. Elizabeth was playing a game on Ley's phone. She appeared to be in awe, despite the simplicity of the game.

"See, Elizabeth?" Ley asked. "It's super easy and fun, isn't it?"

"This is so cool," Elizabeth gasped. "The colors, the noises, even the movements seem so magical."

"If you think that's magical, wait till I show you the new way of gaming," I said. Both Ley and Elizabeth's eyes widened. "Ley, in your time, VR is still pretty new, right?"

"Yeah."

"Well, now the graphics are hyper-realistic, there are gloves that perfectly track your hand movements, and, for the masochists out there, you can turn on a setting to simulate pain if you take damage."

"Sign me up!" Ley squealed. "Well, not for the pain thing, but for the upgraded VR."

"Oh, and that's not even the best part. Most modern arcades have a VR room now. Your arms and legs are strapped into a machine so you can move around."

"I'm so confused right now," Elizabeth sighed.

"Let me go get a few headsets and some gloves," I said. "It'll be easier to show you than to explain it."

Ley was excited to throw on the headset, but Elizabeth was hesitant. When she did put it on, her character appeared. We were in a private chatroom, as I figured a public chatroom or game would be too chaotic. Ley had already switched her character into a fairy. I jokingly made myself into an elf to go with the fantasy theme. Elizabeth's default character was chosen at random and just so happened to be a princess.

"You're right, the movements match up perfectly, and the graphics are so realistic, I almost forgot we're using VR!" Ley exclaimed. "I'm ready to play a game. What about you, Elizabeth?"

Ley and I looked over to see Elizabeth on the verge of tears. Her character disappeared as we heard the sound of her headset falling to the floor. Immediately, we pulled our headsets off and saw that Elizabeth had dropped to her knees, crying.

"Elizabeth, are you alright?" Ley asked as she sat down next to her.

"I'm fine, I-I just… I'm just overwhelmed, that's all," Elizabeth cried. "I need a little time to process all of this."

"I'm sorry," I sighed. "It didn't even occur to me that this may be too much. Anything I can do to make it up to you?"

"For starters, let's leave that thing alone for a while. What did you call it again? A headset?"

"A VR headset. And, yeah, we can find something else to do."

"What do you like to do back home?" Ley asked.

"Well, I like reading," she said. "And sometimes I sneak into the theatre to see a play."

"I can work with that," I said. "I know I promised you two a tour of the base, but why don't we visit the local library first?"

I took the girls down to my car in section three. It was made of the same white metal as section one and was filled with nothing but vehicles. Both of my sisters were beaming with excitement until Ley noticed me reaching for the door to the driver's seat.

"Wait," Ley said. "You're only fourteen, just like me and Elizabeth. So, that means that you don't have a proper driver's license yet, right? Why are you driving us? Have you even started driver's training?"

"My job requires me to drive without having an adult ride with me," I said as I started to get into the car. "Because of that, the higher-ups have provided me and the other agents with a pass. If I ever get caught by the police, they'll get a call as soon as they run my license plate. Less than a minute later, I'm good to go."

"So, you just get off without any punishment whatsoever?" Ley asked as she got into the back seat.

"I wouldn't say that," I said. "You see, if I get caught by the police, it's because I did something stupid, like going forty when I should've been going twenty; not that I ever did that. Once I return to the base after getting caught, I'm usually greeted by someone in a black suit who threatens to give me a fine, suspend me, or even fire me. It honestly depends on their mood and how avoidable my situation was."

"But you *can* drive safely, right?"

"Of course, I can, ya' doofus." I laughed. "I only start speeding when I'm in a rush to, you know, save the world from aliens. Sadly, the police never seem to believe that."

"Gee, I wonder why," Ley said sarcastically.

"This is a car, right?" Elizabeth asked as she sat next to Ley.

"Yes, it is," I said.

"It's more comfortable than I expected."

As I pulled out of section three, I looked in the mirror. Ley looked worried, and I knew why. Section three was underground, so *how would we get out?* I pulled out of my parking space and began driving towards the back wall of the room. Ley's look of panic got worse, making me want to laugh. I pressed my foot down a little harder on the gas pedal. Ley held on to her seatbelt as if her life depended on it. The wall was quickly getting closer and closer… until it lifted, revealing an exit. The "wall" was a door that had been placed above a ramp that led outside. It was set to open automatically whenever a car got close. It worked on the other side, too. To prevent accidents, the door was big enough for two cars and there was a light on the inside that would turn red if a car was coming from the outside.

"I had you worried for a second there, didn't I, Ley?" I laughed.

"That was mean, Linda," Ley said. "You should've told us about that before we left. I honestly thought we were about to crash into the wall and die. You almost gave me a heart attack!"

"Don't be so dramatic," I said. "Face it, the only reason you're ticked at me is because you were on the receiving end of the joke. You would've found it hilarious if the roles were reversed."

"That may be true," Ley said, "but it was still mean of you to do that."

"You're right," I said. "I'm sorry, Ley. I guess I should've gotten to know you a bit more before playing a trick on you."

"Apology accepted," she said. "And maybe by the time Elizabeth and I are done with our crash course from Savannah, we'll all know each other well enough to pull pranks without any issue."

"I sure hope so," I said, "because I'm a prank master."

"Bet!"

***

The next two days were similar: I'd go to school while Savannah gave my sisters a crash course, and I'd hang out with them after. We watched movies, Elizabeth shared more about her life, and Ley started to open up about hers as well. I even broke my own rule and found myself feeling emotionally attached to both girls, something I feared would come back to bite me.

Chapter 5 (Linda)

A couple days later, my sisters were pushing to go to school with me. They wanted to get out of the base for a longer trip, and I didn't blame them. Besides, Savannah had gone over the basics they needed to know to blend in, and the school was safe from the Elements.

"And you're *both* wanting to go with me?" I asked.

"Yes," Ley said. "If Elizabeth gets overwhelmed again, I'll take her to the bathroom to calm her down."

"No. If she gets overwhelmed, get me, and I'll take her back to the base."

"Okay."

"I think I'll be fine, actually," Elizabeth said. "Yesterday, when we went shopping, the sink that turned itself on didn't faze me."

"That's an improvement," I said, "but if you do start to feel overwhelmed, please come get me. I want you to feel comfortable."

"Alright. If the situation occurs, I'll get you."

"Perfect," I said. "Now, I'll need to grab two spare uniforms so—"

"Why do you even need uniforms?" Ley asked. "Do you go to a private academy or something?"

"No, I go to a public school," I said. "There was some huge movement a few decades ago about the 'offensive nature' of certain clothes, and now about nine out of ten schools, public or private, have uniforms. It's honestly not *that* bad, but the whole situation speaks wonders about how soft our society is."

"And why do you have two spare uniforms?" Ley asked. "I get having one as a backup when you're washing the other, but two seems like a bit much to me."

"Every student is highly advised to have a minimum of two spare uniforms. The only issue with that is, they're expensive, even with discounts. So, since most of the agents here attend the same school, and since not everyone can afford two spares, we keep all of our spares together to help each other out."

The girls' school uniforms consisted of a button-up red shirt, a black vest, a black tie, a red skirt, black tights, and black shoes. Elizabeth never verbally said anything, but I could tell from the first time she saw me wearing it that she hated the design and expected something nicer. Still, she put it on. After we all got changed into our uniforms, we went down to the cafeteria. Fortunately, donuts and pastries were being served that morning, allowing us to eat quickly. Once we finished our meal, I noticed that Ley looked a bit anxious.

"Wait, do Elizabeth and I have school supplies?" she asked as we threw our trays away. "We can't just walk in empty-handed. The teachers will be furious if we don't at least have a pencil."

"I already thought of that, Ley," I told her. "I had Savannah pack backpacks for you and Elizabeth days ago. No need to worry."

***

Upon arriving at the high school, Savannah, who drove separately, pulled out maps and handed them to Ley and Elizabeth. Ley still looked anxious, unlike Elizabeth who seemed proud of herself for recognizing some of the different things around her.

"This is a map of the high school; your schedule is on the back," Savannah explained. "I share most of my classes with you, but I didn't manage to fit you into the first two. Luckily, you will have those two classes together, and Ley, you should know the drill."

"High school?" Ley asked. "I'm an eighth grader. Don't get me wrong, I probably *could* pass as a high schooler; I'd even be one if I were born just four or five months sooner, but that doesn't explain why you—"

"I skipped a year a while back," I said. "It's biting me in the butt at the moment, but I'll get through. I'm sorry if some of the classes are ahead of what you've learned so far, but I'm not about to leave you in another building all by yourself."

"That makes sense. What are Elizabeth and I gonna do locker-wise?"

"You and Elizabeth will be sharing with me for now. My combination is written on your schedule. Don't lose it."

"Do you have any classes with us, Linda?" Elizabeth asked.

"A few," I told her, "but for the most part, you'll stick with Savannah, and she always knows where to find me, should something happen. As for your first two classes, you just have each other. Good luck."

Ley looked like she was going to be ill as we walked closer to the school. I gave her a hug to calm her down. "You'll be just fine, Ley," I whispered to her. "And if you want to go home, just let me know."

I understood why she was nervous. If I had been in her position, I probably would've felt the same way. But in the end, how well she did in her classes didn't matter. It's not like she was going to be stuck with me for months or years. At least, that wasn't the plan.

We entered the school with five minutes to get to class. The black marble floors were filthy as usual. Gum, papers, and food painted hideous murals on the tiles. The school did have janitors, but not enough of them to keep up with the sheer amount of mess the students would cause. It was sad, as they were all old enough to know better. I led my sisters to my obnoxiously red locker. After dropping stuff off, Ley looked at the map and escorted Elizabeth down the hallway. Savannah and I went upstairs to Mr. Bradley's math class.

I envied the students who got the "fun" math teachers with colorful rooms. Mr. Bradley seemed to live and breathe the color beige. Everything from the carpet to the desks reflected that. Of course, that didn't reflect how he was as a teacher. I could tell that he genuinely cared about his subject and cared enough about his students to make sure they were all understanding the content. It was just hard for me to learn in an environment that felt as boring as the subject being taught. That's part of why I hated all the white metal used for the Resistance base. Oddly enough, the thought behind it was to "prevent distractions" by making most of the base uniform.

I sat down in the back of the classroom next to one of my fellow Resistance agents, Haley. She was originally part of my main team, but because of her incredible aim, I gave her a position leading her own team of snipers. She was quick-witted and spoke fluent sarcasm, which is probably why we got along so well.

"I didn't expect to see you here so much this week," she said quietly, messing with her dyed red hair. "You're normally busy with missions."

"I'm failing this class, so I have to be here as much as possible," I whispered. "I can't bring my grade up if I'm absent."

"Savannah carried you through middle school by changing your grades, right?" Haley asked. "Can't she do it again?"

"I guess she *could*, but I really do need to learn this stuff," I sighed. "What if I decide to retire from the Resistance? I mean, I don't see it happening any time soon, but if I did decide to leave, there's no way I could get a halfway decent job if I can't understand my core classes."

"Linda Smith, can I speak with you for a moment?" Mr. Bradley called.

"What did you do this time, Linda?" Haley asked with a smirk.

"Oh, shut up," I said with a muffled laugh. "Whatever it is, there's a small chance I'm innocent this time."

"You are so screwed."

I quietly got out of my seat and sat down in front of Mr. Bradley's desk. "What is it, sir?" I asked nervously as I thought back to the last prank I pulled (which may or may not have included the principal, some super glue, and three gallons of pancake batter).

"I've noticed that you've missed a lot of school this month, and your grades are suffering," he said. "It's not too late for you to turn this around."

"Really?" I asked. "You can help me?"

"Yes," he said, "but only if you're willing to put in the effort."

"Of course," I said.

"Well then, I believe it's best that you get to study one-on-one with someone. It's a lot better than those online video tutorials. Would you be opposed to getting a tutor?"

"Not at all. I think that getting a tutor is a great idea."

"Good. I know just the person. He's currently the top student in most of his classes, including math and science."

"Who is he?"

Before the teacher could tell me, John stepped into the room and sat down beside me. His school uniform consisted of a black suit and tie with a red button-up shirt.

"Ah, perfect timing, John," Mr. Bradley said. "I would like you to tutor Linda. You've been doing well in your classes, and I happen to know that you and her get along well. I've seen you two hanging out together outside of school, so I figured you wouldn't mind."

"Sure," John said. "I'd be more than happy to tutor her."

I was completely mortified. John was my best friend, but because he was so smart, I'd always felt embarrassed when the subject of grades came up. I didn't want him to know just how stupid I was. Everything in school seemed to come to him naturally while I struggled to do a single homework problem.

***

"John, you didn't have to agree to be my tutor," I said after class. "I'm sure I can figure most of this stuff out on my own. If I get stuck on something, there are plenty of videos online. Despite what the teacher said, I think they could help me out a lot."

"I'd been waiting for you to come to me for help for a while now," he said, leaning back against a red locker. "I could tell you were struggling because you would always change the subject when I started talking about grades. You only ever change the subject when you get flustered or embarrassed about something. I was hoping that you would eventually feel comfortable enough to ask me for help on your own, but when your teacher asked me to be your tutor, I had to say yes. Why didn't you just come to me yourself?"

"I didn't want you to see me as the idiot I am."

"You're not an idiot," John reassured me. "I've seen you work your way out of some of the toughest situations on missions. Do you really think an idiot could do that?"

"Well, no, but—"

"Just because you don't understand algebraic equations doesn't mean that you're stupid. And if you ever need help with anything, I'm here for you. You're my best friend; I'm not gonna let you fail."

"Thanks, John," I said. I headed down to my locker to get my books for my next class, chemistry. Ley and Elizabeth arrived shortly after. "Hey, how was first block?" I asked.

"Our class went just fine," Ley said. "We're about to head to our world history class."

"Okay, you're all set," I said as I pulled two textbooks out of my locker and handed them to Ley. "I'll see you two in your next class, alright? Try not to fall asleep during the history lecture. I swear they get more boring each day."

I went down the hall to my chemistry class and found myself in what looked like a mystical enchanted forest. My teacher, Mrs. Denton, was a huge fan of the fantasy genre and decorated the non-lab portion of her classroom to reflect that. Fake plants and vines wrapped around the walls, framing the periodic table poster and whiteboard. She even played forest ambiance before class started. It made me feel calm.

I, once again, sat next to Haley. "So, how did Ley and Elizabeth's first class go?" she asked me.

"Ley said it went fine," I replied. "Though I am a bit worried about my sisters being alone."

"Why?"

"I just can't shake this feeling that something's off," I said. "I'm probably just being paranoid."

"Nah," Haley said. "You're new to having sisters; it's only natural for you to worry about them, especially after all the chaos we've had to fight recently. We've had more attacks from the Elements in the past three months than we had last year, though they've never attacked us at school."

"True," I said, "but I think it's more than just general concern for my sisters. Something just feels wrong, and I can't figure out what."

"Whatever it is, I know you'll be able to handle it."

"Thank you, Haley."

After class, I met back up with John in the hallway. I was hoping to set up my first tutoring session with him when I noticed Elizabeth frantically running towards me, alone.

"Linda!" she yelled from across the hall.

"What's wrong, Elizabeth? Where's Ley?" I asked as she approached me.

"She's gone. They took her," Elizabeth said, still trying to catch her breath. "I tried to stop them, but they—"

"Keep your voice down, Elizabeth. Who took her?" I asked.

"This girl she was hanging out with… a-and her friends."

"Describe them to me."

"They were tall, and they all had weird-colored hair, like green, purple, and blue."

"No," I mumbled. "It can't be them, not here."

"Linda, what are you thinking right now?" John asked. "Do you think it could be them?"

"But it makes no sense," I said. "Why would they come here? It's a public place. They could've easily been caught by anyone."

"Who?" Elizabeth asked. "Who do you think took Ley?"

"The Elements."

Chapter 6 (Ley)

"This is a map of the high school; your schedule is on the back," Savannah explained when we arrived at the school. "I share most of my classes with you, but I didn't manage to fit you into the first two. Luckily, you will have those two classes together, and Ley, you should know the drill."

"High school?" I asked. "I'm an eighth grader. Don't get me wrong, I probably *could* pass as a high schooler; I'd even be one if I were born just four or five months sooner, but that doesn't explain why you—"

"I skipped a year a while back," Linda said. "It's biting me in the butt at the moment, but I'll get through. I'm sorry if some of the classes are ahead of what you've learned so far, but I'm not about to leave you in another building all by yourself."

"That makes sense. What are Elizabeth and I gonna do locker-wise?"

"You and Elizabeth will be sharing with me for now. My combination is written on your schedule. Don't lose it."

"Do you have any classes with us, Linda?" Elizabeth asked.

"A few," Linda told her, "but for the most part, you'll stick with Savannah, and she always knows where to find me, should something happen. As for your first two classes, you just have each other. Good luck."

I felt like I was going to be ill as we walked closer to the school. Originally, I felt excited at the thought of getting out of the base for a longer trip, but just seeing the school made me feel anxious. As I soon found out, I didn't hide my feelings very well. Linda was able to see right through me. She gave me a hug to calm me down.

"You'll be just fine, Ley," she whispered to me. "And if you want to go home, just let me know."

We entered the school with only a few minutes to get to class. After dropping stuff off at Linda's locker, I looked at the map and walked with Elizabeth down the hallway to Mr. Johnson's class. Savannah and Linda went upstairs.

"Where exactly are we going, Ley?" Elizabeth asked.

"Looks like we have math first," I said. "According to the school map, Mr. Johnson's class should be the last classroom on the left. It's room 104."

Elizabeth seemed to be even more nervous than I felt as we came closer to the door of the classroom. I didn't blame her. It was a completely different time period for both of us, though the situation was more extreme for her than it was for me.

"Don't worry, Liz," I said as we stepped inside the classroom, "we're only on our own for our first two classes. I'm sure we'll be fine."

"Did you just call me Liz?" Elizabeth asked.

"Yeah," I said. "It's your nickname. Lizzie could work, too. Which do you prefer, Lizzie or Liz?"

"I'd prefer it if you just addressed me as Elizabeth," she said.

"Alright," I sighed.

We walked into the classroom and sat near the back. My eyes caught all the colorful charts and equations posted all over the walls. It felt both welcoming and overwhelming at the same time.

I was able to recognize most of the concepts being taught, even if I wasn't good at them. Elizabeth, on the other hand, seemed lost the entire time. I had to help explain things to her when we were doing group work near the end of the hour.

"I barely understood a word the teacher said," she complained after class. "And this paper he gave us, is this homework?"

"Yep," I said. "Like Savannah explained, you solve all those problems at home and bring them in tomorrow for credit."

"And what happens if I don't?"

"You won't get any credit for that homework assignment," I explained. "One homework assignment won't tank your grade, but if you never do any of the homework, chances are you won't be able to pass the class."

"What!?"

"Yeah," I said. "Homework serves two purposes: one, it gives students extra practice, and two, it works as a buffer for your grade. So, as long as you do all of your homework, you should pass, even if you don't do well on your tests."

"That's absurd," she said quietly. "It'll take me forever to solve all those problems. We better not be stuck here too long. I absolutely hate this place. I would've rather gone shopping again than come here."

"Says you and every other teenager in the history of the world." I laughed. "You'll get used to it: the work, the stress, the tears, the lack of sleep, the anxiety, the depression, the—"

"Ley!"

"What?"

"Could you please stop that? You're not helping me at all. You're actually making me feel worse."

"Oh, sorry."

"So, where are we going now?" Elizabeth asked as she rolled her eyes.

"Well," I said, "we have world history with Mr. Ross next, but we need to stop by Linda's locker first so we can get the textbooks we need."

We retraced our steps to get back to Linda's locker, which was conveniently close to the school's office, making it much easier for us to find. Linda was already there gathering her textbooks for her next class.

"Hey, how was first block?" she asked.

"Our class went just fine," I said. "We're about to head to our world history class."

"Okay, you're all set," she said as she pulled two textbooks out of her locker and handed them to me. "I'll see you in your next class, alright? Try not to fall asleep during the history lecture. I swear they get more boring each day."

Elizabeth and I reached our destination right as the bell rang. There were no empty seats next to each other, causing us to sit separately. Elizabeth sat in the back next to a couple of boys while I sat in the front, right corner. Part of me was worried about her being left on her own, but I pushed those thoughts out of my mind and began studying the room around me. Maps were posted all over the ivory-colored walls, some plastered with notes. The burgundy rug by the door was covered in pieces of paper and dirt from shoes. There was something missing, though, something important: the teacher. The class was full, and yet the teacher was nowhere to be seen. I knew that teachers ran late from time to time, but after fifteen minutes of awkward silence had passed, I began to worry.

"You're new to this school, aren't you?" the girl to the left of me asked. Her red hair was brighter than a firetruck. A small strand fell in front of her unnaturally crimson eyes. Because of her intimidating look, I hesitated before answering her question.

"Yeah, I'm new here," I said nervously. "How could you tell? Am I that obvious?"

"Well, for starters, I haven't seen you around here before. Secondly, everybody knows that Mr. Ross is always late for his classes, and yet you look concerned about him being missing."

"Shouldn't he be the first one here? He's supposed to be our teacher."

"You'd think so, but he's never on time." She laughed. "He's lucky to show up within the first twenty minutes of class. I'm Briar, by the way. What's your name?"

"Ley."

"Well, it's nice to meet you, Ley," Briar said.

"It's nice to meet you, too, Briar."

"I'm sure it must be hard starting in the middle of the school year. Have you made any new friends yet?"

"I haven't had a chance to talk to anyone," I said. "Well, anyone besides my sisters."

"Not gonna lie, that sounds pretty lame. I mean, having a good relationship with your sisters is nice and all, but you really do need some friends besides them. You can hang out with me and my friends if you want. We're planning to meet up after class if you wanna join us."

"I'd love to, but we only have five minutes between classes, right?" I asked.

"Well, yes," Briar sighed. "Wanna skip next block?"

"No thanks," I said. "I'm not comfortable with that."

"So, you're a rule follower. I can respect that. It makes you a much better person than me. Well, since you aren't okay with skipping, can I at least show you our meeting spot after class?"

"It depends on where it is, I guess. Would we even have time for that?"

"My friends and I have a spot in the school where we meet. It's not far from here, and Mr. Ross usually lets us out a bit early even though he's never here on time. You won't be late for your next class, I promise."

"Okay," I said.

Mr. Ross finally arrived with a power drink in his hand. He took attendance before starting the lecture. Elizabeth seemed quite interested in everything that was being taught, and she even asked a few questions. They were dumb questions, but at least Elizabeth was engaged. I, on the other hand, nearly fell asleep halfway through. Briar had to elbow me a couple of times to keep me awake. I found myself starting to focus more on her and the purple cuff she wore on her wrist. She kept fiddling with it throughout class, which was miles more entertaining than anything being taught.

When the lesson was finally over, Mr. Ross dismissed the class even though a few minutes remained. Briar led me out of the room and down the hall. Elizabeth, still depending on me to guide her back to Linda's locker, followed close behind. Three girls stood by a black door at the end of the hall, waiting for us.

"Who's the new girl, Briar?" one of the girls asked.

"Everyone," said Briar as we drew nearer, "this is Ley. Ley, this is Misty, Daisy, and Windy."

Each girl, like Briar, looked a bit off. Misty had dark blue hair that matched her eyes. Her bangs were evenly cut and fell just above her eyebrows. Windy had pale skin and wavy, purple hair, part of which was pulled into a high ponytail. Like Misty, her hair matched her eyes. Daisy had dark skin and emerald green eyes. Her thick, green dreads were put into a high ponytail.

I knew many teens who had dyed their hair, but these girls were different; everything looked natural. The roots were perfectly covered, and their eyebrows matched their hair. It was at that moment that I remembered what John had said the day before about the Elements. Blue could represent water, green could be earth, purple could be wind, and red could be fire. I tried to calm myself down as I had no real reason to believe those girls were Elements.

"Who's the other girl with you, Ley? Is she one of your sisters?" Daisy asked.

"Yes, Elizabeth is my… wait a second, how did you know that I have sisters? I only told Briar about that, and even then, I didn't say one of them was in my class."

"Well, you both just look so… identical," Daisy said hesitantly. "I just assumed you were related."

That was enough to confirm my suspicions; those girls were definitely Elements. I figured they knew Linda was my other sister as they'd have no reason to target me otherwise. While I wanted to know how they knew about me and Elizabeth, I knew that escaping them was more important at the moment. I needed to find a way to leave without letting them know I was onto them.

"It's been nice meeting you girls, but Elizabeth and I should be going," I said.

"We should?" she asked.

"Yes. We should go *right now*," I said, shooting Elizabeth a nervous glance.

"Oh, uh, yeah," she said, catching on. "We're new here and we wouldn't want to make a negative first impression on our teachers by being late, would we?"

"Aw, that's too bad, girls," Misty said. "I wanted to get to know you, but I guess we can do that later. Before you leave, would you at least like to see our meeting spot?"

She pulled out a key and unlocked the door by the end of the hall. Daisy and Windy went inside. Misty gestured for us to follow.

"We'd love to, really, but we have to go," I insisted.

The bell rang and students came out from every direction, giving Elizabeth and I the perfect means of escape.

"Elizabeth, run!" I yelled.

Elizabeth took off down the hall. I followed close behind her. We had almost made it to the stairs when Briar grabbed my arm. I tried to free myself, but her grip was too strong for me to escape. I looked over at Elizabeth, who had just reached the stairs. By the time she realized I wasn't with her, it was too late. More students had entered the hall, pushing her farther and farther away as they fought to get to their lockers. Briar dragged me back to the door and pushed me inside. Much to my surprise, the room was completely empty and had no windows.

"Do you realize how many people just saw that?" I asked.

"They were too busy to notice," Daisy said. "And if they did notice, then they didn't care. They probably think we're trying to ditch class or something."

"Not to mention, Misty is playing lookout at the moment," Windy added. "Anybody who gets curious and tries to get into this room will find themselves stuffed in a locker, if they're lucky."

"This room is a dead end, you morons," I said with an arrogant smirk. "You won't get away with whatever it is you're trying to do. You've messed up big time."

"No, Ley," Briar said as she thrust a small needle into my neck. "We haven't messed up at all. This room isn't a dead end for *us*."

I felt dizzy and nauseous. The room began to spin around me. I could see each of the Elements grinning at me as it got worse. Briar's skin appeared to have turned orange, Daisy's skin looked green, and Windy's skin looked purple. It was hard for me to tell what was real and what was just a hallucination as the room became more and more of a blur. An ear-splitting ring was all that I could hear. My legs went numb, causing me to fall to my knees and then onto the cold floor. I fought to stay conscious, but everything around me slowly faded to black.

Chapter 7 (Linda)

Back in my room at the base, Elizabeth sat on my bed and tried to explain the situation through tears. I couldn't understand much of what she was saying, so I waited for her to calm down before questioning her.

"Okay, Elizabeth," I said after she stopped crying, "run this by me one more time."

"Ley and I went to our history class," Elizabeth explained. "She sat next to a girl with the most unnatural shade of red hair. Her name was Briar, I think. After class, the girl walked off with Ley and I followed them down the hallway. Other girls were waiting for our arrival: Misty, Daisy, and… uh, Windy was the last girl's name, if I remember correctly. All three of them had weirdly colored hair, too, even weirder than Briar's. Ley got this odd look on her face, like she'd figured something out, and tried to leave. The girls wouldn't let us. They just kept insisting that she and I stay. They also knew that I'm Ley's sister, which only seemed to alarm Ley even more despite the obvious nature of us being identical. When the bell rang, she and I made a run for it. Briar managed to catch Ley, but by the time I realized, other students had gotten between us, and I got shoved away. That's when I went searching for you."

"Why would they take Ley?" I asked. "What's so special about her? The only way they'd want her is if they knew she was somehow connected to me, but how could they possibly know that? And you said they knew you're her sister, right? How the heck would they know that? I mean, I know y'all are identical, but I've seen people who look like identical siblings that aren't."

I leaned back against the wall and slid down to the floor. The room went silent. Right after Elizabeth had come to me for help, I went with her to see what was hidden inside the room Ley was taken in, but the room wasn't even there. It was like it never existed in the first place. That was when Elizabeth and I decided to head back to the hideout, ditching the other classes we had.

"I'm sorry, Linda," Elizabeth said, breaking the silence. "I should've tried to use my powers. Maybe then I could've saved Ley, and—"

"No," I interrupted. "There was nothing you could've done besides getting me for help, which you did."

"But, Linda I—"

"If you would've used your powers in front of all those people, the whole world would've found out about what you can do."

"Maybe that isn't such a bad thing."

"Oh really?" I laughed condescendingly. "You think it would be great if everyone knew about our powers? How naïve. If people found out about what you can do, you would become an experiment in a lab, or you'd be weaponized. Maybe even both. Every single country in this world would want you on their side to fight off their enemies. You wouldn't be treated as a person or even a hero. You would be an object."

"Well, even if that *were* the case—"

"It *is* the case."

"Wouldn't you be willing to take that risk if it were for someone you care about?"

"I don't know," I said quietly. "As much as I'd like to say yes, I've never been put in a situation where I had to choose between saving someone or keeping my powers secret. I won't truly know how I'll react until that moment comes. Hopefully, it never will."

"The answer is clear to me," Elizabeth said.

"Really? So, you're saying that the right answer is to not use your powers even if it means someone you care about will be in danger?"

"What? No, that's not at all what I'm saying!"

"Because that's what you did with Ley," I said coldly. "Don't try to act like you're better than me, like you have the moral high ground. We all react to situations differently, even when the right answer should be clear. Nobody is perfect. Not even you, Elizabeth."

Elizabeth's face turned red. I knew I had crossed a line, but I didn't care. She'd watched as Ley was dragged away and then dared to lecture me about taking risks for those we love. I honestly believed that Elizabeth made the right decision, but her hypocrisy made me want to throw something through the wall. I took a deep breath and tried to calm myself down.

"Look," I said, "the truth is, there was nothing you could have done. You were being pushed away from every direction. Even if you did choose to use your powers, how would that have helped? You only just discovered them, and you obviously can't control them. If you had used them, you would've been lucky if you didn't kill Ley in the process of trying to save her."

"You're right," she sighed. "So, what are we gonna do?"

"I'm gonna go find Ley and get her back," I said.

It was around that time when Savannah came back to the base, skipping out on her last few classes. After hearing Elizabeth's story, she told us she believed that the room was part of the Elements' ship disguised by some sort of cloaking mechanism.

"So, if you're correct, how does that help us find Ley?" I asked Savannah in section one.

"Simple," she said as she logged into the large hologram computer on the wall, "the door may be gone, but the ship may not be."

"You're saying that they changed their disguise?" Elizabeth asked.

"Exactly," Savannah replied. "And even if they aren't in that same spot anymore, they can't be too far away."

"What makes you so sure of that?" I asked.

"Boss," she said, "we've been dealing with the Elements for a few years now. Based on their behavioral patterns, it seems as though they are using Ley as bait for you."

"Why her, though?" I asked as I let out a weak, nervous laugh. "How did they figure out that we're sisters? For all they knew, she and Elizabeth could've been transfer students from the other side of the country."

"It doesn't matter *how* they know about Ley being your sister," Savannah said. "What does matter is that they have her, and they may also be after Elizabeth, which puts her in danger as well. I suggest we have her lie low for a bit, at least until I can get the portal open to send her back home."

"We'll worry about me later," Elizabeth said. "Right now, our goal should be rescuing Ley from the Elements. She's in more danger than I am."

"Elizabeth is right," I said, "but I will personally see that her protection comes next. I don't want the Elements going after her, too."

"Okay," Savannah said. "While you're going after Ley, I'll be here trying to access any security footage from the school that could possibly help us. Call me if you need me." She used the computer to pull up the school's camera feed. Elizabeth and I went back into my room.

"So, Elizabeth," I said, "while Savannah is doing that, I'll—"

"Let's go save Ley!" Elizabeth interrupted with a smile.

"Wait, what do you mean by *let's*?" I asked.

"Well, I'm going with you, right? It'll be like an adventure."

"Hold on—"

"I never get to go on adventures, well, not proper adventures," she continued. "I guess technically Marina and I sneak out of the orphanage from time to time, but it's nothing like what this is going to be. When do we leave?"

"You aren't coming," I said.

"Yes, I—"

"No, Elizabeth, you need to stay here."

"Why? Ley is my sister, too."

"One, you'll only slow me down. Two, you shouldn't be going out at all. And three, just because I'm not putting you under some special protection protocol doesn't mean that you should go prancing around on a dangerous mission. That would be risky and incredibly stupid of you."

"But you can't do this alone. You need a partner."

"That's why I'm bringing two members from my team with me."

"So, there's no way I can change your mind about letting me go?" Elizabeth sighed.

"I'm sorry," I said. "I'll make sure Ley comes back, even if I don't. I'm prepared to do whatever it takes to save her."

"Good luck, Linda. Stay safe."

***

After changing out of my school uniform, I went down to section three to meet up with John and Dillan, both of whom had come back to the base with Savannah. We were all wearing the standard unisex Resistance uniforms: black suits with white button-up shirts and black ties.

"I'm hoping that you're both armed right now," I said, "because this mission is going to get messy if you aren't."

"We'd be really stupid if we left on a mission and forgot our weapons." Dillan laughed.

"Says the guy who accidentally placed his gun in the dishwasher and tried to shoot an alien with silverware later that day," John taunted.

"I was on kitchen duty again, and I was working on less than three hours of sleep," Dillan argued. "I'd like to see *you* do better, John."

"I could do better with less than two hours of sleep."

"Oh, really? Wanna bet?"

"Alright boys," I said, tossing John the keys to my car, "playtime is over. Let's go rescue Ley."

"I was actually thinking—" John started.

"You can tell me on the way there."

"No, I think you're gonna want to hear this now."

"What?" I sighed.

"I think we should wait until nightfall to enter the school."

"Why?"

"Well, we're going to have to wait for the school to be empty anyway, right?"

"Yes, but we can go as soon as the staff leave. Why wait until nightfall?"

"Savannah can shut down the power around the area," John explained. "If she does that, we can bypass the school's security systems, and the people who live nearby will be less likely to spot us."

"I guess that could work," I said. "I mean, the last thing we need is the police arresting us for breaking and entering."

"So, we agree, then?" he asked.

"I don't know. You really like to play it safe, don't you?" I asked. "I find that there's always more fun when we're being risky."

"Well, yeah, that may be true," Dillan said, "but being cautious is the reason that John and I are still alive."

"I'm still alive, too," I said.

"For now," he joked.

The three of us headed to the lounge to hang out while waiting for the sun to set. While the guys seemed to be laughing and joking just fine, I found myself feeling increasingly anxious the longer we stayed put. Anxiety always hit my appetite differently, depending on the situation. At that moment, I could've eaten an entire buffet.

"We still have a bit before it's time to leave, so I'm gonna see if I can grab a snack from the cafeteria," I said.

"I have a protein bar on me if you want it," Dillan offered, pulling a cookie dough-flavored protein bar out of his jacket.

"Agent Rollins, remind me to give you a raise," I joked.

"Really, boss?"

"Nah, I need to run all financial decisions by *my* boss, and he probably wouldn't let me do that over a protein bar."

"Okay, but if you *were* able to give me a raise, would you?"

"Only if you admit your hair is dyed."

"It's not dyed! How many times do I need to tell you before you believe me?"

"I'll let you know when you get there."

Dillan's hair had become an inside joke among Resistance agents. It was unnaturally red, like a fire Element's hair. Of course, Dillan was completely human, meaning that his hair had to be dyed (and re-dyed often since his roots were always red, too). Dillan always denied that, which is why we all picked on him.

*****

As the sky grew dark, and the stars began to appear, it was time to begin the rescue mission. I rode shotgun, leaving Dillan to sit in the back. The trip to the school was silent, besides the occasional cough or sneeze. I looked down at my weapon, imagining what I'd do to the Elements once they came into my sight. I was determined to have them begging for mercy or, more specifically, a quicker death.

My team had been butting heads with the Elements since I took over as the leader of the Resistance. While we had taken quite a few of them down, we still lost many lives. Luckily, the specific team of Elements we were fighting happened to be quite small, based on

Elizabeth's description. Not to mention, the mission was a simple rescue op rather than a full-on attack.

The minute we arrived at the school, I contacted Savannah through my wrist communicator. "Savannah," I said, "can you shut down the power at our location?"

"Give me a moment," her voice sounded in my earpiece. The streetlights and buildings within a ten-mile radius went dark. I used the flashlight setting of my phone to see where I was going.

"Thanks, Savannah," I said.

"No problem, boss."

When John, Dillan, and I entered the building, we went to the hall where Ley had been taken away. Sure enough, there was no door where Elizabeth claimed the event took place. I looked down at my wrist communicator. While it looked like a perfectly ordinary watch on the outside, the push of a button revealed that it was both a communicator and a scanner. I scanned the building and sent it to Savannah, who compared it to the real structural layout of the school.

"According to the computer," she said, "there is an added door just upstairs from where you are. That's gotta be the Elements' new location."

"Dillan," I said, "John and I are going to be the first to go in. I want you to stay behind until I signal you. When I give the command, I want you to go inside and get Ley while we have the Elements preoccupied."

"Roger that," Dillan said.

We crept upstairs and approached the door. Dillan went into a nearby classroom with his weapon drawn. I grabbed the handle of the door only to realize that it was locked. I signaled John to stand back before kicking the door down. Nobody was on the other side. There was only an empty room with no windows and no doors besides the one I had kicked down. John and I walked in anyway, knowing that there had to be more to the room than what it appeared to be.

"This has to be it," John said. "This was the only structural anomaly according to Savannah."

"It seems the Elements are toying with us, John," I griped. "There has to be another door in here somewhere. I bet they're cloaking it."

John and I carefully checked each wall, knocking and pressing to find some hidden exit that the Elements could've used.

"Listen to this," John said as he knocked on part of the wall. An echo was given in return. "It's hollow."

"Stand back!" I ordered. "I can punch through it."

"I can punch through that, too," John said. "It's just drywall."

"Yeah, well… I called dibs."

"Oh, you're calling dibs, huh? *Real* mature, Linda."

"Shut up," I said, playfully punching John's shoulder. I threw my fist into the wall, causing a large portion of it to break.

"You know, there was probably a way to open up the wall without breaking it," John said.

"See this face?" I asked. "This is the face of me not caring."

John laughed. I kept punching through the wall and only stopped once there was enough space for both of us to get through. Behind that wall, to my disappointment, was nothing but a large metal pad on the floor.

"What is this, some sort of trick?" I asked.

"I don't think so," John said. "I think it may be an elevator to the Elements' ship. That's the only logical explanation I can think of unless they suddenly learned how to teleport."

"If you're right, we need to find the button to… oh, there it is," I said as I pointed to a small silver button on the wall. "Not gonna lie, the teleportation thing would've been so much cooler." Before I pushed the button to go up to the ship, I called Dillan over. "Change of plans," I said. "Originally, John and I were going to be the diversion."

"Right, and then I was going to swoop in and get Ley while the Elements were distracted," Dillan said.

"But it looks like this is an elevator to their ship. I think we all should stick together instead of trying to enter separately."

"Agreed."

We all stepped onto the metal pad, and I pressed the button. The ceiling and roof of the school opened, allowing the pad to launch upward, and causing me to stumble. John grabbed my arm to keep me from falling off.

"Thanks, John," I said.

"Oh, uh, you're welcome," he said sheepishly as he let go of my arm.

As the elevator went higher above the school, the outline of a large vessel came into view: the Elements' ship.

"Ley better be alive, you monsters," I mumbled, "for your sake and mine."

I woke up in a warm bed with soft, purple sheets. My head was throbbing. I felt disoriented and nauseous. I looked around the room, trying to figure out just where I was. The walls were made of a dark purple metal. There was a blue dresser to my right with a small mirror sitting on top of it. A string of bright lights covered the edges of the room where the walls touched the ceiling and floor. The room felt very welcoming, which only confused me. *Why were the Elements going out of their way to keep me comfortable? Was it possible that I was rescued when I was still unconscious? And did I really get drugged again? That was uncalled for.*

The door to my room opened up and Misty came inside with a tray in her hand, letting me know right away that I had not been rescued. Daisy came in behind her. I noticed that Misty's skin was blue, and Daisy's skin was green, meaning I wasn't hallucinating at school. Misty wore a blue, open-shoulder top with long sleeves and a pair of white pants. Daisy wore a long-sleeve green blouse and brown pants. Both girls also wore a necklace with a square center with eight points. The main four points had a color representing the four elements. The top color was blue for Misty and green for Daisy. Both necklaces were white in the center with two Es back-to-back. The other four points on both necklaces were white, too.

"Why am I here?" I asked. "And why am I still alive? Do you need me for something?"

"We're just here to bring you some food," Misty said, ignoring my questions. She brought me a salad, a roll, and something that looked like chicken noodle soup, though I wasn't one hundred percent sure that's what it was. While I was incredibly hungry, I was hesitant to eat.

"How do I know it's not poisoned?" I asked.

"You don't," Misty said with an ominous smirk. "But don't worry, we need you alive."

I was confused at first as to why the Elements would need me. It's not like I could've given them much information. Then it hit me, the Elements were probably using me to get to Linda. It's the only thing that made sense.

"I'm being used as bait, aren't I?" I asked as I started to put things together.

"Yes, you are," Daisy said.

"How do you know Linda will come for me? I don't think she's stupid enough to fall for a trap like this."

"Your sister and her team never leave one of their own behind."

"How did you even find out that Linda's my sister? Like I said at school, I mentioned to Briar that I have sisters, but I never said their—"

"We've known about you and your sisters a lot longer than you think," Misty said. "Don't you recognize me?"

"What's that supposed to mean?" I asked. "I just got here a few days ago. I know you're one of my kidnappers, and I'm about ninety-nine-point-eight percent sure that you're a water Element, but other than that, how would I know you?"

Misty rolled her eyes and shoved the tray into my arms, causing some of the soup to splash out. The moment she and Daisy turned their backs to me, I sat the tray on the bed, grabbed my salad fork, and tried to attack them from behind. Right as I got close to them, Misty spun around. Chains made of ice came out from the wall and cuffed onto my hands, causing me to drop the fork. The chains started to get shorter, pulling me back to the bed.

"Fighting back is pointless, Ley," Misty said. "You're not strong enough to beat us."

After she and Daisy left the room, the ice chains melted away. I ran to the door, but it had already been locked.

"If only I had super strength, like Linda," I mumbled to myself. "Then I could just kick the door down and escape. If I were like Elizabeth, I could just melt the door. Instead, all I have is a pair of stupid, white wings. What good are wings here? Am I supposed to fly through the door?"

I felt useless, like some damsel in distress. I loved reading those kinds of stories, the ones where the princess needs to be saved by her prince. The issue I had wasn't that the princess needed saving, as *everyone* needs saving sometimes. My issue was that the princess never even tried to help herself; she just sat around waiting for someone to rescue her. I didn't want to be like that. If I had to be saved, I wanted to at least be of use to my rescuer, but I couldn't do that with my wings. I needed to find my other power, assuming I did have one.

Because I knew that using my powers would take a lot of concentration, I started concentrating on all the useful powers I wished I had in hopes that one of them would be my other power. I realized after a few minutes of standing around looking constipated that teleportation wasn't it. *What else could it be?* I tried super-strength next. After all, if Linda and I both had wings, why couldn't we both have super strength? I focused on what I wanted to do before throwing my fist into the wall. I was lucky that I pulled my punch a bit. If I had hit the wall any harder, I would've had some broken fingers. The next power I could think of was shrinking. As I kept concentrating, the room seemed to get bigger. Within a matter of seconds, it got to the point where I couldn't even reach the bed anymore. The room kept growing until I was the size of a bug in comparison. I felt relieved and nervous at the same time. While I knew that shrinking would help me escape, I had no idea how to grow again. I flew over to the mirror to see just how small I was, but I didn't see myself in the reflection. Instead, I saw a ladybug. *I was a shapeshifter.*

I went under the door, ignoring my fear of what was on the other side. Elements were walking all around the ship, but I knew that as long as I could stay a beetle, I'd be fine. I flew through the halls of the ship completely unnoticed until I reached a large room with a platform in the center. The room was supported by eight pillars. Each pillar was made of marble with either lava, vines, water, or dust devils in the center behind glass. They were meant to represent one of the four elements. There were hologram computer systems built into the walls. Three of the computers were occupied by Elements typing information in various languages from Earth.

I was about to fly over to the computers to get a closer look when the platform in the center of the room opened up, bringing Dillan, John, and Linda inside. The three Elements (an earth boy, fire girl, and wind boy) turned around. The earth boy brought vines out of the floor and used them to bind the team.

"I have them where we want them," he said to his fellow Elements. "Go get backup."

"I'm not leaving you, Clay," the fire girl said. "I don't trust them."

After a moment of hesitation, the wind boy ran off. Immediately, Linda used her strength to tear herself free from the vines. She grabbed her gun only for the fire girl to blast it out of her hand.

"Nice move, Amber," the earth Element, Clay, said.

"Thanks babe. Now, what do we do with these Resistance idiots?"

"You start by giving us Ley," Linda said, balling her hands into fists. The Elements laughed. "And then you let Dillan and John go. I'm the one you're after, right?"

"To be honest, I'm disappointed. I didn't think you'd give yourself up so easily," Amber said. "But, yes, you're the one we're after."

I tried to think of something I could do to help, anything. If I could distract the Elements long enough for Linda to get close to them, she could use her super strength to take them out. I landed on the ground next to Amber's foot and focused on changing my body once again. I turned into a mouse and, after noticing Amber was wearing sandals, sank my teeth into her foot.

"Ow!" she screamed before looking down. Clay looked, too, confused as to what was going on. Linda quickly charged Amber and threw her against the wall. She then grabbed her by the hair and threw her into one of the pillars before Clay tried, and failed, to tie her with vines once again. At that point, John and Dillan had managed to free themselves from their vines and quickly drew their weapons. With both Elements preoccupied with Linda, it was only a matter of seconds before they were shot and killed.

"Alright," Linda said, "this area is clear, but it won't stay that way for long. Remember, our only goal is to save Ley. Do not get distracted by anything on this ship."

I ran in front of Linda's feet. I tried to turn back into myself, but nothing happened. Linda started to take a step forward. Despite my urge to panic and run away, I focused on becoming myself again, having my own body back. I shifted into myself just as Linda's foot lowered, causing it to squish my face.

"Ley!?" Linda blurted as she jumped back.

"Yeah, hi, sis," I said as I grabbed my left cheek. "Thanks for not squishing me too much."

"Ley, how did you—" Dillan started to ask.

"We don't have time for questions," Linda interrupted. "We have Ley, and we need to get out of here."

After she helped me up, I noticed that the bodies of the dead Elements had disappeared. I wanted to know why, but as Linda had said earlier, we didn't have time for questions. Linda looked around for some type of button or switch that could power the elevator system but found nothing. Our only option was to find another exit.

"Looking for something?" an Element boy asked smugly as he stepped into the room. "It's kind of hard to escape when you don't know how the elevator works."

The Element's hair and eyes were as red as Briar's, and his skin was pale and orange, letting me know he was a fire Element. He wore a burgundy uniform with orange lines crossing through, like cracks on stone. He hadn't put any thought into his hair as it was sticking out in every direction. His bright red eyes began to light up with flames just like Elizabeth's did in the cafeteria.

"Get down!" Dillan shouted. He ran over to me and knocked me to the ground. Linda and John jumped out of the way just as the Element sent a blast of fire down the center of the room.

"Dillan, you can let go of me now," I said.

"No, I can't," he said, speaking into my left ear. "I have my orders, and I'm not about to disobey them."

Another blast from the Element caused a pillar in the room to fall. Linda picked it up and tried to bash the Element in the head. He ducked, giving an arrogant smirk. The glass of the pillar shattered after hitting the wall, causing water to dump out onto the floor.

"Dillan, please!" I begged. "I can help."

"No," Dillan replied. "Your sister made her orders clear. Our mission is to save you even if it means sacrificing our own lives. I'm going to keep you safe no matter what."

"You would really sacrifice your life for a girl you barely know?" I asked.

"Yes," he said as he held me tighter, "because it's the right thing to do."

"Did you really think *that* would stop me?" the fire Element taunted as he kicked a small piece of the pillar away. "I could've dodged that pillar with a blindfold on!"

"I'd say it worked just fine, dirtbag," Linda said.

"Are you kidding me? That pillar was a mile away," he bragged. "You need to work on your aim." The fire Element's hands lit up with fire once again, but this time, Linda seemed unamused.

"You are *such* an idiot," she said. "The pillar wasn't supposed to hit you. It was meant to distract you from John."

The fire Element's eyes widened. He turned around just in time to see John pull the trigger of a freeze ray. The Element was blasted back into the wall.

"He's not dead, just unconscious," Linda said. "But at least we know that the new freeze ray works."

"I'll have to tell Savannah when we get back," John said. "You know, you missed the opportunity to call the fire Element 'hothead.' Then you could've used 'dirtbag' as an insult against an earth Element."

"Ugh! You're right," Linda said. "That would've been a lot funnier." She and John walked over to where I was. Dillan still held onto me as if his life depended on it, or in that case, mine. "Dillan!" Linda exclaimed. "The fight's over. You can get off of my sister now."

"Right, sorry," he said as his face became red. His dark green eyes locked with mine as he got up, giving me a fluttery feeling that I knew wouldn't end well. He then helped me up and began dusting off his jacket.

"Thank you for saving me," I said. Dillan's face turned an even darker red, and apparently, so did mine.

"Hey, Ley, you better cut that out," my sister laughed. "Your face will be as red as Dillan's hair if you keep blushing like that."

"Nothing is as red as Dillan's hair," John said. "Well, nothing natural at least."

"My hair is perfectly natural," Dillan argued.

"No, it's not."

"Alright, people," Linda said, "we need to get out of here before more Elements show up."

Since Linda and John couldn't figure out how to make the elevator go back down, we were stuck in the predicament of choosing which door to go through to find another way out. There was one door at each end of the room, giving us a fifty-fifty chance of choosing correctly.

"So, which way do we go, sis?" I asked Linda.

"I have absolutely no idea," she admitted. "I could try to scan the ship, but it's so big that it would take at least an hour to complete. That's assuming that the Elements aren't doing anything to block our scanners."

"We're better off guessing at this point," John said. "So, Linda, it's up to you. Do we go left or right?"

Linda hesitated before heading right. The rest of us followed. When the door lifted, Misty was there. Without thinking, John held the freeze ray to Misty's head and pulled the trigger. Misty absorbed the blast through her forehead with a grin.

"That isn't going to help much against me," she taunted.

"Great," Dillan moaned. "Now we gotta deal with the freezy girl!?"

"Freezy girl?" Misty repeated. "There is so much more to me than—"

"Cool story, but did I ask?" Linda interrupted. "John, Dillan, get Ley out of here. I'll follow you after I deal with this glorified snowblower." Misty started to walk closer to us, a layer of frost creeping up from behind her.

"But we can't leave without you, Linda," I said.

"Don't worry about me! Just go!" she shouted.

John and Dillan grabbed my arms and dragged me through the door on the other side of the room.

"Linda!" I shouted as the door closed, leaving my sister alone with Misty. I could hear the muffled sounds of them fighting after we entered the hall, which only infuriated me. "Let me go!" I yelled, trying to fight Dillan and John's grip. "I'm not gonna leave her!"

"Shh," John said as he put his free hand over my mouth. "The coast is clear right now, and we'd like to keep it that way. So, please, unless you want to get us all killed, be quiet." He slowly removed his hand, allowing me to speak again.

"John, my sister could *die* back there on her own," I said.

"You think I don't know that?" John asked. "I care about her, too. She's my best friend."

"Then why aren't you helping her?"

"Because," he said, "she wants nothing more than to get you home safe. If we went back in there and you both died, her sacrifice would be pointless. If she's willing to risk her life, if she's willing to die for your safety, don't let it be in vain."

"Okay, fine. You *or* Dillan go back to help her."

"Yeah, so then whoever stays with you can get ambushed with no backup," John said sarcastically. "Linda may be my best friend, but she's also my boss, and she gave me a direct order. I'm gonna follow it whether you like it or not."

John's grip on my arm tightened as we continued through the halls of the ship. I found it odd that no Elements were walking through the halls. When I first escaped my room back on the other side of the ship, there were Elements around every corner. *So, when exactly did the ship become empty?*

"There," Dillan said as he pointed to the end of the hall. "Escape pods! We may not be in deep space, but we are a few thousand feet up, so there shouldn't be anything to prevent us from using one."

I found myself wondering how they could've gotten to the ship in the first place if it was so high up, but, again, there was no time for… *wait.* If I could keep John and Dillan from taking me home right away, then maybe Linda could catch up to us. I just needed to stall for as much time as possible.

"How did you get up here if the ship is thousands of feet up?" I asked as we drew nearer to the escape pods. "I know you used the elevator, but how were you able to breathe? Wouldn't the air be too thin for you?"

"There's an oxygen field around the elevator," Dillan said. "The Elements need oxygen just like we do."

"How come the ship wasn't spotted by anyone?"

"The Elements have some sort of invisibility field on their ship," John said. "You can see a faint outline of it as you get closer, but nobody on the ground would see a thing."

"Wow, that's cool," I said. "And how does—"

"Ley, quit stalling," he said, his voice turning cold.

Dillan, John, and I got into the escape pod. I looked around but saw no sign of Linda or the Elements. When John reached up to hit the launch button, I grabbed his hand to stop him. I wasn't going to let him leave my sister behind.

"Let go, Ley!" John exclaimed as he pulled his hand away.

"Please can we wait?" I asked. "Maybe Linda is okay."

"She doesn't even know which way we went," Dillan said. "How would she be able to find us?"

"She knows which door we went through," I argued. "She's smart. Surely, she can figure it out from there."

"Ley," John said, "I—"

"Please," I said with tears streaming down my face as I looked John in the eyes, "you said you care about her, too. You said she's your best friend."

John slowly lowered his hand from the launch button. "Five minutes," he said with a sorrowful expression.

"What?" I asked.

"We'll wait for five minutes, and if she isn't here by then, we'll leave."

"Thank you, John," I said.

"Don't get your hopes up," he said as he handed me a handkerchief. "I know your sister is strong, but the Elements are, too. She may not make it."

"But you believe that Linda meeting up with us is possible," I said as I dried my eyes. "Otherwise, you wouldn't be giving her five minutes to get here."

"Ley, just… just don't get your hopes up," John repeated solemnly. "That's how you get your heart broken."

I kept looking towards the other end of the hall. Despite what John said, I knew that my sister would show up. I had it all worked out in my mind. Linda would thank me for buying her time, and we would all head home together. Then I would be able to spend more time bonding with her and Elizabeth. Even though we had just met a few days ago, I already felt connected to Linda, and I wasn't going to let her teammates leave her to die.

John looked down at his watch and then at Dillan, who put his arm around me. I, feeling tired and anxious, leaned on his shoulder. I nearly dozed off as he gently ran his fingers through my hair. I started to feel relaxed in my vulnerable state. Dillan's embrace was warm and gentle, and I soon found myself tightly hugging him. As I wiped more tears from my eyes, I heard the door to the escape pod close. I quickly realized that Dillan wasn't being gentle and kind; he was only distracting me so that I wouldn't stop John from pressing the launch button. I sat up and shoved him away from me.

"What are you doing, John!?" I yelled. "You said that you would give Linda five minutes to get here! You promised!"

"I promised you five minutes, but I gave you eight," he said. "We need to go now. We're lucky the Elements didn't find us and attack."

"Just let me go back!" I yelled as I pounded on the door of the escape pod. "Let me go back and see if she's okay! I'm not gonna leave her! Please, just let me help her."

"I'm sorry, Ley, but it's too late," John said. "We can't go back now, nor would we."

Dillan tried to put his arm around me, again, to comfort me, but I didn't let him.

"Don't touch me!" I snapped, smacking his arm away. "You've killed her! You've both killed my sister! You realize that, right!? Now she's trapped on that ship with no one to help her."

The ride back to the ground was completely silent after that. John and Dillan didn't even try to console me, which was probably for the best. At that moment, I hated them more than anything. I glared at John, who refused to make eye contact with me, and Dillan, who stared out the window. I wasn't just furious with them but with the world in general. I didn't think it was fair for me to lose my sister after I had just found her.

***

The escape pod landed across from the school. After we got out, we headed towards Linda's car. John had the keys and drove us back to the base. I didn't realize until we got there that my hands were tightly clenched. All I wanted to do was throw my fist through the window of the car door.

"Ley, you'll have to go to section four," John said after we pulled into section three. "Dillan can escort you there. I need to report that escape pod's location so we can get it removed."

"Why do I need to go to section four?" I asked with bitterness still lingering in my voice. "And what was even in there again?"

"It's our medical wing," Dillan replied. "Because you were abducted by the Elements, you should be checked out. It's protocol."

"Oh, of course," I said sarcastically, "because the evil space aliens probed me while I was being held on their ship, and there is a slight chance that I could be pregnant with their evil alien babies."

"No need for sarcasm," John said. "This is serious. Even if they didn't physically harm you, it was a traumatizing experience. You were kidnapped, after all."

"The part where we left my sister to die really *helped* with the trauma, I'm sure," I said angrily.

"I've already apologized," John told me.

"And yet, I haven't forgiven you."

"What else do you expect me to do? What do I have to do for you to forgive me?"

"Bring my sister back," I said, holding back tears. "If you bring my sister back, I'll forgive you for everything."

"Ley, you know I can't do that."

"Then I guess you aren't forgiven, John."

"That's not fair."

"Oh, you wanna talk about *fair?* I've been trying to find my family since I woke up on the street with no memories besides my name, age, and birthdate. And just when I finally find my long-lost siblings, I lose one of them. So, tell me, John, what's fair about that?"

John started to say something else but stopped himself before letting me out of the car in silence. Dillan led me downstairs to section four and left me in the care of one of the nurses. I was immediately given a room in the hospital. It looked like a standard hospital room, which surprised me. Once I sat on the bed, I realized it *was* different from hospital beds in 2017 as it was significantly more comfortable and could move without making any mechanical sounds. There were also more buttons on the side of the bed. One of them controlled the holographic image on the wall beside me. Since section four was underground, the holographic image was there instead of a window. I set the image to show a sunset, which seemed peaceful, not that it calmed me down. I was clenching my hands again as I thought back to what happened on the ship.

"How could this all go so wrong?" I asked myself quietly.

A nurse came into my room with a menu. There were plenty of things for me to choose from, things I'd normally eat way too much of on any other day, but I'd lost my appetite.

"I'm sorry, but I'm not hungry," I mumbled.

"Ley, I can only imagine how hard this must be for you, but you have to eat. You can't just—"

"Ley!" I heard someone squeal.

I looked over at the door and saw Elizabeth with a big grin on her face. Before I could say a word, she ran right over to my bed and hugged me. I could feel warm tears dripping onto my hospital gown.

"Savannah told me I could find you here, so I came down to your room as fast as I could," she said as she cried. "I was so worried about you, Ley."

"Elizabeth," I said, "I'm so glad you're alright."

"You're glad *I'm* alright? You're the one who was taken."

"Well, I wasn't sure what happened to you after I was taken away, and I didn't want you worrying too much about me."

"How could I not worry about you?" Elizabeth asked as she hugged me even tighter. "You're my sister."

"I'll leave you two alone for a bit. I don't want to intrude," the nurse said as she set the menu on the tray by my bed. "Let me know when you've decided on something to eat."

"I'm so sorry, Ley," Elizabeth continued. "If I had just…" Her voice trailed off as she choked on her words.

"What're you sorry for?" I asked. "None of this was your fault, Elizabeth. It was mine for not putting things together sooner. After Linda and John told us about the Elements, I should've been on the lookout for them. And even if those girls hadn't been Elements, I still shouldn't have been so trusting of Briar. We were going to school in a completely different century. Becoming friends with anyone outside of the Resistance was risky and stupid."

"I just feel like I could've done something more to help you."

"There was nothing more you could've done."

Elizabeth gave me one more hug before sitting down on the edge of my bed. We were both silent as we tried to collect our thoughts. I, feeling awkward, decided to take another look at the menu the nurse had left while Elizabeth dried her tears.

"Is Linda in one of these rooms?" Elizabeth asked, breaking the silence. "I wanted to thank her for getting you back safely, but I didn't see her upstairs."

I felt my heart sink. Without meaning to, Elizabeth had asked the very question I wasn't ready to answer. I didn't want to face the reality that our sister was, most likely, dead on the Elements' ship.

"No," I said quietly. "She's not here."

"Oh," Elizabeth said, surprised. "I half expected her to pop in here to check on you. Do you know which section she's in?"

"She's not in the base at all."

"Where is she then? Is she alright?"

I could see the grim look in Elizabeth's eyes as if she already knew the answer. I tried to figure out just how to tell her, though I didn't want to tell her at all. Telling her meant accepting the fact that Linda was gone.

"Please, just tell me she's okay," Elizabeth continued.

"I'm sorry, Elizabeth," I said. "When Linda, Dillan, John, and I were on our way out of the ship, we were stopped by Misty. Linda ordered Dillan and John to take me to safety while she stayed behind to fight."

"So, she's still on the Elements' ship?"

"Yes."

"Do you know if she's…" Elizabeth choked on her words before she could finish her question.

"Dead?" I sighed. "I have no idea. They could've killed or captured her. All I wanted to do was go back to help her, but John and Dillan wouldn't let me."

"Do you think there's any chance that she's still alive?"

"I have no idea," I said. "It's a possibility, but it depends on what the Elements want her for."

Elizabeth and I sat in silence until Dillan walked into the room. He appeared to be feeling guilty, as I felt he should. He neared my bed and hesitated before speaking. "…Ley," he said, "I am really, truly sorry for what happened. If there is anything that I can do to earn your forgiveness—"

"Leave," I interrupted. "Leave, and don't ever speak to me again until Linda returns."

"But, Ley, she may be—"

"Yes, I know, she may be dead. If she is, then I guess you just can't speak to me ever again. That'll be the one good thing to come out of this whole situation." Dillan looked hurt. He seemed like a little kid who'd just been grounded for a year. *Was he expecting a different reaction from me?* "What is it?" I asked, curiosity getting the best of me. "What's wrong? Is the guilt too much for you to handle?"

"I just thought that we kinda had a special moment back there on the ship, and, maybe in time, you'd be able to forgive me."

"You think I'm gonna forgive a guy I just met because of one little moment we had?" I asked, rolling my eyes. "Yes, of course, because my burning hot love for you is going to wash away my anger and make everything better." It took everything in Elizabeth to keep a straight face. Her cheeks turned red as she used her hands to cover up her grin. "This isn't some fairy tale, Dillan," I continued, "this is the real world. Now, get your head out of your butt and leave me alone!" After Dillan left, Elizabeth couldn't hold it back any longer. She finally burst out laughing. "Why are you laughing?" I asked. "What's so funny?"

"Your *burning hot love* comment," she said, fighting back more laughter. "It was quite entertaining."

"Yeah, I guess you're right," I chuckled. "I actually enjoyed tearing into him. He had it coming."

"Get your head out of your butt and leave me alone!" Elizabeth exclaimed, imitating me. That only caused us to laugh hysterically for the next few minutes, which was a nice break from crying, though there did end up being tears from laughter. "So, what was this special moment Dillan spoke of?" Elizabeth asked after we finally managed to calm ourselves down. "The moment that he thought would just magically relieve your anger with the power of his *burning hot love* for you."

"You're not letting that go any time soon, are you?" I asked.

"Nope," she said. "Now, come on, answer the question."

"Dillan was just talking about… oh, it was nothing," I said, blushing. "I thought it was kind of sweet until, you know, he left our sister to die."

"Come on, Ley," she said. "What happened?"

"Okay, fine. When Dillan, Linda, and John arrived to rescue me, we were attacked by—"

"Wait," Elizabeth interrupted, "I want to hear the whole story. Tell me everything that happened after the Elements took you."

"Alright," I said. "I sure hope that you're comfortable, Elizabeth. This is a pretty long story."

"I've got plenty of time."

I spent the next hour explaining everything to Elizabeth. When I got done, she was confused, which I expected. What I didn't expect was what she was confused about.

"You mean to tell me that you thought the Elements' ship was like a cruise ship?" I asked, trying not to laugh.

"Well, any kind of ship on water, not a cruise ship specifically," Elizabeth admitted as her face turned pink.

"But how did you imagine the Elements getting to that kind of ship straight from the school?"

"I don't know. Savannah never covered that kind of thing in our crash course."

"Those ships are amazing, but they wouldn't work for space travel. That's why there are spaceships, which is what the Elements use because they're from another planet."

"I guess that makes sense," Elizabeth said. "I never thought about how space aliens traveled. To be honest, I never believed they were real until recently. I also didn't believe the future would be so… strange. I'm sounding like an old lady to you, aren't I, Ley?"

"Kind of," I laughed, "but I don't mind. I think you're pretty cool."

"Really?"

"Yeah, and I enjoy spending time with you."

Elizabeth began telling me stories about her life in the orphanage when one of the nurses came in. "This guy seemed downright insulted that I, a poor orphan girl, had rejected him, a handsome working-class man. He just refused to take no for an answer and started going off on me. Marina snuck up behind him, and—"

"Visiting hours are over," the nurse interrupted

"I'll finish the story later," Elizabeth said as she got up to leave.

"Please don't leave me," I begged, grabbing her hand. "I don't wanna be alone, not after what happened."

"Ley, if you need someone, you can always call for me," the nurse offered. "Elizabeth should go back to her room."

"No," I said. "I just want her to—"

"Would I be allowed to stay the night?" Elizabeth asked the nurse.

"Well, yes, but—"

"Then that's what I'll do," she insisted. Elizabeth brought her nightgown down from section one. After she got changed, she sat next to me. "So, where was I?"

"Marina was sneaking up behind the dude."

"Oh, right." Elizabeth giggled. "She snuck up behind him, pulled his pants down, and then made a scene about how he was being indecent in front of two women. Everyone around started staring. He was absolutely mortified."

"Please tell me you have more funny stories."

"I'm just getting started."

Elizabeth told me more stories about her life and the shenanigans she and Marina were always up to. She told me about her friends and enemies in the orphanage, and she even told me about some of her favorite meals. She then sang a few of her favorite lullabies and folksongs. One lullaby she sang to me sounded just like the one I'd hummed to myself before I went through the portal. When I asked Elizabeth about it, she told me that she'd known that song as long as she could remember, but nobody recognized it. Not wanting to freak her out, I ultimately decided not to tell her that I knew the song.

"One of the things I've always hated about the orphanage is the pressure to get married as soon as possible," Elizabeth said. "Other women have families with money, land, or even animals that make them more desirable. Orphans have nothing. So, the boys are encouraged to work as soon as they can, and the ladies are encouraged to marry the first guy that shows an interest."

"And, let me guess, you want to marry for love?"

"Uh, well, to be honest, I've never had any interest in romance," Elizabeth said. "Of course, nobody listens to me when I say that. I'm told that it's because of my age and that when I'm old enough to marry, I'll be ready. But I know I won't be."

"I'm sorry, Elizabeth," I said. "But look on the bright side, as long as you're here, you don't have to worry about that."

"Yes, I do," she said. "When I get back home, I'll be in trouble for being gone for so long. I'll be lucky if I'm allowed to continue staying at the orphanage. And if I get kicked out, I'll have nowhere to go. Then finding someone to marry truly will be my only way to survive."

"I'm sure it'll be alright."

Elizabeth went quiet for a moment, and I could tell she was fighting tears. All I wanted was to comfort her, but I knew there wasn't anything I could do. She took a deep breath and calmed herself down before changing the subject away from herself.

"So, Ley," she said, "are you going to tell me about *your* life?"

"There's not much to it," I admitted.

"Well, I'd still like to hear about it. If you're comfortable sharing, of course."

"Um, okay," I said. "My foster parents are *always* busy with work or away on trips, so they're rarely home. I wake up every morning, make myself breakfast, get dressed, wish I hadn't woken up to begin with, and then I catch a ride to school. I always feel so alone."

"What about your friends?"

"I don't have any."

"Not even one?"

"Well, technically, I do have one friend, but… if I'm being completely honest, she's been behaving like a bully, so I don't think she counts anymore."

"…oh."

"I've tried talking to other people, but it never works out," I said. "They all think I'm weird. Once, I saw this new girl fall and drop all her things. I honestly wouldn't have noticed her if it weren't for her blue hair. Anyway, she didn't have any friends yet, so I helped her out and invited her to sit with me at lunch."

"And she said no?"

"More or less. She got this weird look on her face and quickly walked off, mumbling to herself. Honestly, thinking back, she kind of reminds me of… of…"

"Of who?"

"Misty… She said she knew about us long before we came here. She asked me if I recognized her."

"You don't think Misty came from your time, do you?"

"I don't know. If only we had our memories. I think that would help me piece this all together."

"Well, whether that girl was Misty or not, she made a mistake by not choosing to be your friend," Elizabeth said. "I'm sure you wouldn't even count this since we're sisters, but I'd like to think we're friends."

"Thanks, that means a lot to me."

"We should probably get some rest now, and it may be worth telling Savannah what you just told me."

"Alright. Goodnight, Elizabeth."

"Goodnight, Ley."

"I love you," I mumbled as I began to doze off.

Chapter 9 (John)

Don't worry about me! Just go!

I woke up in a pool of cold sweat. My dream soon faded from my memory. I got dressed and found myself grabbing my phone off of my wooden dresser to call Linda, only to remember she was gone. Tears began to flood my eyes, but I didn't let them escape. I did what she wanted. I got Ley to safety. Yet I still felt guilty. I scrolled through my voicemails to find the last one Linda left me. I just wanted to hear her voice again.

"Hey, John. I just finished a mission in town and was wondering if you wanted me to grab you some lunch. I don't know about you, but I'm getting tired of the same cafeteria meals each week. Well, anyway, call me when you get this. Bye."

I remembered that day. I ended up going into town to meet her at the diner. We went back later that night to do karaoke as we normally did on weekends, though none of the other agents knew about it. We weren't bad singers, but I wouldn't call us professionals either. Our singing isn't what mattered, though. What mattered was that we had fun. Sometimes one of us would change words or sing in a funny voice to get the other one to crack up.

"I miss you," I said, playing Linda's message again.

Once I managed to collect myself, I decided to head to the cafeteria for breakfast. I didn't have much of an appetite, but I knew I needed to eat something. I decided on pancakes and bacon as my meal, figuring it would be the easiest thing for me to force myself to eat. After I got my tray of food, I ran into Dillan.

"I don't think Ley's ever going to forgive us, John," he said as we sat down at a table against the wall.

"We did what Linda wanted us to do," I said. "We saved Ley. That's enough to clear my conscience."

"We both know that's a lie," Mark, a part-time field agent, said as he sat down at our table. He had only been working for about four months, which is why he was only part-time in the field. During those four months, he managed to get himself placed on a sniper team due to his incredible aim. Linda sometimes borrowed him on her team. "Everyone knows something was going on between you and our boss," he continued, pushing his black bangs out of his face. "Most of us believe you were not-so-secretly dating her for at least three months now."

"We were only friends, nothing more," I said.

"But you certainly *wanted* it to be more than that, didn't you?" Savannah butted in as she, too, joined our table. "It's always been obvious that you like her, even now."

"Come on, you guys, I—"

"Stop denying it, John." Dillan laughed. "You're just making it worse."

"I'm not denying anything," I said. "And I'm surprised you can even joke about this. She's your ex-girlfriend, and she's dead. Aren't you even slightly bothered?"

"Of course I am," he said, his voice becoming stern. "I cared about her, and I can't believe she's gone. Joking about her distracts me from that, believe it or not. It's my way of coping."

"I can understand that," I said, "but I'm not in the mood to joke about Linda right now; last night is too fresh on my mind. So, can we please change the subject to something happier?"

"Of course," Savannah said. "What do you want to talk about, John?"

"Well, I… I don't know. Just anything but Linda's death."

Everyone at the table went quiet for a moment as they tried to determine what to talk about. They all swapped glances with each other but didn't look at me. I didn't mean to make things awkward, but their way of coping with grief was different from mine, and I knew that I was one wrong comment away from breaking. The funny thing is, Linda would've appreciated the joking. That's how she dealt with loss, too. Knowing her teammates were cracking jokes at her expense would've made her happy.

"So," Dillan started, "uh… when will we be getting our new leader? Do we even know who they are yet?"

"We should be receiving word about who our new leader will be sooner or later," Savannah said. "Though I have heard that my name and John's name are on the list for consideration."

"What will happen to Haley's sniper team when we get a new leader?" Mark asked. "Linda made that addition herself. What if the new leader chooses to disband it? I don't want to transfer to another team."

"Her team should be fine," Savannah replied. "I see no reason for anyone to disband…"

Savannah's voice trailed off as I left. Whether my friends realized it or not, they hadn't changed the subject much at all, though them being serious was more comforting to me than their joking around. I threw away what was left of my breakfast and found myself heading downstairs to section four. I knew I needed to talk to Ley after what happened. I needed her to understand why I did what I did and that it was what her sister wanted. Maybe doing that would make me feel less guilty for leaving my best friend behind.

When I entered section four, I was greeted by the nurse in the waiting room. The walls were the same boring, white metal as the rest of the base, but the royal blue chairs added some color. After checking in, I got Ley's room number and quickly made my way down the hall. I walked into her room to see her talking to Elizabeth. Ley's eyes looked red from all the crying the night before. That only made me feel worse. As I came closer, the sisters stopped their conversation and stared at me.

"Ley," I started, "I just wanted to say, once again, that I'm sorry for what happened on the ship."

"I don't want to hear it, John," she said. "I already heard Dillan's pathetic apology."

I figured it would take Ley more time to forgive me since she was present for the incident and was still recovering from the trauma. Elizabeth, on the other hand, should've been quicker to forgive me, at least I thought she should've. As it turned out, I was quite wrong.

"Elizabeth, I'm really—"

"I don't want to hear it either," Elizabeth interrupted as she held Ley's hand. "Neither of us are ready to forgive you, so stop wasting your breath."

"But—"

"Stop pestering my sister and leave us alone," she said coldly, interrupting me once again.

"Just hear me out," I pleaded.

"Okay, John," Ley said. "You get five minutes. Then, you leave whether you're done or not."

"I've known your sister for a long time. She and I were best friends. I stood by her through everything. I was there for her in school. I was there for her during countless missions. I was even there for her when she was ill. I was always there for her, and she was always there for me. So, when she told me—"

"Why weren't you there for her yesterday?" Ley interrupted. "Since you were *always* there for her."

"I'm getting there, Ley. Yesterday, I was there for her whether you realize it or not. You have no idea how important that mission was and how important you were to Linda."

"How could I have been important to her?" she asked. "She didn't even know me that long. I'm nothing."

"You don't know why you were so important to her?" I asked. "Despite some of the things she's said, she's always wanted to find her family. When those blood tests came back, she was in denial at first but was thrilled when she finally realized it was true. Do you wanna know where Linda went while Savannah was taking you to her room? She went to me. Linda came to tell me the big news, and she came back after you and Elizabeth had already fallen asleep. She said that meeting you both was the best thing that could've happened to her."

"Three minutes," Elizabeth said as she stared up at the clock. "Hurry up, John."

"She cared about you, both of you. So, I did what she wanted me to. I saved her family and trusted that she would find a way to save herself."

"If you really cared about her, why didn't you at least call in another team to go get her?" Ley asked me.

"You think I don't care about her?" I asked, raising my voice. "You think that I didn't consider sending a rescue party? I didn't just give you those eight minutes because you begged for it, Ley. I wanted to see Linda catch up with us, too. The Elements have been after her for a long time, because she's the one who runs this place. They used you as bait so they could kill her."

"What if they just wanted information out of her?" Ley asked. "Why didn't you try to contact her through your wrist communicator thing?"

"She would never give them any information about the base or any of us," I said. "Because of that, she's of no use to the Elements alive. And as for the wrist communicator, I *did* try to contact her. I got no response."

"One minute," Elizabeth said.

"Enough!" I exclaimed. "Stop staring at the clock, and listen to me! The Elements were going to kill her, unlike you who they needed alive as bait. So, I knew that if she didn't show up, she was dead. Dispatching agents would've been suicide, and Linda wouldn't have wanted that on her behalf."

"But what if she isn't dead?" Elizabeth asked. "What if—"

"Stop pretending like you've lost your best friend!" I yelled. "Neither of you knew her as long as I did! She and I were best friends. Heck, I always saw her as much more than just a friend, but she never saw me as…"

I stopped after seeing the stunned looks on Ley and Elizabeth's faces. The room went silent for a few minutes as none of us knew what to say next. I was half convinced that the patients and staff in the rooms nearby were eavesdropping, and I couldn't blame them. Without meaning to, I had turned my grief into anger and lashed out at two girls who were grieving, too.

"I… I'm sorry for shouting at you, girls," I said, finally breaking the silence.

"Don't be," Ley sighed. "You have every right to shout at us. We didn't fully understand how close you were to Linda. Elizabeth and I didn't even know her that long, but her reaction to us, like you described, that's how we felt, or at least how I felt. It was a bit overwhelming at first, but I was hopeful that I'd be a part of a family, one that stays instead of frequently abandoning me for business trips. I can only imagine how hard it was for you to leave Linda behind. Thank you for saving me, John, and I'm sorry for acting like such an ungrateful jerk."

"You don't need to apologize," I said. "We're all hurting right now."

"What do we do now, John?" Elizabeth asked. "How do we move on?"

"About a couple of years ago, we lost one of our agents," I said. "Everyone was looking for a way to move on, but nothing seemed to work. That's when Linda said something that helped us all. She said: *A loss isn't something you move on from. It's something you live with. How you deal with the pain you're feeling now is going to impact who you become later on. It's one of life's greatest tests, but together, we will persevere.*"

"That's beautiful," Ley said, grabbing a tissue from the table beside her bed.

"Aw, that's so sweet," sounded a familiar voice, "the three of you crying over me."

Ley, Elizabeth, and I slowly looked towards the door. I couldn't believe my eyes. Linda was standing there with a smile on her face.

"Linda, you're alive!?" Ley squealed.

"Did you really think it was going to be that easy for the Elements to kill me?" she asked.

"Linda," I said, "I'm sorry that I left—"

"You don't have any reason to be sorry, John," she said, cutting me off. "You did exactly what I wanted you to do."

She came closer and hugged me. I was gentle as I put my arms around her, because I wasn't sure what injuries she may have had from her fight with Misty. Even as I held her in my arms, I still couldn't believe that she was alive. *How did she manage to escape the Elements' ship?* In the end, I determined that how Linda escaped didn't matter. What did matter was that my best friend had, in a way, come back from the dead.

"Linda, I'm so glad you're okay," Ley said. "I tried to buy you some time on the ship, but after a while, John and Dillan wouldn't let me hang around anymore."

"Yeah, I know. Dillan told me all about it," she said as she let go of me. "And, to be honest, I'm disappointed in you, Ley. I was willing to endanger my life to save yours. Then what do you do? You put not only yourself but Dillan and John in danger by making them wait for me."

"But the hallway was clear."

"I don't care!" Linda yelled. "What if someone had found you? They could've killed you all before anyone would've had a chance to hit the launch button and escape. What you did was reckless and foolish."

"I just wanted to help you," Ley cried. "I didn't mean to put the rest of the team in danger. I'm sorry."

"I know you are, Ley," Linda sighed. "After everything that's happened, it has become clear to me that you and Elizabeth aren't safe here. So, once Savannah figures out how to get you both back to your own times, I'll make sure that you'll *never* be able to come here again."

"Don't you think that's a bit harsh?" Elizabeth asked.

"I'm doing this for your safety," she replied. "I will not apologize or even feel guilty for wanting what's best for you." Linda grabbed my hand and dragged me out of the room, leaving Ley and Elizabeth alone in tears.

Chapter 10 (Elizabeth)

I tried to come up with some way to console Ley. I was hurt by Linda's decision, too, but Ley seemed to be taking the news even worse. I put my arm around her and brushed a small strand of hair out of her face.

"We may not be able to see Linda anymore once we've been returned to our homes, but we can still see each other," I said as I handed Ley a tissue.

"How?" she asked. "It's not like we can open up a portal on our own. And if you're sent back to the 1800s, you'll die before you reach my time. We'll never be able to see each other again."

"Come to the orphanage with me," I begged. "It's not an ideal way to live, but at least we'd be together. Maybe we could find work and get a home. We'd find a way to be free to live our lives how we want."

"You really want me to go back with you?" Ley asked. "I'd need some time to think about it. Permanently living centuries in the past is a pretty big decision."

"Or I could go with you and live centuries in the future," I suggested.

"No. I couldn't ask that of you. You have a friend. I have neglectful foster parents and a bully. The only thing good about my time is the technology. If we stick together, then we're both going to the orphanage. I just… I need to think it over."

"And you have plenty of time to do so," Savannah butted in as she walked into the room.

"What's with her always popping up out of nowhere?" Ley mumbled to me, almost causing me to laugh.

"I couldn't help but overhear your conversation," Savannah continued. "Your sister can make demands all she wants, but it won't make the process quicker. I still haven't found a way to open the portals." She came closer to the bed to hand Ley a light blue paper and a pen. "By the way, Ley, the hospital is finally releasing you. Here's the form. Your sister already signed off on it, but your signature is needed, too."

Ley signed her name on the form and handed it back to Savannah. It surprised me that Linda decided to release Ley after the conversation that had just taken place. I half expected her to keep Ley in the hospital longer out of sheer spite.

Ley changed back into her regular clothes, and the two of us went to the cafeteria for breakfast. She seemed off to me, but I dismissed it at first because I figured she was just hungry. After she had eaten about half of her meal, it became more apparent to me that something was bothering her. I began to worry. I knew that she was either anxious about Linda sending us home or she was dealing with the trauma of her abduction. I was about to ask her about it when she spoke up on her own.

"Elizabeth, did you think Linda was acting a bit strange?"

"Well, I think she overreacted a bit," I told her, "but I wouldn't necessarily call it strange. After what she'd been through to save you, I'm sure she thought her harsh words were justified. Not that I agree with what she said."

"It's not her anger that was strange to me," Ley continued. "I completely understand her reasons for being upset. What I found strange was that she didn't bother to ask how I'm doing. She didn't even ask about anything that happened to me while I was being held captive on the Elements' ship."

"I guess that *is* a little odd," I agreed.

"It's more than just a little odd. John had just explained all those things that Linda told him about us and how happy she felt when we arrived here. John said that saving me was important to her, and yet she didn't care enough to ask how I'm doing?"

"Perhaps John was exaggerating when he described our sister's reaction," I said before taking a sip of my orange juice.

"Maybe," Ley said, "but I can't shake this feeling that something's not right with her. She just seemed so different compared to how she acted a few days ago."

"She was angry."

"Well, yes, but just because you're angry with someone doesn't mean that you don't love them or care about their wellbeing anymore."

"She said she was sending us away for our safety."

"Yes, she *said* that, but I don't think she meant it," Ley said. "Her tone was off. Just trust me when I say something's wrong with her."

"If it will ease your conscience, I'll keep an eye out for any strange behavior from Linda," I offered.

"Thank you, Elizabeth."

***

After Ley and I finished our pancake stacks, we looked for something to do. We would've considered doing something with Linda, but she was still angry with Ley. So, we needed to find something else to do to pass the time on our own. Ley suggested that she continue showing me all the cool features on her phone, which she'd accidentally left in Linda's room the day she was captured. I liked the idea, so Ley and I went up to section one. As we approached the door to our sister's room, we could hear Linda talking to someone whose voice we couldn't recognize.

"Have you managed to get any information out of her?" Linda asked.

"Not yet," the voice said. "She isn't being the most cooperative, but we'll break her soon enough. We're willing to do whatever it takes."

"We could always threaten to hurt her sisters."

"That's not the plan."

"What plan are they talking about?" I asked.

"Shh! I'm trying to listen," Ley said.

"Speaking of the sisters," the voice continued, "aren't they gone already?"

"Not yet," Linda said. "Nobody in this base knows how to open the portals to send them home. Do you want me to do it myself?"

"It would look too suspicious if Linda magically knew how to open the portals. So, get involved in the effort, and do your best to steer the team in the right direction. Let me know when Ley and Elizabeth are gone."

"Understood," Linda said. "And even though we don't intend to harm them, we can still make Linda think that we will."

"I'll pass that idea along to Briar."

And with that, the conversation ended. It took a few seconds for me to even process what I just heard. Ley gave me a nervous look, which I returned.

"So, the reason Linda has been acting so strange is because she isn't Linda?" she whispered.

"B-but how is that even possible?" I asked.

Ley and I heard Linda walking towards the door. We bolted for section two, but by the time Ley put her hand on the scanner, Linda's door had already opened.

"How long have you two been outside my door?" the fake Linda asked before we could reach the stairs.

"We have no idea what you're talking about," I lied as Ley and I spun around to face her. "Ley and I were just having a conversation out here in section one."

My lie wasn't fooling anyone. The nervous look on my face and Ley's gave us away. The fake Linda pulled out a gun.

"Get in my room, now," she ordered before pointing the gun at our heads and leading us into our sister's room. "Get on your knees, put your hands behind your head, and interlace your fingers."

"What is this, one of those late-night cop shows?" Ley asked. "If you're going to hold us hostage or kill us, then you at least owe us an explanation. Who are you and what did you do with our sister?"

"Dramatic explanations seem a bit cliché, don't you think?" she asked. Her skin slowly turned green, revealing that her face was a mask. She peeled it off along with her wig, revealing her thick, curly hair. "I don't even know why I'm still holding this," she laughed as she tossed the gun onto Linda's bed.

Ley and I had our backs turned to the Element but could hear her pressing buttons on her communication device. This time, someone else answered. After hearing the situation, she was ordered to do what she thought was necessary. Unfortunately for Ley and I, the Element found it necessary to kill us.

"Kill me and let Elizabeth go," Ley pleaded. "She's from the 1800s. Her technology is extremely outdated compared to the technology here, so she'd have no way to return or even send a message to anyone from this time. I'm the one that needs to be killed, not her."

"I can't let you do that," I told her. "I can't let you die for me, not after all you've done to make me feel at home here."

"She won't have to die for anyone," the Element interrupted, "because I'm killing you both. To be honest, I didn't understand why you'd be kept alive to begin with. If you got here once, you can get here again. Any last words?"

"Ley," I said, "I didn't know you for very long, but I know we would've grown quite close. I'm glad I had a chance to meet you."

"Elizabeth," Ley said, "I wish we had more time together. I was seriously considering going to the orphanage with you. Now, it seems our happy future is *going up in flames*." She gave me a wink, and I then realized what she meant. Ley wanted me to use my powers, or at least try to. I couldn't control my powers too well, but I knew that it was our only chance of escaping the Element.

"Get up!" she yelled.

Ley and I obeyed. I took a deep breath, tried to concentrate, spun around, and sent a fiery blast towards the Element. Unfortunately, the flames went out before they could reach her.

"Well, that wasn't exactly the rescue I was hoping for," Ley sighed. "Thanks for trying, though, Elizabeth."

The Element raised her hands to use her powers, but before she could do anything, the door opened, and John entered the room.

"Hey, Linda, I was just wondering if you'd like to—" John said, becoming speechless when he saw what was happening.

He reached for his weapon, but the Element turned and sent a giant thorn deep into his side. While her back was turned, Ley and I used the opportunity to attack her from behind. Ley took the gun off Linda's bed and shot the Element, killing her instantly. The look of shock and horror on Ley's face was unforgettable, but it only lasted a moment before she sprung back into action.

"John, are you okay?" she shrieked as she ran up to him.

"I need to get to section four," he groaned as Ley examined his wound.

"Is there anything I can do to help?" I asked, staring back at the body.

"Yes," Ley answered. "You can start by getting a doctor. I'm going to need some help moving John down to section four. And hurry. He needs immediate medical attention."

Chapter 11 (Ley)

I sat by Elizabeth in the waiting room of section four. Even though many hours had passed, she was still freaked out about the incident with the Element. I didn't blame her. While she wasn't really our sister, it was still disturbing to see her dead body. Neither of us had an appetite after that.

"How am I going to make it around here?" Elizabeth asked, burying her face in her hands. "The Elements want us dead, our sister is gone, John was hurt, I can't properly use my powers, and I just want to go home! What am I gonna do, Ley?"

"Don't panic, Elizabeth," I said. "Everything will be fine. We'll figure it all out soon enough."

Around that time, one of the nurses came out to speak to us. She and the rest of the medical staff were the only ones who appeared to be over eighteen. It made me wonder if they got recruited later than the agents.

"John will be just fine," the nurse said. "His recovery may take a while, but he'll eventually be able to work again with no long-term damage."

"That's great," I said.

"Tell him I'm glad he's alright," Elizabeth said.

"You can tell him yourself," the nurse continued. "He would like to speak to you both."

She led me and Elizabeth to John's room. John was sitting up in his bed eating a cup of jello. All the color was drained from his face. He looked as pale as a sheet, and his blond hair was messy like he'd just woken up from a nap.

"How are you feeling, John?" I asked him.

"Even with the medicine they gave me, I'm in a lot of pain," he said. "But that's not why I wanted to talk. I just want to know if the imposter mentioned anything about what happened to the real Linda. I figured that would give me some closure. I miss her so much."

Looking into John's pale, blue eyes, I found myself almost feeling guilty for crushing on him after we first met. It was obvious his feelings for Linda went beyond just a crush, and while I figured she'd deny it, I knew she felt that way about him, too.

"Well," I said, "Elizabeth and I overheard the Element's contact saying something about Linda refusing to cooperate. She's alive for now. I think they need her for information."

John let out a sigh of relief. "So, they didn't kill her. I've never been so glad to be wrong. Now that I know she's alive, I've got to get her back. They could be doing anything to her right now. I'm not gonna let the Elements hurt her." He started to get up, but Elizabeth stopped him and gently pushed him back onto the bed.

"You were injured, John. You need to rest," she told him. "You're no help to Linda in the shape you're in right now."

Savannah came into the room, looking down at her watch. She seemed almost emotionless as she approached John's bed.

"Oh, hey Savannah," I said. "Where'd you come from? And why are you here?"

"Someone had to clean up Linda's room," she said, sounding monotone. "Anyway, I decided to come in here to check up on my teammate. That is okay with you, right?"

"I'm sorry, I didn't mean it like that," I said. "I was just curious."

"How are you doing, John?" Savannah asked, ignoring me.

"I've been better," he said, "but I'm happier now that I know Linda is still alive."

"She is?"

"Yes, and I'd like to be a part of the rescue op."

"You can't help with an injury like that," Savannah insisted. "I'm sure I can find a suitable extraction team without you."

"Who exactly would be on this team?" John asked.

"Well, I'll need at least four people. Dillan has been on the ship before, so he'll be going. I'd also consider Mark, Haley, and, of course, myself. So, there's no need to worry. This mission is in good hands."

"Elizabeth and I can join you," I offered as I put my arm around Elizabeth. "I've been on the ship before, too, and Elizabeth can help by using her powers to defend—"

"That's completely out of the question," John interrupted. "Remember why I kept you from leaving the escape pod, Ley?"

"John, we know for sure that Linda is alive now," I argued. "Back on the ship, none of us knew that, which was one of the reasons why you said going back was too risky. Why can't I help out now?"

"Because if you're killed, everything Linda did for you will be for nothing."

"John, I'll be fine. Now that I know that I can shapeshift, I think I can be of use to the team. I want to help save my sister."

"Me, too," Elizabeth chimed in.

"No. Both of you are to stay here in the base," Savannah said. "That's an order."

"I thought our sister was the leader here, not y—" Elizabeth started.

"In the event of your sister's absence, I take control until a new leader is chosen or until your sister returns," Savannah said, cutting her off. "So, as of right now, you take orders from *me*."

"Last I checked, we don't work here," I argued. "So, no, we don't take orders from you, Savannah."

"And last *I* checked, you and Elizabeth are dependent on me to get home. I highly doubt that the two of you could figure out how to open the portals yourselves."

Elizabeth started to open her mouth to say something again, but a sharp look from Savannah caused her to go quiet. For the next few minutes, nobody in the room dared to say a word. The tension was unbearable. After a while, Savannah finally left to gather the members of the extraction team. The room remained silent a little longer before anyone attempted to speak.

"I'm glad that's over," I said as I let out a sigh. "Savannah really knows how to make people feel uncomfortable, doesn't she?"

"You'll get used to it," John said, "depending on how long you stay here."

"You mean she's always like that?" Elizabeth asked.

"Yep." John laughed. "She may occasionally crack a joke, but she's normally pretty serious when it comes to her job. I guess you could say she's married to her work. She's also a very logical thinker and doesn't always think about the feelings of others, which is why she comes across as mean sometimes."

"I guess I kind of understand that, though I don't know what her deal is about me and Elizabeth," I complained. "What's the point in having these special abilities if we can't use them to help people?"

"You and Elizabeth are just learning to use your powers, right? You can't expect to be allowed on a dangerous mission without any training. Savannah, regardless of her personality, is very good at her job. She and her team will do whatever it takes to get Linda back."

"Yeah, I guess you're right," I mumbled.

Elizabeth grabbed my arm and quickly led me out of the room. "Come on, Ley, let's go," she whispered in my ear. "If we're going to help Linda, we can't have John overhearing us. He'd just report us to Savannah."

"How are we gonna help save Linda if Savannah won't let us?" I asked as we went back upstairs.

"Your other power is shapeshifting," Elizabeth said with a mischievous grin.

"Yeah, and?"

"Does that mean you can turn into *anything*?"

"Well, I don't know for sure, but I think I can turn into anything."

"That's all I needed to know."

Elizabeth had a plan but didn't bother to tell me what it was. She just kept grinning all the way to section one. When we got there, Savannah was in the middle of briefing her team. The look on her face became one of anger once she noticed us.

"Excuse me," Elizabeth interrupted, "but I still think I could be of use to you."

"I already said no," Savannah grunted. "Now, get out of here before I have one of my teammates force you out."

"Technically, you said no to Ley's proposal," Elizabeth continued, ignoring Savannah's threat. "I have one of my own."

"I *said*—"

"Please just hear me out?"

"Fine. I'm listening," she said.

"Since I can wield fire, I *should* be immune to Briar's attacks," Elizabeth said. "I could be a human shield for you and everyone else on your team."

"What about Ley? Are you going to ask me to let her join, too?"

"No. She'll be staying right here where it's safe. While her shapeshifting may be helpful, she's already been through enough. Why put her through another traumatic experience?"

"Wait, but I—" I started to object, but Elizabeth stomped on my foot, signaling me to shut up.

"Elizabeth, stay up here for the rest of the briefing," Savannah said. "I'll decide whether or not you can join us afterwards. Ley, you won't be needed on this mission. Please find somewhere else to go while we talk."

I sat by the stairs in section two until the meeting was over. I couldn't figure out why Elizabeth had turned on me. *How could she leave me at the base when I could be of use to the team?* Twenty minutes later, Elizabeth rushed over to me with a smile on her face.

"I managed to convince them to let me go on the rescue mission," she told me, only rubbing salt in the wound. "They think my powers could be quite useful. So, now you'll just need to go to—"

"But Elizabeth," I interrupted, "you can't control your powers. Why are they taking *you*?"

"They had their doubts, sure, but all it took was a little bit of confidence to convince Savannah and the others that I'd be fine. Even if I can't properly use my powers, I should still be immune to any fire Element attacks. Like I told them, I'm a human shield."

"What about me?" I asked with a cold tone. "Did you convince Savannah to let me go, too?"

"Of course not," Elizabeth said. "That wasn't part of the plan."

"Why would you do this to me!?" I jumped. "Why would you lead me to believe that you would get Savannah to bring me on the mission only to get her to take you instead? I thought that we were a team, Elizabeth."

"Ley, please lower your voice," she begged. "You don't understand."

"Fine then, enlighten me. What do I not understand?"

"I figured that Savannah would say no if I asked about you, so I planned to have you shapeshift into something small. That way I could take you on the mission with me."

"…really?"

"Yes."

"That's brilliant!" I squealed. "Thanks, Elizabeth. I'm sorry I jumped at you."

"It's alright. I probably should've told you my plan before executing it."

"So, what exactly do we do now? When are we supposed to leave to go on the mission?"

"Savannah wants me and the rest of the team to meet her in section three in five minutes," Elizabeth told me. "Let's go into Linda's room so you can shapeshift without anyone catching you."

We went into our sister's room and sat down on her bed. Once we knew for sure that we were in the clear, I shapeshifted into a small, blue hair clip. It was strange being something that couldn't move around, but it was the best option we had. Elizabeth hesitated before gently lifting me up and placing me in her hair.

"I hope this works," she said before taking off to section three.

"You're two minutes late," Savannah complained when we arrived. "You're lucky we didn't leave you behind."

"I'm so sorry, Savannah," Elizabeth said. "I just wanted to say goodbye to Ley before we left. She's still crushed about not being allowed on this mission." I was shocked that Elizabeth could come up with such a convincing lie on the spot, especially considering the paper-thin lie she came up with when we faced the Element.

"Next time, though I doubt there will *ever* be a next time, we'll leave you behind if you don't show up at the exact time that I have specified," Savannah said. "Understood?"

"Yes, Savannah."

Chapter 12 (Elizabeth)

I sat in the back of the car with Mark and Haley by my side. Savannah was driving with Dillan riding shotgun. I kept looking at my reflection in the car windows to make sure the hair clip, Ley, was still there. I feared that I'd lose her somehow, but she seemed to be keeping her cover well. As the car accelerated, I found myself taking deep breaths to calm myself down. The speed alone made me uncomfortable, but I was also nervous about the mission. I couldn't back out, though; it was too late. Not that I would've left even if I could've. Linda needed me.

When we reached our destination, Savannah hit the brakes, causing us to jerk forward. We got out of the car and began unloading weapons from the back. Haley took a long-range gun, as did Mark. Dillan and Savannah took regular pistols and weapons they called "plasma pistols." They gave me one of each. Haley and Mark each took a plasma pistol, too, as backups to their other weapons.

Mark and Haley were the only agents that I hadn't been properly introduced to. Mark was tall with black hair and green eyes. Haley had hair almost as red as Dillan's, except her brown roots were visible, matching her eyes.

"I'm ready," Savannah said. "Let's go."

"Wait. How exactly do I use this?" I asked, gesturing towards my plasma pistol.

"Have you ever used a regular old handgun before?" Dillan asked. "I'm assuming they exist in your time."

"Well, yes, of course, they exist in my time," I said. "I've never had to use one before, but I do know how to use a handgun if needed."

"Using a plasma pistol is just like that, but with more damage," Dillan said.

Looking at the weapon, I still had my doubts. The plasma pistol was very different in appearance compared to a basic handgun. The handle was wider and more rounded, and the barrel was longer. It was also white with a purple muzzle and black panels on the sides.

"Honestly, those things look like hair dryers if you ask me," Haley joked, "but they are effective."

Savannah stared blankly as hologram screens projected from her glasses. After messing around with the screens, power to the alarms was shut off. I wanted to understand how it worked, but I was afraid to ask given the mood Savannah had been in. In the end, my curiosity got the best of me, and I asked, "How did you do that?" Savannah ignored me, rolling her eyes.

Dillan led us into the high school where the platform was. "We'll have to use the escape pods on our way back," he warned. "Because we don't know how to properly operate it, this elevator only goes one way."

"Noted," Savannah said. "Alright everybody, let's move."

Dillan waited for all of us to gather on the elevator before pressing the button. After he did, we began to rise, and the ceiling opened up. We were lifted into the sky until the faint outline of a large vessel could be seen. I was in awe, but that only lasted a moment as my fear of heights kicked in.

"This thing is safe, right?" I asked. "We're *really* high up."

"Yes, it's safe," Savannah groaned.

"You're afraid of heights?" Dillan asked me.

"Yeah," I said. "And this situation is especially bad because we're on some magical, flying platform."

"It's not magic."

"That doesn't make me feel any better," I said. "Wait, what will happen if someone on the ground sees us?"

"They won't," Savannah said. "There's an invisibility field around the elevator, based on John and Dillan's report of Ley's rescue mission."

"What's an invisibility field?" I asked.

"I regret taking you on this mission already," Savannah sighed. "Your constant questioning of every little detail is becoming incredibly annoying. But, if it'll shut you up, an invisibility field prevents people outside of it from seeing what's inside of it. So, nobody looking up at the sky tonight will see us; they'll just see the stars as they usually would."

When we arrived on the ship, only three Elements were there. They were all staring at the glowing panels on the walls until the elevator stopped, causing them to turn around. The one in the middle, a fire Element girl, was taken out before she could react. The other two, a water Element boy and an earth Element girl, began their attacks. The earth girl caused a giant flower to grow from the floor. Its center opened up, revealing many sharp teeth. As the girl used the flower to attack the team, the water boy turned the floor to ice, making it hard to move without sliding or falling.

"Elizabeth, do something!" Mark yelled.

I slipped, and as my hands landed on the ice, steam began to rise, leaving two hand-shaped sections of the floor without ice. I tried touching more areas of the floor with my hands, but I knew that I couldn't thaw it fast enough like that. I needed to do something else.

Ley fell out of my hair and slid across the room. Her body seemed to turn into black sand before taking the shape of herself and going back to normal. Her clothing remained on her body as it did before she became a hair clip. She was behind the Elements and remained unnoticed. I wanted to call out to her, tell her to run, but before I could, a large vine wrapped around me and pulled me to the flower's mouth. My plasma pistol fell to the ground, leaving me with nothing to defend myself besides my uncontrollable powers.

Time seemed to slow down in that moment as I realized that this was it. I was about to die. How could I have been so foolish to think I could handle this? Did I really think I could go on an alien ship and survive? I was so naïve, and I had brought Ley into danger with me. All I could do was hope that she would escape as the flower opened its mouth and pulled me closer. Its teeth looked more like thorns when up close, but as large and thick as they were, I figured they were just as powerful as the real deal. Dillan, who spotted Ley, slid his plasma pistol over to her before putting his hands in the air to act like he was surrendering. The water boy blasted him in the head with ice, laughing as he fell to the ground. I couldn't see what happened after that as I was soon inside the flower's mouth. It was just as dark, wet, and terrifying as I imagined it would be, though the smell was surprisingly pleasant. I tried to relax and accept my fate as I prepared to be chewed up and swallowed. I felt a falling sensation and heard the team calling to me after. As I found out later, Ley had taken Dillan's weapon and used it to shoot both Elements from behind.

"Elizabeth!" Dillan yelled. "Are you in there? Can you hear me?"

"I'm here!" I shouted back.

The team worked together to open the flower's mouth, allowing me to crawl out. My right arm got caught on one of the thorns, leaving behind a large cut that tore through my shirt sleeve. I didn't care, though. I was alive, and everyone else was, too. That's what mattered most. I looked over to where the Elements had stood, but they were gone. Even their bodies were nowhere to be found.

"T-thank you for saving me," I stuttered, still processing what had happened. "Is the coast clear now?"

"It is at the moment," Savannah said, "but I'm sure it won't be long until more Elements arrive."

"And we'll be ready for them," Dillan said with a grin.

"But first things first, Ley shouldn't be here. Dillan, get her back to the hideout."

Dillan started to grab Ley's arm, but she punched him in the nose. He fell to the ground, bleeding. Haley and Mark drew their weapons on Ley to defend their teammate. I drew my weapon on them to defend my sister only to be stopped by Savannah, who drew her weapon on me.

"Guys, this isn't going to get us anywhere," Ley said as she slowly lifted her hands above her head. "If you want to save Linda, and I know you do, you'll let me stay because you need all the help you can get. After all, I just saved you by shooting those two Elements, and you can't afford to send one of your teammates away just to take me back to the base."

"Stand down," Savannah ordered her team as she lowered her own weapon. Haley and Mark followed. I hesitated before doing the same.

"Thanks," Ley said. "Now, let's stop standing around awkwardly. My sister needs us."

"I hope you know just what you're signing up for, Ley," Savannah said grimly. "Before we go any further, I think you should know that we would've been fine without you. I don't see you as an asset to this mission, just an extra body to protect. But as long as you're here, you might as well lead us to where you were being held captive. That way you can truthfully say to your future children, if you survive to have any, that you weren't completely useless."

"You know, you weren't this mean when I first showed up."

"And you weren't this stupid when you first showed up, but here we are."

Ley rolled her eyes and quietly led the way. She mumbled something under her breath, but I couldn't quite hear what.

"Savannah shouldn't have been so hard on you," I whispered to her.

"She's just angry," Ley said, "and she has every right to be, though you'd think what I did back there would count for something."

"Yeah," I said. "I would've been compost if it weren't for you."

"I'm going to head back down to Earth soon," we heard an Element say from around the corner of the hallway. "Do you wanna come with me, Daisy?"

"We're gonna need a detour," Ley whispered.

We went into the nearest room, which turned out to be a closet. Ley was pinned next to me and Dillan. Dillan's nose wasn't bleeding anymore, but it was caked with dried blood. Even though it was Ley who caused his injury in the first place, Dillan still looked at her apologetically. Ley wouldn't even meet his gaze.

Savannah pressed her ear to the door, listening for the Elements. Once she believed the coast was clear, she led us back out into the hall. As we continued through the ship, I noticed that the walls and floor were made of some type of purple metal. Lights were at the bottom and top of the walls in the spots where they met the floor and ceiling. I had never seen anything like it before. It was strange, yet beautiful.

"I don't understand," Ley said as she came to a stop by an empty room. "This is the room where they held me. If this isn't where they're keeping Linda, then where is she?"

"When we overheard the Element talking to her contact, it sounded like they were trying to get information out of her," I said. "If that's truly the case, then they probably have her held somewhere a little bleaker."

"I believe you're right about the room, Elizabeth," Savannah said, "but that doesn't give us a specific location. Maybe we can trace Linda's wrist communicator."

"Only if it's still on her person," Mark added. "The Elements could've easily removed it."

"I know for a fact that Linda doesn't have her communicator on her," Ley said. "John tried to contact her, but got no response."

"So, that means that the Elements did remove it?" I asked.

"I'm sure they did," Dillan said. "Why would they risk letting her keep it?"

"Even if Linda *did* have her wrist communicator, I'm sure the Elements would block our scan," Mark added.

"The wrist communicators run on a special frequency that I helped John develop," Savannah explained. "The Elements may be able to block our scans of the ship, but they can't prevent us from locating other Resistance communicators. Let's just hope that this leads us to Linda's general location."

Savannah used her wrist communicator to run a scan. The hall remained silent until more Elements started to come through, forcing all of us to get back to the closet we were in before. I caught myself holding my breath. Ley seemed to be doing the same. Dillan tried to comfort her, but that only resulted in him being punched in the arm.

"So, assuming Linda's wrist communicator is still close to her," Savannah said, "she should be on the floor directly above us. There's got to be an elevator or a staircase somewhere around here. Follow me."

We went through the halls of the Elements' ship, occasionally stopping to hide until we found another elevator that took us to the next floor. Things seemed to be working in our favor until we were caught by a tall wind Element with wavy hair. Everyone drew their weapons, but he didn't seem afraid at all. He seemed to find the situation humorous.

"There's no need for that," he said. "I'm here to take you to Linda."

"How'd you know we're here?" Ley asked. "And why aren't you hurting us?"

"Well, after we found what was left of the Elements you killed, it wasn't difficult to figure out where you were going and where you could be hiding," the wind Element said. "And whether or not I end up hurting you is entirely dependent on how you behave. So, why don't you all put down your weapons? If I have to disarm you myself, things will get messy."

Savannah nodded, silently signaling for the team to obey. Once everyone's weapons were put away, the wind Element led us to a large room filled with cells. Each cell had some sort of translucent light covering it, and only one was occupied. Linda's cell. It was at the very end of the room. Linda's face was covered in bruises. Her suit jacket and white shirt were torn to shreds. Her left arm appeared to be covered in minor burns going all the way up to her shoulder and around her back. Her wrist communicator was laying on the floor right outside her cell. The strap was broken, implying that it had been violently ripped off of Linda's wrist instead of simply being unfastened.

"Linda!" Ley exclaimed. "Are you alright?"

"Forget about me," she said. "Are *you* alright? Why are you even here?"

"They're here to say goodbye to you," the wind Element said. "They'll be free to go so long as they leave you here."

"What?" I asked. "What makes you think we'd just leave her?"

"She's the only one we want. If we have her, all of this can end."

"Can we please have some privacy?" Ley asked. "I'd rather not say my goodbyes with the enemy still in the room."

"Of course," he said, "but don't try anything funny. If Linda leaves her cell, you won't escape alive, I promise."

Once he left, we got to work. We weren't about to let the Elements scare us into surrendering. Linda was coming home with us whether they liked it or not.

"Don't worry, Linda," Ley said. "We're gonna get you out of here."

"No! You have to go back to the base without me," Linda insisted. "Didn't you hear what that Element said? I'm the only one they want."

"But why, though?"

"I'm not quite sure. The Elements who interrogated me kept mentioning something about a prophecy."

"Prophecy?" I asked. "So, this whole thing is over a superstition?"

"It doesn't matter how ridiculous the concept is," Linda said. "What matters is that you all can go without getting hurt."

"And leave you here?" Ley asked. "No way. You rescued me. So, now it's my turn to rescue you."

"Don't do this. Don't go risking your life for me, I don't deserve it."

"We came here to get you out," I said, "and that's exactly what we're going to do."

"Elizabeth—" Linda started, eyeing the cut on my arm.

"We're not leaving without you, boss, and that's final," Savannah said.

Before Linda could get another word in, Savannah walked over to a hologram computer at the end of the room and began messing with the settings until the light covering Linda's cell went away. I was confused as to why she didn't just walk through it in the first place, but I had no time to ask questions. The moment Linda left the cell, a hoard of Elements barged into the room. I felt my heart racing.

"You absolute morons!" Misty exclaimed. "Linda was the only one we wanted. I guess now we don't have any other choice but to kill you all."

Haley and Mark began taking out Elements in the back of the room. An earth Element attacked Dillan and Savannah. Vines wrapped around their arms and legs. They tried to free themselves but failed. The earth Element tried to attack me next, but I managed to dodge. While I was distracted by him, Misty sent an icy blast straight into my chest, sending me flat on my back. My body ached as chills spread across my skin. Linda charged at Misty in an attempt to help me.

Misty sent another blast, but Linda barely managed to dodge it. She punched Misty in the face with her super strength, causing Misty to fly back into the wall so hard that a dent was left behind. I stood back up, ready to fight. A ball of fire flew by my head and hit Linda in the shoulder, letting me know that a fire Element had entered the fight. A wind Element boy charged at Ley.

"Stay away from her!" I shouted as I launched a ball of fire at him.

I successfully hit him, but another Element came at me from behind. Vines began climbing up my arms and legs until I could no longer move. I fell down. I watched as Ley grabbed my plasma pistol off the floor and pointed it at Misty, who had stood back up. Misty, while holding her left hand on her head, blasted the gun out of Ley's hand. Next, she bound Ley with chains of ice and dragged her away. Misty pinned Ley against the wall. A band of ice wrapped around Ley's neck and began to tighten. Large icicles were pointed at her from every direction. Ley was barely able to get her hands to her neck as she fought to breathe.

"If you even try to shapeshift, I'll run you through," Misty said as the icicles drew nearer to Ley.

"Why are you doing this to me?" Ley gasped. "What did I ever do to you?"

"Exist," Misty answered as she tightened the thick band of ice around Ley's neck even more.

As I heard Ley's desperate gasps for air and saw her face begin to turn blue, I felt my heart accelerate. My blood was boiling through my veins. I felt like I was about to burst. I blasted my way through the vines and stood up. My hands were engulfed in flames just as they were when I had first discovered my powers. The flames grew larger and larger; my anger seemed to be fueling it. The flames grew to be so large that I couldn't control them any longer. Before I could warn my teammates, fire and stone launched out of my body in every direction. The ice around Ley was shattered, and the team managed to duck just in time. The Elements, who were too busy fighting my teammates to notice me, were caught in the blast, and knocked unconscious.

"Elizabeth!" Ley exclaimed as she ran up to me. "You did it. You saved me from Misty. Thank you."

"Well, I certainly wasn't going to let her kill you," I said, hugging Ley. "I love you, Ley."

"I love you, too, Elizabeth," she said. "And I've made my decision."

"Decision about what?"

"What you were offering this morning."

"Oh, right, I almost forgot about that. Well, what did you decide? Will you come home with me?"

"If Linda tells us that we can't come here again, I would love to go with y—"

Ley stopped mid-sentence and let go of me. Her eyes widened and filled with tears. I was incredibly confused as to why she had stopped speaking. Her face became one of shock and pain. She looked like she had been stabbed.

"Ley, what's wrong? What is it?" I asked. "Are you alright?"

Before she could answer, or attempt to answer, I saw it. A large ice spike was sticking out of Ley's back, and Misty was trying to get back up off the floor. Ley fell down on her side, her eyes empty. It all seemed to go in slow motion until Linda took my arm.

"We need to get out of here, now," she said.

"What about Ley?" I asked, looking down at her lifeless body.

"She's gone," Linda replied, "and we will be, too, if we don't get out of here. I'm not going to lose two sisters today."

"No, we can't leave her body here!" I yelled. "We need to take her back with us!"

Linda, feeling the same way, went to pick up Ley's body. Before she could lift Ley's arms off the ground, a huge wave washed the body away to the end of the room. Misty had gotten up once again.

"Were you really going to take away my trophy?" she asked as she wiped blood from her face.

She was barely able to stand, but that didn't matter. She was able to use her powers just fine, leaving all of us in immediate danger. Still, her calling Ley a trophy went right through me.

"Did you just call Ley's body a trophy, you heartless monster!?" I screamed. "Ley was a living, breathing person who—"

"Yeah, cool story. But did I ask?" Misty taunted.

Linda was enraged, and I'm sure she would've fought Misty one-on-one again if she were alone, but because the team and I were there, too, she didn't risk it. Instead, she grabbed my arm and ran. The rest of the team followed. Dillan eventually got in front of us so he could lead us all to the escape pods.

"After them!" Misty shrieked at the other Elements who had started to wake up. A stampede of Elements began their pursuit. We ran through the halls of the ship, following Dillan's lead.

"Dillan, how far are we from the escape pods?" Linda asked, trying to catch her breath.

"Well, the escape pods we used before were downstairs, and I'm not quite sure how to get back there," he said.

"Are you telling me that we're lost?"

"Not exactly," Dillan continued. "I think there may be escape pods on each floor of the ship."

"And if you're correct?"

"If I'm correct, then the escape pods on this floor should be in the same area as the escape pods on the floor below us."

"And how far is that?"

"Not too far. Just keep following me."

The Elements could still be heard behind us, their footsteps getting faster and louder as we followed Dillan blindly through the halls. We ducked as ice and vines flew over our heads. Linda and Haley occasionally turned back to shoot down a couple of Elements, but neither dared to slow down. As we turned to our right, the floor became ice. I tried to keep my pace, knowing that attempting to slow down or stop would cause me to slip.

Just as Dillan had suspected, there were escape pods on our floor. Savannah, Haley, and Mark went for one, and Dillan, Linda, and I went for another. The six of us got inside the escape pods just in time. A huge wave, just like the one that got Ley, came crashing down the halls towards us. Linda hit the launch button of the escape pod right before the water could reach us. Clear doors sealed us off from the ship, and for a moment, I could've sworn I saw two glowing blue eyes in the water on the other side. Before I could get a better look, a second set of doors closed. A thin layer of frost started to creep around the door just as we took off.

"That was *way* too close for me," I said.

Linda didn't respond. She fought back tears, not wanting to cry in front of her teammate. I was in shock at what happened, too. Ley had been in my arms, alive, only a few minutes ago. So, even though I saw what happened to her, even though I saw her body hit the ground, it was still hard for me to accept that she was dead.

"I'm so sorry for your loss," Dillan said, fighting tears himself.

"Thank you," I said.

Linda remained silent, refusing to even make eye contact with me or Dillan, but, eventually, it became too hard for her to hide her emotions completely. "It should've been me," she said after a few minutes had passed. "Ley didn't deserve to die like that."

Chapter 13 (Linda)

After changing into my tank top and being briefed on everything that had happened since my capture, I went to visit John in section four. John was oblivious to what took place during the mission, which was good for me. News of Ley's death had already spread around sections one and two, causing everyone to give the typical "I'm sorry for your loss" speech that I honestly didn't want to hear any more of. It's not that I didn't appreciate the thought. I was just tired of hearing it over and over from all of my coworkers. I didn't like being treated differently. Having dealt with loss before, I determined that going back to business as usual was best for me because it would force me to move forward despite my grief. Sadly, none of my coworkers understood that, which is why I wanted to see the one and only person I knew of who wasn't aware of Ley's death.

"I'm so glad you're back," John said when I entered his hospital room, "but shouldn't you have your own room here? It's protocol to—"

"I don't need to be checked into the hospital, John," I said. "The Elements just kept asking me about my attack plans and about some prophecy thing, which I didn't even recognize. When I refused to tell them anything, partially because I didn't know some of what they were asking me for, they beat and burned me. Nothing too serious."

"Beat and *burned* you?" John asked. "You should get that checked out by a doctor."

"I'm fine. The bruises can be easily covered up, and the burns aren't that bad. Second-degree at worst. They're also mainly on my upper back. The Elements needed me alive, so they never would've inflicted any fatal wounds."

"You're so stubborn," John said. "You know, Elizabeth and Ley were worried that they wouldn't see you again, and, well, so was I." John's words pierced my heart, though I knew he didn't mean it. My thoughts drifted back to Ley, causing my eyes to sting with tears. "What's wrong?" John asked. "Are you alright? Is it something I said?"

"I…" Instead of answering, I hugged him. He seemed caught off guard for a moment before gently hugging me back. His arms were warm, which helped to comfort me. My tears dripped from my face onto his shoulder.

"Are you alright?" he asked again, hugging me a little tighter before letting go.

"No, I'm far from alright," I said.

"Do you want to talk about it?"

"To be honest, John, all I want right now is a distraction."

John looked concerned. He brushed a strand of hair out of my face and used one of the tissues on his tray to gently wipe away my tears before gesturing for me to sit down next to him. I found myself not only sitting beside him but also leaning over as he put his arm around me, doing his best to stay clear of any burns.

"I'll be fine," I said. "I just need something to distract me, anything. Surely there's something you've been dying to tell me. Maybe some new invention in the lab?"

"There is something I wanted to ask you about," John told me, "but I don't think it's appropriate considering your current state."

"Please, John," I begged. "I need this more than anything right now."

"Whatever happened back there, I'm sure it was bad, so I don't think I should—"

"John, I don't care if it's a fart joke. I need something to take my mind off of what happened back on the ship."

"And what exactly happened?"

"I'd rather not talk about it. Not yet, anyway. Please, just tell me something that isn't mission-related."

"Alright, then," John said as his face turned pink. "I was wanting to ask you if you'd like to—"

"Boss!" Mark interrupted as he entered the room. He gave John a slight smirk as soon as he spotted the two of us curled up next to each other. "Sorry to intrude. I've been looking for you everywhere."

"What is it, Mark?" I asked.

"Elizabeth was asking about doing a memorial service for Ley. I told her you'd need to approve it."

"Right," I said. "Of course, I'll approve it. I'll even help her plan it. Just give me a moment alone with John, alright?"

"Okay. I'll let her know," Mark said as he left. "Sorry again for the intrusion. And nice job, John."

"Shut up!" John called after him before turning back to me. "A memorial service? What's Mark talking about? Where's Ley?"

"Ley and Elizabeth managed to get themselves involved with the mission," I said. "Elizabeth nearly died in a giant plant, and Ley… Ley got pierced in the back by Misty. She didn't make it. That's what I wanted to be distracted from."

"I'm so—"

"Please don't say it," I said, covering John's mouth. "I've already heard it a million times tonight. Could you please get back to what you were saying before Mark came in?" I moved my hand, and John held me closer for a moment like he was trying to silently finish what he was saying before.

"I think I should hold off," he said. "I don't think it's an appropriate thing to discuss right after Ley's death."

"Please?" I begged. "I need this."

The room went silent for a moment as John looked into my eyes.

"Okay, fine," he said. "I was wanting to know if you'd be interested in having dinner with me sometime."

"John, are you asking me out on a date?" I asked as I felt my face turning bright red. "Again?"

"Yes, I am."

"John," I sighed, "don't you remember last time? You asked me out, and I said no because—"

"Because you didn't want to ruin our friendship," John finished. "I was hoping that your feelings about that would've changed by now. You don't have *any* romantic feelings for me?"

"Of course, I have romantic feelings for you. I've liked you like that for a while now, going back to before you first asked me out."

"If you felt that way about me for so long, then why won't you give us a chance?" he asked.

"Because I don't want to ruin what we already have," I said. "I love our relationship as friends, and I don't want it destroyed with a romantic relationship gone wrong."

"Oh, come on, *nothing* could ruin our friendship," John insisted.

"You don't know that," I said. "If we started dating and our relationship ended horribly, why would we stay friends? The only reason I chat with Dillan is because he's my coworker; if I had my way, we'd never speak again."

"Just let me take you out on one date," John bargained. "If things don't go well, then we forget all about it and go back to the way we were before. That way we won't risk ruining our friendship. If things do go well, maybe we could try a second date and explore our feelings a little more."

I thought about it for a moment. I was worried about ruining our friendship, but I also knew John's feelings for me wouldn't be changing any time soon. He *had* helped me by giving me a distraction like I asked, and to some degree, I felt like I owed him for all the things he'd done for me. Once, when I got an awful stomach bug, he stayed with me and held my hair back. He also helped me clean up some nasty messes and even made me soup. It almost felt like he was treating me like his girlfriend, even though I was dating Dillan back then. Come to think of it, John had never had a girlfriend before, as far as I was aware. It was almost like he was waiting for me.

"John, can I ask you something?"

"Anything," he said.

"Have you ever had a girlfriend before?" I asked.

"No."

"Why not? I've seen some of the girls around here flirting with you."

"I'm not interested in dating them."

"Why?"

"Because I have my heart set on someone else."

"And who would that be?" I asked, already knowing the answer. John just stared into my eyes. "Fine. I'll promise you one, and *only* one, date. And I'm only agreeing to that because you distracted me for a bit like I asked you to."

"Thank you," he said.

"And, if this doesn't work out, you better find yourself a girlfriend. I don't want to see you grow up to be a lonely old man."

"Knowing your track record, I think you'd become a lonely old woman," John said. I rolled my eyes. "And," he continued, "you'd probably become senile, marry me, and then we would become bitter together and yell at the neighborhood kids to get off our lawn."

"Sounds great to me." I laughed. "Kids will be afraid to even walk past the Davis house."

"Which means we won't have to worry about buying Halloween candy."

"Not true. We'd be buying it for ourselves and eating it until our teeth rot."

"We don't have real teeth anymore, remember? All agents got free implants last year."

"Oh, yeah… well, I could always find a candy sticky enough to rip an implant out." I laughed.

For a moment, I forgot why I had been crying. For a moment, things seemed lighthearted and fun. But that moment faded as I slowly began to remember what happened. As much as I just wanted to stay with John, I knew Elizabeth needed me more than ever, and I felt guilty for leaving her alone.

"I should go see Elizabeth about the memorial for Ley," I said. "Right now, I'm the only friend she has, not to mention the only family she has."

"I understand," John said. "And, I know you're sick of hearing it, but I'm sorry for your loss. If you want to come back later and talk about it, or if you just need another distraction, I'll be here."

"Thanks, John."

Elizabeth was also in section four, but she didn't have her own room since she just needed a few stitches for that cut on her arm. She was in the ER section of the floor, which was filled with hospital beds. I found where she was and sat down beside her. Her eyes looked red and puffy from crying. Her chin and neck were still drenched in tears.

"I see you haven't gotten the stitches yet," I said. "What's the holdup?"

"I wanted to wait for you."

"Oh. I'm sorry," I said. "If I'd known, I'd have been here sooner." Elizabeth kept staring down at the ground. I realized that small talk wasn't going to cut it. We needed to talk about the mission, about Ley. "So," I said gently, "how are you holding up?"

"How do you think?" she asked. "I lost Ley, got her back, lost you, got you back, and then lost Ley again within a week. And on top of that, I still can't get back home. I'm barely hanging on right now."

"We'll make it through this together," I said as I gently put my arm around her. She leaned on me and began to cry once again.

"It's my fault, Linda," she said.

"How is it your fault?" I asked.

"I had Ley shapeshift into a hair clip so I could sneak her onto the Elements' ship. Her death is my fault."

"Savannah shouldn't have let you go in the first place," I said. "And it was Misty who put that ice in Ley's back, not you."

"But—"

"No buts, Elizabeth. This isn't your fault."

"But I still feel so guilty," Elizabeth cried. "Ley was going to go back to the orphanage with me. That way we could still stay together even if you chose to send us back without a way to open the portals ourselves."

"Elizabeth," I said, "I finally found my family. Did you and Ley really think I was going to send you away? Don't get me wrong, you probably should get back home, but I would've figured out a way to contact you. I would've come up with ways for us to visit each other."

"Really? You would've done that?"

"Of course," I said. "I… I love you."

"I love you, too, Linda."

Elizabeth started to get choked up again, so I held her in my arms as she tried to calm herself down. I felt like crying again, too, but I held my tears back. I felt that crying in front of Elizabeth would only make things worse. She needed me to stay strong.

"So, what are we going to do for Ley's memorial service?" Elizabeth asked. "We don't have a body or any pictures. The only thing we have that belonged to her is her phone."

"She left her phone here?" I asked.

"Ley was coming to get it when we overheard the Element disguised as you talking to her contact. After that, we found out about you being alive, and she focused only on saving you. I-I grabbed it from your room before coming down here."

Elizabeth handed me the phone, and I pressed the home button. Ley's phone lit up, revealing a snowy background. The phone had no password protection, allowing me to get in with no trouble. I went through Ley's gallery, trying to find pictures that could be used for the memorial. Sadly, there were very few pictures of Ley herself. Most of the pictures were of her backyard or of notes from school. She had a couple of pictures of one friend, but the timestamps on them showed that they were taken in 2015. That told me that Ley didn't have much of a social life.

"I think Ley would've wanted you to have this," I said as I handed the phone back to Elizabeth. "Though you didn't know each other long, I think you were the best friend she's ever had."

"But, because of the incident, Ley didn't get to finish showing me how this thing works. How do I use it? Savannah didn't get into all the details in our crash course."

"I can show you," I said, "but let's get those stitches for you first."

I could tell Elizabeth was uncomfortable the entire time, but she managed to hold still and keep quiet. Once she was taken care of, I took her up to my room in section one. There, I spent the next hour showing her how to use Ley's phone after quickly teaching myself how to use it since it was incredibly old. I started by showing Elizabeth how to make calls and how to text. I then showed her how to charge the phone and how to use some of the other basic features, like the camera.

"And I use this to contact you if I need you?" she asked.

"Well, yes," I said, "but you can also use it if you just want to talk."

Elizabeth broke down crying again. I couldn't fight it anymore. I started crying, too.

"There's got to be some way to…" Elizabeth choked on her words, leaving me to fill in the blanks.

"No," I said. "I'm sorry, Elizabeth, but there's no way to bring Ley back."

"That's not what I was going to say," she said. "I was going to say that there's got to be some way to get revenge. There's got to be a way to stop the Elements from killing more people."

I thought of something that had never been done before, something incredibly dangerous. "I could infiltrate the Elements' ship by disguising myself as one of them," I said. "Give them a taste of their own medicine."

"That's genius!" Elizabeth exclaimed. "What would we need to disguise ourselves?"

"A wig, colored contacts, body paint, new clothes, and… wait, did you say *we*?"

"Yes, we," Elizabeth said. "You and I are going to work together to get revenge on the Elements."

"No," I insisted. "I can't let you. I already lost Ley. I'm not gonna lose you, too."

"Linda, please."

"It's a suicide mission, Elizabeth."

"All the more reason for me to go with you," Elizabeth insisted. "You are the only family I have left. If you go on this mission, I go with you. If you die, I die with you. We do this together no matter what happens."

"No, Elizabeth, you should—"

"This is my choice to make, not yours."

"So, I guess there's no stopping you." I chuckled. "It seems you and I share the same stubbornness."

"Indeed, we do, sis."

"Fine, then," I said. "You can come along."

"Thank you," Elizabeth said. "You have no idea how much this means to me."

"You're welcome," I said, gently squeezing her hand.

"How long will it take you to get what we need?"

"I should have it by tomorrow morning," I said. "Some of the things we need for our disguises can be found in storage from previous undercover missions, though those missions weren't anything like this. I'll have to go shopping for the rest of the items, like the body paint and the colored contacts, but I know for a fact that a few stores have those things leftover from Halloween."

"And we'll infiltrate the ship after that?"

"Yes," I said. "And from there, we'll take those alien scumbags down."

Elizabeth and I slept well that night knowing that the Elements, or at least Briar's team of Elements, would soon be no more.

I woke up the next morning before the alarm went off. All I wanted to do was go back to sleep under the warm comforter, but I couldn't. I was wide awake, and my mind kept wandering to the mission to attack the Elements, the suicide mission. I looked beside me to see if Linda was still asleep, but she was already gone. The gray sheets were flipped up from her leaving the bed; I was surprised that didn't wake me. I grabbed clothes from the dresser drawers before getting changed. Spotting a black brush in front of the dresser mirror reminded me to brush my hair before heading downstairs to the cafeteria. When I got there, Linda was on her way out. We nearly ran into each other.

"Oh, you're awake," she said.

"Hello, Linda," I said. "I'm surprised you're awake, too. Did you have trouble sleeping?"

"I guess you could say that," Linda said. "Since I couldn't go back to sleep, I decided to drive to the store. After I got back here, I went down to the cafeteria to grab some food for John. I was going to wake you up myself since the alarm clock startles you so badly, but I thought I would bring John his breakfast first."

"Don't the nurses take care of that?" I asked.

"Well, they do, but John isn't allowed to have any *real* food just yet, so I'm smuggling this into his room like the good friend I am."

"You said you went to the store," I said. "Does that mean you have our disguises for the mission?"

"Yes, and I'll show them to you in a moment."

I followed Linda down to section four and into John's room. He looked much better than when Ley and I had visited him before. There was more color in his face, and it looked like he had managed to comb his hair. The moment John spotted the food Linda brought him, he smiled.

"You didn't have to do that for me," he said.

"What kind of friend would I be if I didn't?" Linda asked as she handed over the bag of food.

"How are you holding up?"

"Not well. I'm still blaming myself for everything."

"It isn't your fault," John said.

"Yes, it is," Linda said, much to my surprise. "If I hadn't agreed to take Ley and Elizabeth to school in the first place, none of this would've happened. Ley trusted me to keep her safe, and I failed her."

"Did you already forget what you said to me last night?" I asked Linda.

"That's different," she sighed.

"How? You had no idea that the Elements would be there."

"I should've. According to the school's records, those girls: Briar, Daisy, Windy, and Misty, have been there since the start of the school year. They've had a lot of absences, but they were registered nonetheless."

"How could you have possibly known they were Elements until they attacked?" John asked. "They can disguise themselves as humans."

"Which is why I shouldn't have been so dumb as to think that the school would be safe," Linda said. "Just because they hadn't attacked there before didn't mean that they wouldn't ever try. This is my fault, and I'm going to make it right in the only way I can. I'm going to stop the Elements from hurting any more innocent people."

"And how do you plan on doing that?" John asked.

"I think what Linda meant to say was: *we* are going to stop the Elements from hurting any more innocent people," I told John. "Together, she and I are going to infiltrate the Elements' ship, because we will only feel better after we know that everyone is safe from those monsters."

"That's practically a suicide mission," John argued. "You're really doing all of this because of Ley?"

"It's not *practically* a suicide mission, it *is* a suicide mission, John," Linda said. "And this isn't just about Ley. What about the other people who have lost their loved ones because of the Elements? We need to show these aliens what happens when they mess with the people of Earth."

"Are you *this* desperate to get out of our date?"

"You're going on a date?" I asked. "I didn't realize you two became a thing. I'm glad you did, though. You make a cute couple."

Linda blushed. "John and I aren't exactly a couple, Elizabeth," she said. "I promised John one date, which we haven't gone on yet. And, before you ask, no, I'm not trying to get out of it."

"Look," John said, getting us back on track, "there's got to be some other way to take out the Elements, something safer than what you've got planned. You've got to think rationally here."

"I stopped thinking rationally a while ago," Linda said. "You can't change my mind on this."

"You're too emotionally invested in this, which is why—"

"Which is why I'm the one who can take things as far as they need to go."

John and Linda continued arguing about the mission. I, feeling awkward, ignored them and looked around the room. Because section four was underground, there were no windows, just a hologram on the side of the wall that could be changed to display whatever outdoor scene the patient wanted. John had it set to a lovely garden scene. I looked at the wall across from John's bed. There was a thin black panel with a piece of glass in the front. It took me a moment to remember the word for it, TV. While I knew what it was, I had never used one myself. I found the controller on John's tray and pressed the red button, turning the TV on. I started playing with the buttons on the controller to see what each one did, but after accidentally turning the sound up all the way, the nurses came in and took the controller away from me.

"Well then, since I can't convince you to let this madness go, good luck with your mission," John sighed. "Even though I think it's stupid, and even though I know I'd probably die, I'd still go with you if I could."

"I know you would, John," Linda said.

John and Linda looked at each other like they wanted to say or do something more, but couldn't. Whatever the case, they were wasting time, and I was becoming annoyed.

"You can stare into each other's eyes later," I complained, breaking the silence. "Let's go already."

***

Linda led me back to her room in section one and roughly shoved my disguise into my arms. "Here ya go," she said, sounding slightly annoyed. "One red wig, orange body paint, red contact lenses, and a black dress. Don't worry, there are shorts to go under the dress just in case you get into a fight. We wouldn't want you flashing yourself to the Elements, would we?"

"So, I'm going undercover as a fire Element?" I asked.

"Well, that makes the most sense considering your powers," Linda said. "I, on the other hand, don't have any elemental-type powers. So, I'll be going as a water Element just because I can. Oh, and take this." Linda handed me a switchblade with a sleek, black cover.

"A knife? Really?" I chuckled.

"Well, a gun would be harder to hide, and it would look suspicious since the Elements just use their powers. A knife, however, is easy to slip into a pocket, which your dress has, by the way."

"Thanks, but I won't be needing a knife. I have powers, too, remember?"

"Powers you can't control."

"…fine," I said, reluctantly taking the knife. "What about you?"

"I always have a knife on me, see?" Linda held out her own knife.

"Looks like you gave me the bigger one," I said.

"It's not the size that matters; it's how you use it."

"Huh?"

"Never mind."

Linda put her knife away and began setting the pieces of our disguises on top of her dresser. I was confused until she explained that Savannah ran a new scan of the school. The Elements' ship wasn't there anymore. Presuming it was still nearby, Savannah was running a scan of the entire city, which could take hours. In the meantime, Linda went to get breakfast for me and herself. I stayed in her room and sat on the bed. Ley's phone was sitting on top of the dresser next to my disguise. I unplugged it and pressed the home button.

After unlocking the phone, I decided to look through Ley's photos. Most of the photos didn't have Ley in them, but they still made me tear up a little. The phone and the pictures were all I had left of her. Though I didn't know her long, she had quickly managed to become my friend. She was a very kind and funny person who I wanted to get to know more. I closed my eyes and tried to replay everything in my head: my arrival, going shopping, even visiting Ley in section four. I didn't want to forget a single detail of our time together.

***

I heard singing in the distance, a *child's* singing. Curious, I made my way out of Linda's room and found myself in a different bedroom. The walls were light blue with pink butterflies painted on them. I could see flashes of lightning outside the barred window, followed by loud rumbles of thunder. A tall bed with blue sheets was centered against the wall facing the right. A toy box was at the foot of the bed, and a black mirror stood on the other side of the room.

The singing continued, drawing my attention to a young girl with long, brown hair. She sat on the bed, swinging her legs as she sang. Her face was swollen and covered with cuts and bruises. It looked like she had been beaten up. I sat next to her on the bed. As lightning illuminated her face, I realized I knew her.

"Ley?" I asked.

The child looked over at me and smiled. "You should sing with me, Elizabeth."

As the singing grew louder, I almost didn't hear the footsteps outside the door. Ley froze as soon as she heard them. I found myself freezing, too, though I didn't understand why. My heart began accelerating, and I felt my hands start to sweat. *Was I in danger?*

"Pretend to be asleep!" Ley blurted to me, but it was too late, the door was opening. She ran to the window, fighting tears as a tall, ominous man walked in. He held a needle in his right hand. As he approached Ley, she started to scream for help.

"Leave her alone!" I shouted.

"Elizabeth," I heard a voice echo from afar.

I ignored the voice and threw myself in front of Ley. I wasn't going to let the man hurt her. He grew closer to us, causing Ley to cower down. As my eyes met the gaze of the man, I felt a familiar feeling of dread, like I knew what was about to happen to me, when in reality, I was completely oblivious as to what the man was planning to do.

"Who are you?" I asked.

A flash of lightning allowed me to get a better look at him. He had black hair and crystal blue eyes. After noticing his perfectly chiseled face, a name popped into my head.

"Davis," I mumbled.

Everything around me went black, like I was trapped in a void. The only other thing in the void was a mirror. I walked up to it and quickly realized that the reflection wasn't my own, at least, not my current reflection. It was me as a child.

"Do you remember?" the child asked.

"Elizabeth!" I heard a faint voice echo again.

I ignored it just like before. I knew I was dreaming, that much was clear, but something felt off. It felt like more than just an ordinary dream. It was like a distorted memory that I'd stored away.

"Remember what?" I asked. The mirror shattered, leaving me alone in the void. "What do you want me to remember!?" I heard nothing but my own echo in return.

"ELIZABETH!" I heard Linda yell, causing me to wake up.

"How long have I been out?" I asked, still half-asleep.

"I'm not sure," Linda said, "but when I came in here, you were screaming: *Leave her alone!*"

"Sorry, Linda," I said. "I wasn't trying to freak you out. I just had a bad dream, that's all."

"Do you want to talk about it?"

"I saw this little girl," I said. "She was screaming for help. The poor thing had obviously been abused. Her face was swollen. She was trying to escape from this shadowy man, who I think is the one who abused her. The thing is, I knew both the girl and the man. I recognized them."

I knew that there was more to the dream than what I had told Linda, but I couldn't remember it. Just like that, it was gone. The names of the girl and the man, *what were they?* I tried to remember, but nothing came to my head.

"Dreams can be weird like that," Linda said as she handed me a plate of eggs, bacon, and toast. "Your mind could've easily been pulling faces from your subconscious. Maybe the child was a little girl you saw here in the city on the way to school. Maybe the man was a teacher you saw walking in the hallway between classes. Either way, none of it was real."

"You're probably right," I said, "but I just can't help but feel there's something more to it. It all seemed so familiar to me. The girl's face, her clothes, her room, even her voice. I swear I know her from somewhere. And the man, too, there was something about him that made me more afraid than I've ever felt before."

"Don't let it get to you, Elizabeth. It's just a dream. Though, come to think of it, Ley had something weird like that, too. When she first arrived, she asked me if I was the girl from her dream."

"Do you think it's possible that Ley remembered you?"

"Maybe," Linda sighed. "I've had times where I started to remember things, just blurs, but as I told Ley, they always cause a headache and then fade away. These blurs aren't dreams. They're normally triggered by déjà vu, and most of them happen while I'm talking with John. He's been so kind in trying to help me remember things. He even has a journal of some of the things I remembered so I wouldn't lose it later. He keeps it somewhere in the lab."

"So, you don't remember any of these blurs now?" I asked.

"Not really."

"And you've never had a strange memory dream?"

"Nope, at least, not to my recollection. I do remember waking up with a sense of dread or waking up feeling depressed. I even woke up in tears before, but I couldn't remember why I was crying."

"What about—"

"Look, I'm sorry to disappoint, but that's all I got. I *want* to remember you. I *want* to remember Ley. I just can't, no matter how hard I try."

"I want to remember, too," I sighed.

Linda and I sat on the bed and ate our food in silence. I couldn't stop thinking about the mission; she clearly couldn't either. She kept checking her phone for messages. After a few minutes, Savannah sent something to her. I tried to look over Linda's shoulder to see it, but she turned away from me as she sent something back.

"What did the message say?" I asked. "Has Savannah found anything yet?"

"Yeah," Linda said. "Briar was found leaving the park in her human form. Savannah thinks that's where the ship's elevator must be hidden."

"Wait, so does that mean that the scan isn't done?" I asked.

"No," she said. "Savannah is having trouble getting anything from the downtown area, which is where the park is located. The signal is being blocked."

"Which means the Elements must be there, right?"

"Yes, though Savannah doesn't have the exact location. Luckily, we shouldn't need the exact location if we're in the general vicinity. There's one minor problem, though. If we go in our disguises, we won't go unnoticed."

"What are we gonna do if someone spots us?" I asked.

"We proceed with the plan. It'll be embarrassing, and we may have to find a way to explain ourselves, but it shouldn't blow our mission. Not that many people are out in the park this time of year anyway with all the snow and ice on the ground."

"Okay," I said. "Let's take those space monsters down!"

"Go ahead and get ready," Linda said. "I've ordered Savannah to bring you to the park and stay with you until I can get there. I'll meet up with you as soon as I can."

"Wait, why are you sending me ahead of you?"

"The sooner we find the elevator to the ship, the better," she started. "And also, I have something I need to do before I go out on a suicide mission."

"Can't I just stay back with y—"

"It's private!" Linda jumped.

"Oh," I said quietly. "My apologies."

"…I'm sorry. I shouldn't have jumped like that. I'm just feeling stressed."

Linda and I stared at each other awkwardly. We didn't look away from each other until we began to change into our disguises. I put on everything from the body paint (avoiding the bandages over my wound) to the colored lenses for my eyes, which I needed help with. Linda only put on her clothes and left her blue wig, body paint, and colored lenses on the bed. She wore a blue sweatshirt and matching pants.

"I should leave," I said quickly. "I'm sure Savannah is waiting. What time should I expect you to arrive?"

"It's about ten o'clock now," Linda said, checking her phone. "I should be there by eleven-thirty, and I'll even bring some food so we can have an early lunch. Nothing big, of course, just something to keep our energy up."

I started for the door but then stopped as I thought about why Linda would stay behind. It suddenly occurred to me that maybe her private reason for staying longer was John. I turned to Linda and gave her a loose hug, making sure not to get orange body paint on her.

"I'm sure John will be just fine," I said, causing my sister to blush.

"Thanks, Liz."

"What did you call me?" I asked as I let her go.

"Oh, uh, Liz is short for Elizabeth," Linda said. "Lizzie would work, too; it's a nickname."

"Ley wanted to call me that," I said, "but I didn't like it at the time."

"I'm sorry, I should've asked before I—"

"No, it's okay," I said. "I was wrong before. Liz has a nice ring to it."

Linda gave a faint smile before doing a double take at my outfit. "Oh, crap. I didn't realize the dress was sleeveless," she sighed. "I can lend you a coat."

"I'll be fine," I insisted.

"Liz—"

"I grew up in a drafty orphanage. Trust me when I say I'll be fine."

"You'll regret not bringing a coat."

"I doubt it."

...I would regret not taking the coat.

Chapter 15 (Elizabeth)

I stood under a shelter in the park with Savannah, waiting for my sister. Except for a few dirty looks, I hadn't been noticed, but my chances of causing a scene increased the longer I stood out there. It was already half past one, officially making Linda two hours late, and causing me to become angry.

"Where are you, Linda?" I mumbled to myself.

"She'll be here, Elizabeth," Savannah said, looking down at her phone. "There's no need to worry."

"At this point, I don't know if I'm more worried or annoyed," I said, "…or cold."

The temperature had only dropped since our arrival. A thick layer of snow and ice covered the sidewalks. I was surprised to see that there was a decent-sized crowd. Parents were helping their children build snowmen and snow forts. A group of kids had gotten into a snowball fight near the shelter I was in. One of the kids accidentally hit me in the shoulder with a large snowball, making me hate myself even more for not taking the coat. My regret only grew as the cold wind blew on my bare arms and legs.

Savannah, who was smart enough to wear a nice winter coat, kept messing with her phone, ignoring me and everyone else around her. She was becoming visibly annoyed, probably because she was out in the cold longer than she was supposed to be.

"Elizabeth, do you think you'll be fine on your own?" she asked me. "I have to get back to the base. I've got an important call to make."

"Can't you just make your call here?" I asked.

"It's classified, so no, I can't just make the call here. This is a public area."

"But what if Linda doesn't show?"

"She'll be here soon, I'm sure of it," Savannah insisted. "You have Ley's phone now, right? You can send Linda a message if you're worried."

"Well, if your call is so urgent, then I guess I'm alright with you leaving," I said. "I'll be fine here."

"Thanks," she said.

After she left, I decided to call Linda. There was no response, so I tried again. Still no response. I left her a voicemail and sent at least six text messages asking her where she was, but still received nothing in return. I looked around the park and noticed that more people were staring at me, causing me to panic. Linda originally said that being spotted by the public wouldn't be that big a deal, but she was also under the impression that hardly anyone would be around.

It was at that moment that something caught my eye. A girl with red hair, pale skin, and blood-red eyes walked through the park and into the girls' bathroom. I waited a few minutes to see if she would emerge, but when she didn't, I took a deep breath and went inside. All of the stalls were open except for the large one at the end of the room. Though the door was shut and locked, I couldn't see any feet from the space under the stall. The floors and walls closer to the toilets were visibly filthy, and the smell was atrocious. Though it seemed like a nasty and unladylike thing to do, I swallowed my pride and slid under the door of the locked stall. After I got back up, I saw the elevator leading to the Elements' ship. It was awkwardly placed in front of the toilet. Gross.

I quickly checked Ley's phone for notifications. Linda still hadn't sent a thing, not even a message to say she was running late. It was like she had forgotten about me. With the rancid smell of the bathroom burning through my nostrils, I went to leave through the stall door, only to find myself accidentally pressing the button of the elevator.

"I guess I'm on my own," I said to myself, trying not to panic.

When I arrived on the ship, I realized that Linda never told me her plan. She had only talked about infiltrating the ship, nothing more. That meant that I couldn't even get a head start. I was completely useless. I tried to focus on my breathing. Panicking would only cause me to be easily spotted and caught, which was the last thing I needed. If I got caught, it would only complicate Linda's plan, whatever it was.

"Hey!" I heard someone shout. I spun around and saw Briar. As she approached me, her skin turned orange. She looked furious.

"What's your name?" she asked me.

"My n-name?" I asked nervously.

"You do have a name, don't you?"

"Of course, I do. Who doesn't?"

"Well, what is it then?"

I let out a nervous laugh as I tried to come up with something that sounded Elemental. I didn't want to come up with something too obvious because I feared it would make me stick out. I thought back to the names of people I had met when I snuck out of the orphanage.

"I'm waiting," Briar said.

"My name is… uh, Eldrid," I said.

"Well, Eldrid, what did I say about walking in your natural form in broad daylight!?" Briar yelled. "Do you not remember the speech I gave to everyone before we arrived on Earth? There are

Resistance agents all over this city. You could've compromised our location."

"I'm sorry, Briar," I said. "It won't happen again, I swear."

"I know it won't," Briar said as she grabbed my arm and began leading me down the hall, "because I'll be locking you in one of our cells until we get back to Elahntra. Once we return, you'll have to answer to the council."

I began to internally freak out. If Briar locked me away and Linda didn't show up, I knew I would be found out and killed. I had to escape. I just needed a diversion.

"Briar!" Misty shouted as she ran up to us. "Briar, where the heck were you?"

"Since you found the ourathian, I went to check up on some of our old friends who've been stationed in this city," Briar said. "I figured they'd want an update on our progress."

"Well, I'm glad you're back," Misty sighed. "We thought we found her, but we were wrong. We need your help."

"Can't you see I'm busy here, Misty?" Briar asked as she glared at me. "This Element, Eldrid, was waltzing around on Earth in her natural form."

"I know that's a major offense, but this is more important right now," Misty argued. "We need all hands on deck if we want to catch that little brat."

"Fine," she groaned. "Eldrid, I'm assuming you were notified about our not-so-little issue."

"Yes, of course," I lied.

"If you help us capture the ourathian, I'll refrain from reporting you to the council," she said. "Do we have a deal?"

"Yes, Briar," I said.

Briar released me and ran off with Misty. As long as they were after whoever escaped, I was in the clear. I decided to further explore the ship while I waited for my sister to arrive with her plan. I was still angry about her being late, but I was also angry with myself for clumsily pressing the button, leaving me stranded on the ship alone. I figured Linda would probably be mad, too, once she found out I had gone on without her.

I went through the hallway and entered a large, two-story room. The ceiling had the colors for each element as well as two E's back-to-back in the center. It was beautiful. The pillars supporting the second story of the room also represented the four elements, with each having a different thing in the center just like the ones near the elevator. I heard footsteps in the distance, causing me to become alert. I turned around just in time to see Briar and Misty.

"See, Briar? I told you I recognized her," Misty said. "There is no Element named Eldrid on this ship. That girl is Elizabeth."

"Well, I wish you would've recognized her sooner!" Briar shouted.

While they were arguing, I took the opportunity to run. Just as I was about to reach the hallway, a large wall of ice formed in front of me, causing me to stumble backwards and keeping me from going any farther.

"You didn't think we were going to let you get away again, did you Elizabeth?" Misty asked.

"No, this can't be happening," I mumbled. "Where are you, Linda?"

"You know, I just gotta admit, I'm impressed you could make up a name so quickly," Briar said. "Too bad a new name doesn't change your face. Only an *idiot* would've fallen for your lie."

"Well, it fooled you, didn't it?" I retorted. "So, based on your statement, you're the idiot. You wouldn't have caught me if it weren't for Misty."

"You little twirp!" Briar shouted as she lunged at me.

I got up and moved out of the way just before she could pin me. Her hands and eyes became engulfed with flames as she sent a fiery blast my way. Thinking that I would be fine, I allowed it to hit me, but I quickly learned that my human shield idea was wrong. The blast knocked me back into one of the pillars. Misty and Briar began to laugh.

"Did you see that?" Briar cackled. "She didn't even move! And she thinks *I'm* the idiot?"

"But I'm immune to fire attacks," I said. "Since I can wield fire, I can't get hurt by fire, right?"

"No, sweetie," Misty laughed. "I can understand where you would draw that conclusion, but no, you aren't fully immune to fire. Fire attacks from other Elements can still hurt you, depending on how strong they are. Briar could easily kill you right now if she wanted to."

"Fine, then," I said through clenched teeth. "*Kill me.*"

"Why would we?" Misty asked. "We still need you, for now."

Briar and Misty laughed as I tried to sit up. I slipped my hand into the right pocket of my dress and felt something cool touch my skin. *The knife.* Quickly, I pulled it out and lunged towards Briar. She managed to block it with her hand, but to my surprise, the blade didn't go through; it didn't even cut her. Instead, the metal began to glow red as it melted before my eyes. Briar grabbed the plastic handle from me and melted that, too, with a smirk.

"Pathetic," she said, "but I applaud you for trying nonetheless."

"B-but how?" I asked. "How did you—?"

"Aw, poor little Elizabeth doesn't understand how my powers work, how *her* powers work." Briar laughed.

I'd never felt so hopeless. I found myself wishing for Linda to not find the elevator. I just wanted her to be safe, even if it meant my death.

Chapter 16 (Linda)

After Elizabeth and Savannah left for the park, I went back to check on John. I walked into his room and found him asleep with the last of his breakfast still sitting on his tray. I knew I should've gone on with Elizabeth, but I wanted to say a proper goodbye to John first in case something happened to me during the mission, which I fully anticipated. I started to gently run my fingers through his hair, causing him to wake up.

"Linda, you startled me," he said as he sat up and put his glasses on.

"How'd you know it was me without your glasses?" I asked. "You're literally blind without them."

"I doubt any of the nurses would be playing with my hair, and I'd find it creepy if it were anyone other than you anyway." John laughed. "So, why exactly are you here? I thought you and Elizabeth were going on that crazy suicide mission."

"I wanted to see you alone before leaving," I told him. "Ley's rescue mission nearly cost me my life, and I know this mission will be even more dangerous. So, I wanted a chance to say goodbye just in case I don't make it back."

"Don't do that," he said. "Remember our first mission together?"

"Yeah. How could I forget it?"

"I didn't know at the time what you could and couldn't do when it came to your powers. I spent most of the time trying to protect you when you didn't need protecting at all."

"It's the thought that counts." I laughed. "Though, to be honest, we all need someone to protect us sometimes no matter how strong we are. There have been plenty of missions where you saved my life."

"That's not the point," John said. "The point is, I know now what you're capable of, and I believe that you'll make it back to me in one piece. You may be injured, but you'll be alive."

"If this is how you really feel, then why did you object to me going in the first place?" I asked.

"Because I didn't want you to take the risk," he said. "I care about you, and I don't want to see you get hurt because you felt the need to take reckless vengeance."

"This is about more than vengeance," I said. "It's about proving to the Elements that the human race is a force to be reckoned with. If we show them how hard we're willing to fight back, maybe they'll finally leave us alone."

"Well, you're certainly the woman for the job." John chuckled.

"Thanks, John," I said as I gave him a quick kiss on the cheek.

"What was that for?" he asked as he started to blush. "Not that I'm complaining."

"That's for just in case I miss that date of ours," I said. "Because you and I both know that there is a chance I don't make it back alive."

"I've never known you to fail, and I've known you your whole life," John said, turning red when he realized what he had just admitted.

"Known me my whole life? John, we didn't meet until well after I came here. So, how… unless you knew me before I lost my memories."

John stared down at the white sheets on his bed, refusing to look up at me.

"What are you hiding from me, John?" I asked, fighting to stay calm.

"I-I…"

"*John?*"

"Don't be mad. I just didn't think it was the right time to tell you."

"Tell me what?"

"I knew you when we were kids. Your sisters, too. We were best friends. I know how and why your memories were erased, but I didn't tell you because I knew you'd ask questions. I thought it would be easier to show you than to try to explain it to you, so I've been working on a way to restore your memories in the lab. I thought you and I could go searching for your sisters after that, but then they showed up here on their own."

"But, John, if we were such good friends, how come you and I never spoke when I first arrived at the base? We didn't start talking outside of work until you knocked me over in the cafeteria six months after I started working here. Is that the only reason we're friends now? Were you going to avoid me until you found a way to restore my memories?"

"Yes," John said, still avoiding my gaze.

"Why?"

"I was afraid that maybe I wouldn't like the new you or that maybe the new you wouldn't like me. Every time I saw you walk by, I saw my childhood friend, but I knew that you didn't recognize me. It hurt… it *really* hurt. I wasn't going to speak to you socially until I could restore your memories because then I'd be reunited with the you I knew before, the old you."

"So, what you're saying is, you don't like who I am now?"

"What? No!" John blurted. "I-I was afraid that I wouldn't, but I was pleasantly surprised. Please don't be mad at me."

"Don't be mad!?" I shouted. "You knew about my past, you knew I have sisters, and you hid it from me! Then you had the nerve to act oblivious! I remember when you first asked me about my powers, about my wings. I remember you asking me about my family and my childhood as if you didn't know that my memories had been wiped."

"I would've told you the truth about everything once I figured out how to restore your memories. I promise you, I would've."

"How can I trust you now, John?" I asked. "How in the heck am I supposed to trust you? Our friendship was built on a lie, and if we had started dating, our relationship would've been built on a lie, too. Even as your boss, I'm not sure how I'm supposed to trust you."

"I'm sorry."

"No, you're not sorry for what you did; you're only sorry that you got caught," I said. "And you can forget about that date. I only go out with men I can trust."

"Linda, please—"

"Goodbye, John."

I ran to my room in section one, fighting tears. John was my best friend, or at least I thought he was. I felt like I could let my guard down around him. I felt like I could let myself be vulnerable around him. After realizing that John had lied to me, I felt like I was going to be sick. He knew me before I lost my memories, he was my friend even then, and yet his solution was to hide from me until he could find some way to restore everything that I'd forgotten. *What if my memories couldn't be restored?*

I checked the time and decided to take a quick nap. There was no way I could focus on a dangerous mission in the emotional state I was in. Unfortunately, I had a horrible nightmare, causing me to wake up in a pool of my own sweat. The first thing I did after calming myself down was check the time. To my horror, I was already two hours late. I'd forgotten to set an alarm.

By the time I was ready, another half hour had passed. I knew Elizabeth would be ticked at me if she hadn't already died of frostbite from being stuck out in the cold. I drove to the park as fast as I could without risking getting pulled over by the police. When I arrived, Elizabeth was nowhere to be seen, and neither was Savannah. I checked my phone and saw that Elizabeth had sent me a few messages. One was to inform me that Savannah had left. The others were her asking where I was.

"Look, there goes another dumb cosplay freak," a lady said to her son as I walked through the park.

"Another?" I asked as I turned around. "You saw another girl here?"

"Yeah, she looked like you, but orange," the lady said. "She ran into the bathroom, and I didn't see her come back out. Maybe she decided to wash that stupid body paint off. I will never understand kids these days with their cosplays. What exactly are you supposed to be anyway? Your outfit is the dumbest thing I've ever seen."

"Oh really?" I asked. "Have you looked in the mirror lately?"

I ran into the bathroom before the lady could get in another word. The stalls were grungy and empty, as park bathrooms usually were. The only stall that appeared to be taken was the large one at the end. I couldn't see any feet under the stall, but I did spot some orange body paint. Elizabeth had been there. I slid under the stall door and saw the elevator. Without hesitation, I pressed the button.

"Don't worry, Elizabeth," I said, "I'm coming."

As soon as I entered the ship, I tried to figure out which direction Elizabeth went. I only had two choices, the door in front of me or the door behind me. I guessed the door in front of me and ran as fast as I could. I wasn't sure when Elizabeth had arrived or where she was, but I hoped that she wasn't too far ahead. I used one of the internal elevators to go upstairs. When I entered the main hall on the second floor, I found myself looking another water Element in the eye.

"Oh, um, I'm sorry," she said, sounding nervous. "I was just trying to find the, um, the library. Any idea where it is?"

"No, sorry," I said. "I'm new."

"Oh, uh, so am I," the girl said.

"By any chance has a fire Element been captured or has a new fire Element arrived?" I asked.

"Um, I think I heard Briar saying she was taking somebody to the cells."

"Thanks," I said. "Good luck finding the library."

Something about that water Element seemed familiar, but then again, I had fought many water Elements before. Maybe I fought one of her family members. Whatever the case, I didn't have much time to think about it as I had more important business to take care of.

I remembered where the cells were located based on my last visit, but the moment I stepped into the room, I realized that I was expected. Briar stood by Elizabeth's cell with a smirk. I began to feel nauseous. Before I could run, Daisy stepped behind me.

"Just as I suspected," Briar said. "As soon as Misty and I caught Elizabeth, we knew you couldn't be too far behind. Nice water Element disguise, by the way."

"After you captured me before, you made it clear that you were willing to let Elizabeth live as long as you had me," I said. "So, take me and let her go."

"It's too late for that," Daisy said. "She's already proven that she can find our ship with the help of your team. What would stop her from coming back to rescue you again?"

"Why don't you just move your ship again or take me back to your planet?" I asked.

"No!" Elizabeth shouted before Briar or Daisy could answer. "I wouldn't let them take you. I would find a way to chase after them."

"Elizabeth, you aren't helping," I sighed.

I was locked into the cell next to Elizabeth's. I felt completely hopeless. Ley was dead, Elizabeth and I were captured, and nobody was coming to rescue us. It's not like I thought that outcome was impossible, but part of me thought that I'd at least be able to do some damage first, or that I could at least help Elizabeth escape with her life.

"I'm sorry I went without you," Elizabeth said from her cell. "I wasn't trying to. I accidentally pressed—"

"It's okay," I sighed. "I'm sorry I was late. And I'm sorry I even brought you on this mission. I should've stuck with my instincts and left you at the base."

"Linda, I chose to be here with you. If I had a chance to do this all over again, I would still choose to be here with you."

"Thanks."

"My eyes are getting itchy," Elizabeth complained.

"Yeah, mine, too. The air in here is pretty dry," I said. "Just be careful if you start rubbing your eyes. I spent a whole five dollars on each pair of colored contacts, and that's *with* the post-Halloween discount. I'm still shocked at how much was left this close to Christmas."

"Is five dollars a large sum of money around here? I haven't been paying attention to how much things cost in this city."

"No, Liz, I was making a joke," I sighed. "Five bucks is nothing."

"Bucks? I thought you said dollars. Am I missing something here?"

"You don't understand, both can be used… you know what? We'll have a more in-depth talk about American currency later. We need to find a way out."

"You're in luck. I already found one."

"What do you mean, you already found one?"

I couldn't see what Elizabeth was doing, but it sounded like she got up, charged towards the force field, and fell flat on her back.

"B-but the wall is made of light!" she exclaimed.

"It looks like it, but it isn't," I said. "A force field is a solid surface. I'm surprised you didn't realize this sooner."

"Briar decided to stay and wait for you, so that's why I didn't try to escape earlier."

"Trust me, if you could escape by running through the force field, someone would still be guarding us both."

"So, what do we do?" Elizabeth asked.

"We come up with a plan B, and hope that we aren't stuck with plan C."

"What's plan C?"

"It involves a few Elements dying, but we go out with them."

"I think I prefer plan B, whatever it is."

"Either way, we are very lucky that they didn't search my pockets."

"Well, they've seemed pretty distracted about something. Briar and Misty were talking about an 'ourathian girl,' whatever that means."

Elizabeth and I tried searching for a way out when we heard footsteps heading our way. I felt my heart accelerate as two male Elements stepped into the room. One of them was an earth Element, and he entered Elizabeth's cell. The other, a fire Element, entered mine.

"If you're here to ask me the same questions as before, I'm afraid my answers haven't changed," I said.

"Oh, but they will," the fire Element said. "How long have you been in contact with your mother?"

"My mother? The one who abandoned me? Yeah, never met her."

"Are you the prophesied weapon?"

"I don't even know what that means."

"So, you want to be stubborn? Fine then. Maybe your sister will convince you."

"Huh?"

The earth Element brought Elizabeth out of her cell and in front of mine. Vines were tightly wrapped around her neck, but she still had a little room to breathe.

"Where is your mother hiding?" the fire Element asked.

"I DON'T KNOW! I SWEAR I DON'T!" I yelled. "Just, please, let Elizabeth go; she doesn't know either."

"We'll kill her."

"NO! If you're going to kill someone, kill me. Not her, ME!"

The vines around Elizabeth's neck tightened, causing her to gasp for air. I wasn't sure what to do. If I lied, they'd probably be able to tell, especially since I had no clue what they were asking me about. But telling the truth wasn't working.

"Please," I begged, "let her go."

"Then give us answers," the fire Element insisted, walking closer to me. "If hurting your sister isn't enough, we can always hurt you, too."

I realized that he intended to burn me, but unlike my previous experience, there weren't other fire Elements to keep me from fighting back. As soon as he took one step closer, I lunged towards him. I grabbed the back of his head and slammed it against the wall of my cell repeatedly. The earth Element dropped Elizabeth before entering my cell to defend his teammate. A long, thick vine shot out of his hand, pinning my arms to my waist. I ripped my right arm free of the vines before grabbing hold of what was still attached to the Element's hand. His eyes widened as I took the vine and used it to sling him against the wall. He fell to the ground, holding his head.

"Now answer me something," I said as I approached him. "Why are you so obsessed with my family and my people?" The Element just laughed. "Answer me!"

"Because you're monsters, all of you. Monsters!"

"Screw you."

Without hesitation, I stomped his head, leaving a bloody mess. It reminded me of the first time I saw Element blood, the first time I killed. It was almost disturbing how quickly I got used to it. I looked out of my cell to see Elizabeth on the other side with a look of disgust on her face.

"A-are you alright?" she stuttered.

"Yeah," I said. "Not the first time I've killed an Element, and I'm sure it won't be the last. How about you? You alright?"

"Uh, yeah. I'm alright, I guess."

I looked down to see the earth Element's body and blood turn into leaves, something I had seen many times but still wasn't used to.

"What happened to him?" Elizabeth asked.

"This is how Elements die," I said. "They become something related to their powers."

"Does that mean the fire Element is still alive?"

"Yeah," I said before killing him, too, "and now he won't be able to terrorize anyone else." His body went up in flames and quickly burned out, leaving scorch marks behind. "Now that that's taken care of, can you access the computer?"

"I can try," Elizabeth said.

"Okay, while you attempt to figure that out, I'll keep trying to find a way to bust out from the inside."

I looked down at the pile of leaves again and noticed a thick purple cuff that had been partially buried. I began thinking about how the Elements were able to cross through the force field so easily and decided to test out a theory. I put the cuff on my left wrist and walked through the force field.

"Linda, how'd you do that?" Elizabeth asked.

"I picked this up from the earth Element's body," I said.

"So *that's* how they could cross through without hitting their heads."

"Here," I walked back into the cell and grabbed a scorched cuff, "you can have one, too." I quickly tested it to make sure it was still working. Once I realized it was, I handed it to Elizabeth. "I'm not sure if we'll need them again anytime soon, but it doesn't hurt to have them just in case."

"Thanks," Elizabeth said. "So, now that we're out, what do we do? You never told me a plan."

"We're going to blow this ship up along with all the Elements on it," I said. "It's time to let the Elements know what happens when they screw with the people of Earth."

Chapter 17 (Ley)

I woke up on the floor of the Elements' ship. My back was killing me. At first, I feared that maybe I had been paralyzed, but I was proven wrong as I began to move my feet. I held my breath and clenched my teeth as I pulled the ice out of me. I felt warm blood pour onto my hands from the wound. The bleeding didn't feel bad enough for me to panic, but I knew I'd still need medical attention sooner or later. I took off my jacket and tied it around me as tightly as I could to help stop the bleeding until I could find a doctor. I looked around the room and realized that my sisters were gone. The rest of the team and the Elements were gone, too. I guessed that they thought I was dead, which meant that I had to find my own way out of the ship.

"Well, I managed to get one of them, Briar," I heard Misty say in the distance. "I killed Ley."

"Nice job, Misty," Briar said. "Where's the body?"

"She's by the farthest cell against the wall on the right side."

I quickly shapeshifted into an ant and crawled through one of the small holes in the metal grated floor just as Briar and Misty entered the room. I hadn't seen Briar since I was abducted. She, like Misty, had changed out of her school uniform. She wore a white dress, with black side panels that stopped a little above her knees. She had a necklace much like Misty's except the top color of hers was red and the bottom was blue.

"Well, where is she then, Misty?" Briar asked. "Why don't I see a body anywhere?"

"I-I," Misty stuttered, "she was right here! I stabbed her in the back with ice and washed her body over there against the wall. Look, there's even blood on the floor, and ice is right next to it."

"Did anyone else come through here? Could someone have moved the body?"

"I'm afraid not."

"You should've made sure Ley was really dead before running off, you frostbitten halfwit!"

"I thought I could catch the others. What did you expect me to do instead? Stand guard over the body?"

"Well, no," Briar sighed, "but I'm still mad that your attack failed to kill her. You should've put a piece of ice through her head after she went down."

"You're right, Briar, and I'm sorry," Misty said.

"Whether she's dead or alive, she's still on this ship since the team left without her," Briar said. "We'll send an alert to all Elements on board and then put the ship on partial lockdown; Elements can enter the ship, but nobody can leave."

"Where do you think Ley could be? There aren't *that* many places to hide."

Briar got down on her knees and began searching the grated floor. I stood as still as I could, figuring that movement would only cause Briar to spot me sooner. She continued to crawl on the floor, looking through the holes. Her blood-red eyes were less than a centimeter from me, but I blended in with my surroundings well enough to fool her.

"What the heck are you doing on the floor, Briar?" Misty asked.

"Ley's a shapeshifter. She could be hiding anywhere, even on the floor. It's grated, which would make it the perfect spot for her to hide."

"I could fill the space underneath the floor with water," Misty suggested. "It would block some of the vents, but it'll be temporary."

"Go ahead."

As soon as the water got close to where I was, I turned into a small water bug and tried once again to squeeze myself in between two of the holes in the floor, keeping me out of Briar's sight by a hair.

"I still can't see her anywhere," Briar complained. "We'll just have to keep an eye out for anything out of the ordinary: new crew members, Earth insects, *anything*. It's in Ley's best interest to get off this ship, so she can't hide away forever."

"I have an idea," Misty said. My heart stopped as her body turned to water and poured under the grated floor. Two glowing, blue eyes appeared, making the rest of Misty's translucent body visible. I could tell she hadn't spotted me yet, and I wanted to keep it that way. Slowly, I swam towards Briar's feet. I turned back into an ant, crawled onto the floor, and then crawled onto the underside of Briar's right heel.

After a few minutes of searching, Misty came back up from the floor. A large pool of water took the shape of her body before turning solid. It made me wonder if any of the other Elements could transform their bodies like that.

"Did you find anything?" Briar asked.

"No, but I guess it's possible I looked something over. The room is still spinning a bit from—"

"From you getting your butt handed to you? Doesn't surprise me," Briar scoffed as she stood up, nearly causing me to fall off her heel.

"We'll find her, Briar, so just calm down," Misty said as the water under the floor started to go away. "She'll slip up eventually. She's a stupid ourathian after all."

"Need I remind you of what that *stupid ourathian* is capable of?"

"…no."

"Then let's take this search seriously rather than counting on Ley slipping up."

After Briar and Misty started searching in another part of the room, I crawled back under the floor and kept moving until I reached an empty hallway. Then, I came out from under the floor and shapeshifted into a water Element. I began searching for the medical wing of the ship. I knew that nobody in the medical wing would hesitate to treat me since I disguised myself and Briar hadn't alerted anyone yet. The only issue was my clothing. While most of the Elements wouldn't have thought twice about it, anyone who fought me earlier would've recognized my blue jacket and my jeans, which would have caused them to attack me. I figured that once I reached the medical wing, I would be able to steal another patient's clothing. I just needed to avoid being noticed on my way there.

To avoid any conflict, I hid in the closest room I could find whenever I heard someone walking in the hallway. Most of the rooms I ran into were empty, but that changed when I heard someone talking from around the corner, prompting me to dive through a door to my right. Much to my disbelief, I found myself in a forest.

"Hi," a wind Element girl said as she approached me.

Her hair was cut short overall, but the hair on her right side was significantly longer. It was as if she had shaved the left side of her head but was trying to grow it back out. She wore a cropped purple top with high-rise pants and a long-sleeved jacket. All were various shades of purple. The top and jeans were darker than the jacket. I noticed that her skin was a deeper purple than Windy's, and her hair matched her top.

"Hello," I said. "I'm new to this ship. Where exactly am I?"

"You've never seen a simulation room before?" the girl asked. "I find that hard to believe."

"Oh, this is a *simulation* room." I laughed nervously. "I thought the ship added a new… uh… greenhouse."

"Heck no!" The girl cackled. "We're not adding another greenhouse to this ship. If the earth Elements want more plants, they can grow them in their own rooms."

"That's a relief," I lied. "I was really worried for a second there. I mean, if you cave on one thing, what will stop the earth Elements from demanding more?"

"I know, right?"

"So, anyway, as I was saying before, I'm new here," I said. "Could you tell me where the medical wing is?"

"Of course," the girl said. "I just came back from being stationed on Earth a few months ago, so I understand how easy it is to get lost. As soon as you leave, take a right, and keep going straight until you reach the end of the hall. Then turn left. You'll see a large sign pointing you in the right direction from there. You can't miss it."

"Thanks," I said.

I began to wonder just how long the Elements had been on our planet. I figured it had to have been for a while since none of them seemed to speak an alien language. *Did they even have their own language?*

When I finally found the medical wing, I was greeted by a tall earth Element nurse standing by a purple desk with hologram computers. Her thick, green hair appeared to be made up of vines, which she had tied into a messy French braid. She had brown eyeshadow and dark green lipstick on her face. She wore thick, white glasses and brown scrubs. She also wore a necklace like some of the other Elements. Her necklace's colors matched Daisy's.

"Hello, my name is Flora," she said. "How can I help you?"

"Oh, um," I started, trying to come up with my story, "I got in a fight with one of my fellow water Elements, and it went a little too far. I ended up with ice in my back, which I managed to pull out, and I'm in a lot of pain."

"I see so many cases like this, it's not even funny," the nurse said. "Those water Elements are real twirps, in my opinion… no offense to you. Anyway, just fill in this form while I set up a room for you to stay the night in."

"Oh, I don't need to stay the night, I'm just here because of—"

"Is this your first trip away from Elahntra?"

"Yes."

"Well, allow me to fill you in. Upon entering the medical wing, a patient is given a room and is required to stay for at least one night for any illness or injury. It's standard policy when visiting another planet. Unlike diseases on Elahntra, Earth diseases take time to show symptoms, and injuries can make you more susceptible to them."

"But—"

"No buts. I can't change the policy, and I won't make any exceptions."

I reluctantly took and filled out the medical form, which wasn't as hard to fake as I feared it would be. I needed to make up a name, so I went with Brooke. I was brought back to my room and immediately changed into a hospital gown. The room had a deep purple bed with green sheets. It appeared to be hovering over the blue metal floor. There were medical posters all over the walls, reminding me of doctor's offices back home. Two bright red chairs sat against the right wall, and a small vent was at the bottom of the wall to my left.

I began to grow anxious the longer I was there. I knew that Misty and Briar were searching for me. It was only a matter of time before they would think to search the hospital, and they knew that I could shapeshift. All they would need to do is ask for a demonstration of my powers to prove that I wasn't an Element.

"Attention all Elements," Briar's voice sounded throughout the ship, "Ley Smith is loose on this ship. We are on lockdown until she's found. Report any suspicious behavior to me."

I waited about an hour for my doctor and soon learned that Elemental fights, usually done for fun or to show dominance, were common. Elements with opposing powers (fire vs. water or wind vs. earth) were constantly fighting each other when they weren't fighting their own. At least, that's what I understood based on what I managed to hear from the nurses via eavesdropping. I tried to avoid asking questions directly, as that would make me look suspicious.

When my doctor came in, he didn't say much besides telling me I shouldn't have pulled the ice out on my own. He looked at my back, disinfected the wound, gave me some stitches, and then gave me some pain medication. Luckily for me, the ice didn't go nearly as deep as I thought it did. I figured that was because Misty had just been slammed against the wall by both Linda and Elizabeth before attacking me.

Once the doctor left, I determined that it was safe to sneak out. The only problem was, doctors and nurses were constantly walking throughout the place. I started by unhooking myself from all the machines before shapeshifting into a beetle. The doctors ran in, saw that I was gone, and began their search for me. After they left my room, I snuck into the next patient's room. I made sure they were asleep before turning back into a water Element and stealing their clothes. I also stole the patient's bag to store my real clothes inside. Before I could leave, I ran into Flora, who looked incredibly annoyed.

"It looks like we'll be adding security to your room, Brooke," she said as she escorted me back, not noticing the stolen bag of clothing. "We wouldn't want you to sneak out again, would we?"

Once again, I became extremely anxious the longer I was trapped in my room. Briar and Misty had plenty of time to search the rest of the ship, making them sure to discover me sooner or later. I looked around the room, desperately seeking a way to escape. Though, as much as I needed to escape, part of me just wanted to sleep. I was worn out after all the fighting that had taken place a few hours prior. On top of that, drowsiness was a side effect of the pain medication I was given.

As I tried to come up with an escape plan, I spotted a small spider crawling out of a vent. I figured that it must've come in on one of the Elements' clothing if not my own. I soon came up with a grand idea. I pressed a small red button on the side of my bed to alert one of the nurses.

"What do you need, Brooke?" Flora asked as she came into my room. "And please hurry, I have other patients waiting."

"I found the shapeshifter!" I exclaimed, pointing to the spider. "I wasn't able to use my powers because I—"

"Don't worry about your powers; it's a side effect," Flora explained. "Certain pain medications and sleeping drugs can cause us to lose control of our powers or temporarily lose them altogether."

I hadn't known that but was relieved that Flora thought that was what I meant. I was going to make up some pathetic story about my injury causing me to be too weak to use my powers. Thanks to Flora interrupting me mid-sentence, I knew one of the Elements' weaknesses, though it wouldn't do me much good if I couldn't get access to extra pain medication and a syringe.

As Flora went over to grab the spider, it crawled away into the vents, only making my lie seem more real. She tried to reach it using vines, but the spider was too fast and went out of sight. Flora immediately contacted Briar and warned her that the enemy was leaving the medical wing vents. I knew it would take time for Briar and Misty to find the spider, let alone figure out that it wasn't me. Because of that, I felt that it was safe to get some sleep.

***

I woke up the next morning when a fire Element nurse came into my room with breakfast. Unluckily for me, she brought an Elahntran breakfast. It looked like oatmeal, but it was pink with purple, red, and brown chunks. It was also much thicker in texture than the oatmeal I was used to. I was given a greenish juice to drink with it. I, not wanting to blow my cover, forced myself to eat and drink what was given to me. The juice was good. It tasted like kiwi with a hint of peach and banana, almost like a smoothie. The oatmeal, however, tasted kind of like birthday cake mixed with bad grape cough syrup and that cherry-flavored numbing stuff that dentists use. To make things worse, the texture of the oatmeal almost made me gag.

I was held in the medical wing a few hours longer before the nurses even considered releasing me. I was relieved when I was given a simple cheese sandwich with a bag of chips for lunch. As it turned out, the Elements stationed on Earth had gotten used to eating Earth food rather than the Elahntran food they had grown up with. I found out from more eavesdropping that cheese sandwiches, chips, and donuts were some of the Elements' favorite Earth foods. After hearing that, I almost felt bad about not being able to stay for dessert.

While Flora was changing something out in my room, I managed to grab a syringe from her pocket. I didn't know the Elahntran health policy concerning syringes, so I couldn't tell if it had been used or not. Not that I cared. It wasn't like I was planning to use it on myself.

After I was finally released, I got dressed and then went into the same patient's room that I had gone to before. The patient was still asleep. I searched their room for sleeping or pain medications that I could use in case I got caught. I found a small glass bottle that had rolled under the bed. Before I could read the label, I heard nurses talking nearby. It sounded like they were getting closer to me, so I used the syringe to suck the medicine out of the bottle and then ran out of the room.

I left the medical wing and went back into the main hall. I was about to go through the door at the end when it opened, and another water Element stepped through. She almost bumped right into me. I freaked out as I tried to come up with a story on the spot.

"Oh, um, I'm sorry," I said, sounding nervous as I hid my syringe. "I was just trying to find the, um, the library. Any idea where it is?"

"No, sorry," the water Element said. "I'm new."

"Oh, uh, so am I," I said.

"By any chance has a fire Element been captured or has a new fire Element arrived?" she asked.

"Um, I think I heard Briar saying she was taking somebody to the cells," I lied.

"Thanks," she said. "Good luck finding the library."

There was something familiar about the water Element's face and voice that I just couldn't place. It was as if I knew her, but that was impossible. The only water Element I knew by name was Misty.

As I continued walking through the hall, I started to panic. What I had told that water Element was a lie. If the fire Element she was looking for wasn't in the cells, then she could've suspected that I was an imposter. I had to hurry. Instead of going forward, I waited for the other water Element to leave before turning left and going deeper into the halls.

I heard footsteps nearby, making me think that maybe I had been found out already. I had gone through too much to be caught so soon and so easily, so I ran through the open door to my right. I found myself in an Element's bedroom. The walls were painted blue, and the bed was covered with white sheets, making me suspect that the room belonged to another water Element. I pushed the bag with my real clothes into a corner of the room that was already piled up. After doing that, I tried to find a place in the room to hide, a place that was safe. I found a fish tank across from the bed. I turned into a fly, hovered over the tank, and then turned into a bright blue fish. A water Element boy walked into the room. He looked to be only sixteen or seventeen years old. He immediately walked over to the fish tank and dumped a couple scoops of fish food in.

"Wait a second," he said as he looked into the tank. "I only had one blue fish."

His eyes widened, letting me know that I had been found out. I jumped out of the tank and turned back into myself. I was sprawled out on the floor, drenched. The syringe fell out of my pocket and rolled to the boy's feet. His eyes narrowed, as he picked up the syringe and tossed it away from me. Then the boy quickly closed and locked his bedroom door.

"Please don't kill me," I begged. "I don't want to hurt anyone. I just want to get back to my sisters."

"Really?" he asked. "What's the syringe for then?"

"I don't even know what's in it," I said, "but I can assure you that I was only planning to use it in self-defense."

The boy extended his hand and helped me up. "You don't *look* evil," he said as he studied my face.

"Thanks, I guess," I said. "Look, I need to get off this ship. So, if you could help me by showing me the way to the exit, I'd be very grateful."

"You're an ourathian, so why would I help you?" he asked. "You may not look evil, but that doesn't mean I trust you. You're the enemy."

"Okay, so I'm an ourathian," I said, putting together that the word ourathian meant human. "Why does that automatically make me bad?"

"Well, I don't know," the boy said. "We were all told from the time that we were little that all ourathians are evil, that we have to stop them."

"I know there are evil people of my species, but that doesn't make us all bad," I said. "I was told that Elements are evil and hostile, but you don't seem all that bad to me." The boy still didn't seem to trust me. I looked around for a weapon just in case I needed to defend myself but found nothing. I was completely at the mercy of the boy. "I've only told you the truth," I said. "If you don't believe me, then kill me or call for Briar."

The boy stared at me for a bit, trying to determine just what he wanted to do. "You really want peace?" he asked. "I've been waiting for this war between my people and yours to end for a long time now."

"Of course, I want peace," I said. "If you want it, too, then help me escape. I'll try to get the people on my side to set up a meeting with your people. Maybe then we can end the fighting. No more blood needs to be spilled on either side."

"Okay, but I'm going to need something to make sure you don't double-cross me."

"I don't have anything of value on me right now, but you could take my—" Before I could finish my sentence, a sharp band of ice wrapped around my left wrist.

"If that meeting you mentioned isn't set up within a week, I'll use that ice to slit your wrist," the boy said. "And don't even attempt to melt or shatter it. I can refreeze it the very moment you try, even if you're miles away."

I grabbed the bag with my clothes as the boy went to unlock his bedroom door. While his back was turned, I also grabbed the syringe as a precaution. I was so distracted by the ice band that I forgot to shapeshift into an Element again. The boy led me through the hall and towards the elevator to the floor below us. From there, we headed to a large room similar to the one where the main elevator was kept, just minus the pillars. I felt relieved. Not only would I escape, but I had a chance to end the fighting between humans and Elements.

"What's your name?" I asked the boy.

"Delta," he said. "And you're Ley, right?"

"Wow. It seems like everyone on this ship knows my name," I joked. "It's like I'm famous or something."

"You kinda are, but that's not a good thing."

"…oh." I wanted to ask what exactly I did, but I figured the answer would be the same one Misty gave me. *Did my existence really pose a threat?* "You know," I said, changing the subject, "the agents on my sister's team couldn't figure out how to make the elevator go back down."

"That's probably because the elevator to go down is in this room and the one they came up in is in the next room over," Delta laughed.

"What?"

"Yeah. The elevator they used only takes people up," he explained. "Having two separate elevators helps with traffic. So, the only time that elevator goes down is after it's been idle for so long or if somebody down below called for it."

"Have any people other than Resistance agents found the elevator before?" I asked.

"No, but they could if we wanted them to," Delta said. "We're pretty good at keeping it hidden. It also helps that your average person doesn't have access to high-tech scanners."

"Why did you let us find Linda?" I asked. "I mean, you didn't even change the location of the elevator."

"We weren't trying to let you find her," Delta said. "That was an accident. We created the disguise for our agent, Rose, which we figured would keep you from pursuing us. Needless to say, we got a bit cocky. After the remains of our data analysis team were found, we decided to go ahead and let you find Linda."

"I still can't believe you all thought we'd leave at the expense of my sister," I said.

"It sounds fair to me; lose one to save the rest," Delta said.

Just as we got close to the down elevator, a huge wall of ice formed, blocking us off. Delta tried using his powers to break through it, but an icicle went through his head before he could shatter it. The band of ice he had created around my wrist melted away. I turned around and saw Misty.

"You know, I hate to give you any credit, but you're pretty clever, Ley," she said. "That whole spider thing had us fooled all night. We finally caught it this morning. It wasn't until we tried to interrogate and torture it that we realized it wasn't you."

"Why did you kill him? Why did you kill Delta?" I asked, looking at his body. "He was just a kid, and he was one of your own." Delta's body began to turn to water. It looked like he was melting. "What's happening to him?"

"His body is reverting to its elemental form," Misty explained. "He's part of nature now, nothing more. That's the price of our powers."

"You did this to him!"

"No, *you* did this to him by convincing him to help you. But don't feel too bad about it, Ley. He's much older than he looked, and you wouldn't have escaped anyway. The down elevator and the escape pods have been disabled at the moment."

"Please don't kill me, Misty," I begged. "Just let me get back to my sisters."

"Oh, I won't *kill* you, not yet anyway, but I won't free you either," Misty said. "I'll lock you up and have you tortured for information." She grabbed my arm and dragged me away. Using my free arm, I pulled out the syringe and shoved it into Misty's shoulder. She backed away from me before I could push the plunger. I watched as she pulled the syringe back out and inspected the liquid inside. "You thought this was pain medication, didn't you?" she asked.

"Clever plan, but poorly executed. I'd need to ask one of the doctors to confirm, but I'm pretty sure this is a vaccine."

I wasn't sure what to say. To be honest, I didn't have much of a plan, even if I did manage to neutralize Misty's powers. I felt my heart sink as Misty grabbed me once again.

"So, what exactly is your grand plan?" I asked.

"Originally, we just wanted Linda," Misty said. "We determined after studying you and Elizabeth that you two were mostly harmless. We were going to let you live, but then you both planned an attack on us to get Linda back, and we realized that we couldn't let any of you go free."

"You were gonna let me and Elizabeth live, huh? What about that imposter? Rose, was it? She tried to kill us before Elizabeth and I did any sort of attacking."

"There must have been a mistake then. She was only supposed to send you back through the portals, even if you *did* discover what she was. Killing you wasn't even an option."

"Who gave her the order?"

"I don't know. Maybe one of the leaders of the Elemental Council. One of them wasn't exactly okay with the plan to keep you and Elizabeth alive."

"What's the Elemental Council?"

"On Elahntra, we have a council of four Elements, each representing one of—" Misty quickly cut herself off. "I've already said too much. You're supposed to be my prisoner, not my friend. I shouldn't humor you at all, even if the information is harmless."

When we arrived at the cells, I noticed that one of them at the end had a large pile of leaves and some scorch marks on the ground. It looked like an earth Element and a fire Element had gotten into a fight or something, but the look of panic on Misty's face let me know something bigger had happened.

"No," Misty said. "They got away."

"Who did?" I asked.

"Your sisters believe that you're dead, if you haven't figured that out already. They came here to get revenge," she explained, humoring me once again. "We locked them up and sent two members of our team to get information out of them. Now they're gone."

I felt relieved knowing my sisters were okay, but that feeling didn't last long as it was soon replaced with pain. The medicine I had been given was finally wearing off, causing my wound to ache. I let out a groan, getting Misty's attention.

"It hurts, doesn't it?" she asked.

"Yes," I said. "Not that you'd care."

"I'm sorry about the ice," she said. "We've been watching you and your sisters for years now, and you've always been my favorite." Despite her kind words, she locked me in one of the undamaged cells and created an extra barrier of ice to prevent my escape.

"Misty, you don't have to do this," I said. "I don't want to hurt anybody. My sisters are only fighting you because you're after them. I'm not sure who drew first blood, but clearly, there was a misunderstanding."

"Don't act so innocent," Misty said. "I'm not as gullible as that boy. The fact that you were clever enough to delay your capture proves just how dangerous you are."

"No, you don't understand. Just hear me out," I pleaded as Misty started to walk off. "I'm begging you. Listen to me!"

Chapter 18 (Elizabeth)

"Okay, Linda," I said, "tell me what the plan is, and I'll do whatever it is you need me to do."

"We need to find the heart of the ship," Linda said. "If we blow up the heart of the ship, the whole thing should go down, killing all the Elements on it."

"What about the people in the park? Won't they be in danger?"

"Mark and Haley are working on clearing the area as we speak. I also had them alert the higher-ups so that they can begin working on a cover-up."

"How much time will we have to escape the ship?" I asked.

"Once I activate the explosives, we'll have five minutes to get out of here," Linda said. "It isn't much time, but it should be just enough for us to escape as long as we can avoid getting caught. It also ensures that the Elements won't have all day to diffuse the bombs if they're discovered."

"And what if those five minutes *aren't* enough for us to escape?"

"We die, but we take those alien freaks out with us."

"Was plan C blowing ourselves up in the cells?" I asked.

"Yeah," Linda sighed. "I figured that if we couldn't escape, we were as good as dead anyway. Might as well take a few Elements with us, right?"

"Fair point," I said. "So, how exactly will we find the heart of the ship?"

"If I could get access to a computer, I could look up a map and see for myself where the heart is."

"Alright then. Let's find a computer."

We continued walking through the ship in silence, only pausing to hide from nearby Elements. I found myself thinking back to the last thing Ley had said to me. We could've stayed together if it hadn't been for Misty. She was willing to give up the life she knew just to stay with me. Though, if I was being honest with myself, I was starting to believe Ley and I would've been stuck in the future forever. When I first met Savannah, I truly believed she was capable of opening the portal to send me home. After I got to know her more, I doubted she even understood how the portals worked. She was cold, condescending, and cocky. It still bothered me that she called Ley stupid, and it bothered me even more that Ley died so soon after I met her. Finding out I had sisters was overwhelming, but in a good way. I was happy that I had found my family. Ley's death turned that happiness into despair. Even if Ley had lived, and even if Savannah were able to open the portal home, I still expected things to be… complicated. Linda had mentioned the idea of us visiting her, but I worried that she was lying. She seemed like the type of person who would do anything to keep the people she loved safe, even if that meant avoiding them. I worried that once I was able to go home, *if* I was able to go home, there was a chance I would never return.

I wondered why Linda was the way she was. She had been damaged, that much was obvious. *Did it have something to do with her job?* I thought back to what she said after Ley was abducted from school.

"Linda," I said, "remember when Ley was taken and you said that, if I revealed my powers, I would be weaponized and treated like an object?"

"Yeah," Linda said. "Why?"

"Were you talking from experience?"

"Yes," she said quietly. "My earliest memories are of me being trained by my foster parents to use my powers to fight. They told me it was for self-defense, and I was stupid enough to believe them. I was guaranteed my government job from the time I was eleven. By the time I was twelve, I was a fully trained soldier. Yet, even knowing it was all a lie, I still miss them sometimes. And you know what's even worse? I *shouldn't* miss them. They didn't truly love me. I know because I asked them the day I was taken to live at the base. I asked my foster mom if she or my foster dad loved me, and she looked me in the eyes and said no. That's when I realized I was never really viewed as a daughter, let alone a person."

"I see you as a person," I said, "and I'm sure all your friends do, too."

"I don't have a lot of friends. I have a group I hang around occasionally, but, deep down, they all fear me, except for Savannah and John."

"Is that why you like spending time with John so much?" I asked. "And is that why you're going on a date with him?"

"We are getting *way* off topic, Liz," Linda said, obviously flustered. "We didn't come here to socialize."

"I'm sorry if I made you uncomfortable."

"Me? Uncomfortable? Nah! I'm just… well, it's just that we're kind of busy, you know, saving the world right now."

"*Right.*"

We found a staircase that led us back to the first floor. As we continued searching the halls, we found ourselves wandering into the large, two-story room I had been in before.

"To find a computer, we may need to ask for help," Linda sighed. "I don't want to do that, but the plan won't work if the bombs are placed anywhere else. The shields would protect the ship from crashing."

"Wait, but our disguises are pointless now," I said. "Asking for help would be incredibly risky."

"I warned you this is a suicide mission before we came," Linda said. "You can stay here if you want, but you wouldn't be much safer, especially without backup. Briar, Misty, and Daisy are the only living Elements who spotted us in our disguises anyway. They'd only be able to describe us to everyone else, so there's a chance we may find an Element who doesn't know who we are and would be willing to help us."

"I'll come along with you," I sighed. "I just wish we had another way."

To make her outfit a little different, Linda took off her blue sweatshirt and tied it around her waist, revealing a white undershirt. She then proceeded to rip the straps off my dress, much to my dismay, and tied them around my wounded arm, making the bandages look like a cuff.

I reluctantly followed Linda through the ship, fully knowing that she had no idea where we were going. We wound up in the ship's library, where we found a wind Element with a side part reading a gardening book with a bright, red cover. It took him a moment to notice we were standing there.

"Can I help you ladies with anything?" he asked.

"Yes, actually," Linda said as she came up with her story. "We've been stationed on Earth for quite some time, and the ship isn't the way we remember it. Needless to say, we're lost."

"Oh, I understand," the boy said. "These new models are so much bigger and more complex than the old ones. I could give you a tour if you'd like."

"We appreciate the thought, but we don't have time for a tour of the whole ship."

"My apologies, I didn't realize you were in a hurry. Where exactly are you trying to go?"

"We're trying to find the… the console room," Linda said.

"I can show you the way," he said. "It's not that far from here. My name is Bayu, by the way. What are your names?"

Realizing that my fake name, Eldrid, had likely been compromised, I knew I had to come up with something else. Flame? No, that wouldn't work, and it wasn't even a name. Candle? Candle-ah? Candela.

"I'm Candela," I said. "And this is my friend Ana…hita. Her name is Anahita."

"She's always had trouble with my name," Linda joked, covering my mistake.

Bayu led us through the ship and into a small room with hologram computers. Each one had a bluish tint. "As I'm sure you've noticed," Bayu said, "we've updated our hologram computers to the latest model. Aren't they gorgeous?"

"Yes, they look so much better than the old ones," Linda said, continuing the charade.

"They work better, too," he bragged. "Well, I better get back to the library. If you ladies change your minds about that tour, let me know."

"Thanks," I said. "We will."

"We won't," Linda mumbled to me after Bayu left, causing me to giggle.

Elements were working at each of the hologram computers, which kept them from noticing us, but it also prevented us from accessing a computer. Linda and I waited for one of the Elements to leave. To our horror, Daisy stepped into the room. Linda and I turned so that we weren't directly facing her and hoped that she wouldn't notice us. The Element using the computer closest to her got up, and Daisy waited a moment before taking the spot. Knowing that she hadn't noticed us, Linda and I let out sighs of relief and continued to wait for a computer to open up. After a few minutes had passed, the Element to the right of Daisy got up and left their station.

"Don't tell me you're thinking about taking that hologram computer, Linda," I whispered. "Daisy is right there. What if she spots you?"

"Elizabeth, we've been waiting here for too long," she said quietly. "I need to do this before we draw attention to ourselves. Daisy might not notice me anyway since she's currently preoccupied with whatever the heck is on her computer."

I held my breath as Linda took the open hologram computer. She carefully brushed some of her hair over the left side of her face to help prevent Daisy from noticing her. The computer scanned the cuff Linda stole from the earth Element before displaying a box that said 'Welcome, Phoenix' with the same message written in Spanish, French, and Mandarin underneath it. After she found the map of the ship, Linda carefully slipped out her phone and took a picture of it. Daisy still hadn't noticed her, causing me to feel a little less tense. Linda quickly logged off and got up just as Daisy finished what she was doing at the computer.

"Stop right there, you ourathian scumbags!" she yelled upon seeing us.

Linda and I ran out of the room. Daisy and the other Elements from the console room followed. A thick layer of vines began climbing the walls. They tried to grab me, but Linda pulled out her knife and cut them away.

"Boy, am I glad you have your knife," I said. "Briar melted mine."

"Yeah, well this isn't doing much," Linda said. "Speaking of things we have, isn't there something you can do with your powers?"

"I don't know," I said. "They never work right for me, remember? The only time I managed to do something grand was when I got really angry."

"And why did you get really angry?" she asked.

"Because Misty was hurting Ley."

"Well, let's hope your hunch is right."

"Hunch? What hunch? What are you—"

She shoved me out of the way as more vines lunged at us. They wrapped around Linda's waist and began pulling her back towards Daisy. I tried to launch a ball of fire, but it didn't work. The flames barely made it two feet, which was nowhere near where the Elements were. As rage and desperation began to build up inside me, my hand brushed up against the wall, and a stone barrier formed between Linda and the Elements. The vines were completely cut off. Once again, I had managed to successfully use my powers to save someone I cared about, even if it didn't go as planned.

"I knew you could do it," Linda said as she got up and pulled the remaining vines off of her waist. "Now, let's find the heart of the ship and turn these Elemental dirtbags to dust."

"But I didn't… I didn't even mean to—"

"Come on, Liz, we have to keep moving."

Linda and I followed the map to a large room with a blue metal door on each end. The walls were glass. The ship wasn't high enough for us to be in space, but we had a beautiful view of the sky and the city below us. I stared in awe.

"It's breathtaking, isn't it?" Linda asked.

"I've never seen a view so astonishing," I said. "I wish we could stay here for a while."

"I do, too, but we can't," Linda said. "You should probably take some pictures with your new phone if you want to remember it, because this view is about to be blown away with the rest of the ship."

As I took pictures of the room, she pulled out four semicircle-shaped devices. Each had a red screen on the center and small lavender pods covering the sides.

"What are those things?" I asked.

"They're explosives," Linda said. "They may look kind of small, but they can do a lot of damage. Do you see these little pods on the side? Each one contains a highly flammable chemical. When the timer finally reaches zero, the device detonates, setting off each of the pods. One of these devices alone could easily take out two full streets of a small town."

Linda set up each of the devices in the four corners of the room. Before starting the countdown, she and I checked to make sure that the coast was clear. The last thing we needed was to be captured and stuck on the ship as it blew up.

"For Ley," Linda said.

"For Ley," I repeated just as she activated the devices.

Linda and I checked the map again and darted for the escape pods. Just after we left, an alarm sounded. The bombs had been discovered already.

"Do the Elements have an escape plan?" I asked. "We may be able to cut them off somewhere or trap them on the ship."

"I don't know," Linda said. "It seems like they have escape pods on each floor, but trust me when I say there aren't enough for everyone on the ship, especially after the team took some of them. They also have the elevator, but only so many Elements can use it at a time, and I haven't seen it go down before."

"We could always launch some of the empty escape pods," I suggested.

"That's a great idea, Elizabeth," she said. "You seem to be adjusting to the future quite well."

"Thank you."

When we reached the escape pods on our floor, Linda and I launched each pod one by one until there was only one left for us to share.

"Going so soon?" Linda and I turned to see a wind Element standing behind us. His deep purple eyes complemented his creepy smile. "If I'm going to die here," he said, "I'm taking you both with me."

With a wave of his hand, a strong, straight-line wind blew towards him, pushing me and Linda away from the escape pod. Quickly, Linda pulled out her knife and lined it up with the wind Element's head before letting go. It ended up going through his neck, and the wind died down as he dropped to the floor. Linda grabbed my hand and pulled me into the escape pod just as the Element's body became cloud-like and blew away.

"I can't believe we made it," I said.

"We're not out of the dark yet," Linda told me as she pressed the launch button. "The ship should blow any second now. Brace yourself."

I closed my eyes and found myself fighting a panic attack as I expected to be caught in the ship's explosion. As it turned out, the only thing I needed to brace for was the landing; the ship was perfectly fine. Linda and I looked at each other in shock as we got out of the escape pod.

"You watched me set those explosives, right?" she asked.

"Yeah, you set the timer and everything," I reassured her.

"I can't believe we failed…"

Linda sat down on the ground and buried her face in her hands. I stood frozen, not knowing how to comfort her.

"I risked my life, *your* life, for nothing," she sighed.

"It wasn't completely for nothing," I said. "We did take some Elements out, didn't we?"

"Yeah, but that's not worth dying for."

"We're not dead," I told her as I extended my hand to help her up. "Thanks for taking me along with you on this mission."

"I shouldn't have, but since you're alright, I'm glad I did," she said. "If the ship isn't going to explode, we should probably head back to the base."

"What about the escape pods?" I asked.

"Once we return to the base, I'll call them in, which is what I did last time. Then our salvage crew will take any parts they can use for gadgets and destroy the rest."

"When we get back to the base, I could really use a shower."

"Same. After all the running we've been doing, this body paint has started to clump up, and these contacts are hurting my eyes."

Chapter 19 (Briar)

After Ley's capture, I decided to relax in the ship's recreation room. The recreation room had a hot tub, a pool, a massage parlor, and rooms set aside for meditation. My favorite place to visit was always the hot tub. Once I finished changing into my black, one-piece bathing suit, I got in. Except for a couple of my teammates in the pool, I was the only one in the recreation room, allowing me to relax even more. My work was always stressful, but it had gotten worse ever since my team was ordered to hunt down the ourathian triplets. I was losing sleep, my friendships became strained, and I even found a few white hairs. Being able to relax in the hot tub was one of the few things that allowed me to keep my sanity. When I was there, it seemed like nothing could stress me out, but then the ship's alarm went off.

"Briar!" Windy shouted as she came running into the room. "I'm sorry to interrupt your relaxation time, but there are explosives in the central viewing deck. We don't have time to disarm them."

"D-don't worry, Windy, I'll handle this," I said, trying to stay calm.

I reluctantly slipped out of the hot tub and snatched a towel. Knowing that I didn't have time to get dressed, I tried to dry off my bathing suit and my hair as I ran to the central viewing deck. When I arrived, I spotted multiple explosives that had been placed with less than a minute before detonation. I knew that I could absorb the fire from the explosions, but part of me worried that I'd crumble under pressure. The whole crew was counting on me to save them and the ship.

"You can do this," I mumbled to myself. "Just remember your training."

When the explosives went off, I managed to hold the flames of the explosion in place. At first, I had trouble absorbing them. I tried to keep myself calm, knowing that if I got too emotional, it could cause my powers to spiral out of control.

"Briar, are you alright?" Misty called as she arrived. "Can you hold it long enough for us to evacuate? I can get another fire Element to help you, or I could try to use my powers to put out the flames."

"You can't put this fire out," I said. "It's already in the beginning stages of absorption. I'd have to let go for you to do anything to it, but that would risk the ship going down."

"Okay, so that's off the table. What about the other options?"

I tuned Misty out as I thought back to my training. The three keys to using elemental powers for defense were emotional balance, confidence, and concentration. I focused all my power and energy on the flames that appeared to be frozen in time as I continued to hold them in place. Slowly, the flames came towards me and were absorbed through my fingertips and chest. The more I absorbed, the faster the flames came to me and the more refreshed I felt. Absorbing all that fire was like taking a power nap, which I desperately needed.

"No need for evacuation, Misty," I said as I finished absorbing the flames. "I think I've taken care of it."

"When did you learn to absorb large amounts of fire?" Misty asked. "Did you get into a training program or something? That's an advanced skill."

"After I graduated from basic elemental training, I went into a special combat program," I said. "Advanced absorption is one of the skills I learned."

"At first, I didn't even consider going into a program like that, but I completely changed my mind after my friend, Arana—"

"Misty," I interrupted, not wanting to hear the rest of the story, "give me an update on the Ley situation."

"Oh, right," Misty said. "Ley is contained for now. I don't think we should proceed with the plan without contacting the council first. The Resistance attacks have caused us to change plans so many times, I've almost forgotten what the end game is."

"Please tell me that's a joke," I scolded. "We are trying to prevent the ourathian prophecy from coming true, because if it comes true, an entire planet will be invaded, and its species will be destroyed."

"Yes, I know, Briar. I was just joking," Misty grumbled. "You know, you and I used to be good friends."

"And we still are."

"Are we? Really? Because you've been rude to me throughout this entire mission."

I really had been. I tried to justify it by telling myself how important this mission is and how costly her mistakes were, but I'd be lying if I said I didn't make similar mistakes in the past. The weight of leadership had turned me into something I never wanted to become, and I determined right then and there that I wasn't going to let it get in the way of my friendship with Misty.

"You're right, Misty," I sighed. "I've been an absolute jerk, and I'm sorry. I'm just under a lot of pressure right now. You know what's at stake."

"I do," Misty said, "and I'm sorry I screwed things up. Just, please, promise me you'll try to stop being so harsh with me and the rest of the team. All it does is make the situation worse."

"I promise."

After I changed out of my bathing suit, Misty and I met up with Daisy and Windy in the communications room of the ship. There was a large, round console in the middle with four hologram computers meant for video chats. After logging in, I started a holographic chat with the Elemental council. The leaders: Evian, Venus, Azar, and Zephyr answered almost immediately.

"Hello, Briar," Evian said. "I'm assuming you have some good news for us."

"After much hard work, yes," I said. "We have Ley captured and secured."

"I thought I told you to get Linda!" she yelled. "She's the one we need!"

"Calm down, Evian," Zephyr said. "There's no need to panic so soon. Ley may still be of use to us."

"Alright then," Azar said with a raspy voice. "Get information from Ley by *any* means necessary. Report to us once you have something useful."

"But don't let that distract you from capturing Linda," Evian said.

"Understood, ma'am," I said before ending the call.

"So, which one of us gets the pleasure of torturing the ourathian brat?" Windy asked. "I could suffocate her, Daisy could strangle her, or Misty could waterboard—"

"No, Windy," I said, cutting her off. "I'll do it. I am the leader of this team, after all."

I marched down to Ley's cell, excited to break her spirit. When I arrived, I was pleased to see that she hadn't escaped. It appeared as if she hadn't even tried. The only thing she had done was change back into her real clothes, leaving the ones she stole in a pile on the floor. Ley was curled up in the corner of her cell with her head down, hugging her knees. She slowly looked up as I got closer. She looked tired, lonely, sad, and ready for it all to end. I knew at that point that breaking her wouldn't be too hard.

"I'm assuming you want information about Linda," Ley said. "Am I right?"

"Yes, but there's more than that," I said. "So, why don't you make this easy for the both of us? If you tell me what I need to know, I'll make sure you get treated well in whichever Elahntran prison you're sent to before you're executed."

"Executed!?" Ley shouted. "What exactly did I do? Last I checked, *your* teammate tried to kill *me*. Any violent acts I committed were in self-defense."

"At first, I thought you and Elizabeth were oblivious," I said. "The plan was to send you two back to the time periods you were sent to five years ago. After all the attacks, I realized that you both know more than you were letting on. Because of that, you will most certainly be executed when this is all over."

"I have no freaking idea what you're talking about, Briar," Ley said. "Elizabeth and I attacked you because you kidnapped our sister, who had done nothing wrong."

"Nothing wrong? Oh, just spare me the lies." I laughed. "I'm not going to fall for your little act anymore. I can't believe I was foolish enough to believe it was just Linda who was corrupt. It seems that all three of you have been working for your mother for quite some time now. What are her plans concerning the prophecy? Is she using Linda's army? Is it true that Linda is the prophesied weapon?"

"We're orphans!" Ley screamed. "We don't know who our mother is because she and our father didn't bother to stick around. She may have been the one that separated us for all I know! And I haven't heard of any stupid, freaking prophecy!"

"What?" I asked, floored by Ley's statement. I could see it in Ley's teary eyes, she wasn't lying. She had no idea what I was talking about, and she didn't know about her mother. She was innocent and very confused.

"If you want information, good luck," she continued. "I don't know anything, and even if I did, I would never tell you. You're a monster!" She buried her head again as she began to cry.

"You don't know, do you?" I asked. "You really don't know what you are?"

"I'm some sort of mutated human, last I checked," Ley said. "What does that have to do with anything?"

"Do you still have that gap in your memory?"

"How did you know about that? And, yes, I do. Did you expect me to magically remember the nine missing years of my life?"

I entered Ley's cell. As I approached her, she jerked her head up and began breathing heavily. I think she was expecting me to hurt her, and just a moment ago, that's exactly what I would've done. Instead, I sat down next to her and gave her a hug. I used my powers to create a gentle warmth around her in hopes that it would help calm her down.

"I am so sorry," I said, "for all of this."

"What is this? Some new interrogation trick? You think befriending the enemy will get you information? I'm not falling for it, though I'll admit it *is* a pretty clever tactic."

"This isn't a trick, Ley. I'm sorry for everything I've done and for everything my team has done."

"But, you're the bad guy," Ley said. "Bad guys don't feel bad for being complete jerk-wads. That's why they're called bad guys."

"You don't understand," I said. "Neither of us are bad guys. There's been a major misunderstanding between the Elements and the Resistance. We've been fighting each other when we should've been working together."

"What do you mean?"

"Ley, why were you fighting us?"

"You mean besides the whole kidnapping thing?"

"Yes."

"Well, the Elements are trying to invade Earth, and as a human, I feel the need to defend my planet."

"Now ask me."

"*Okay*," Ley said, looking skeptical. "Why were you fighting us?"

"The Elements are trying to protect the people of Earth from the ourathians. We also change the seasons on Earth like we've done since the beginning of time."

"Wait, you mean 'ourathian' isn't the Elahntran word for human?"

"No, it's not," I explained. "The ourathians are a very evil and hostile species. They've been after Earth for ages."

"There must be some sort of mistake then," Ley laughed, "because I was called an ourathian many times by you guys even though I'm a human."

"Ley, there is no mistake," I said quietly. "I'm sorry, but you've been living a lie."

"No, that isn't true!" Ley yelled as she started to cry again. "You're lying! I'm not an ourathian. I can't be. I'm human. I've always been human."

She shoved me away from her and started hugging her knees even tighter than before. I felt bad for her even if she was my enemy. She hadn't been pretending to be human, she believed she *was* human. She was only fighting my people because she thought that the human race was being attacked. She was noble, not evil. I tried to think of the right words to say to Ley. Simply apologizing wasn't enough. I needed to make things truly right with her, and I knew just where to start.

"I'm going to get you out of here, Ley," I said. "Just hang on a little longer."

"Briar," she mumbled, "are you telling the truth?"

"Yes," I said. "Why would I lie about this?"

"To gain my trust."

"Okay, how do I prove to you that I'm telling the truth?"

"Do the Elements have any way to restore memories?" Ley asked. "I'd trust you if you found a way to—"

"I'm sorry," I interrupted. "We don't have anything like that."

"For five years, I've had no idea who I am," Ley said. "I still don't know who I am. All I remember from my past is my name, my age, and my birthday. About a week ago, I had to deal with the fact that I have two sisters who I don't remember meeting before, even though we shared a womb. Two sisters who, like me, were ripped off when it came to their childhoods since neither of them can remember it. Now you're here in front of me, telling me that I'm an alien, that my species is evil, and that the only thing I was sure about has been a lie."

"I'm sorry," I repeated, not knowing what else to say. "I can't even imagine what this must be like for you."

"It's terrifying," she said. "Absolutely terrifying. Why? Because I still don't know who I am even now. I still don't know who my sisters are. As much as I want to know about my past, as much as I've longed for answers, part of me is afraid of what I might find. What if we really are the monsters your people have been fighting?"

"I… may know a bit about your past."

"What?"

"It's a long story, and—"

"Please. You have to tell me," Ley begged. "I need to know who I am."

"I don't have time to tell you everything, and I honestly think you'd be better off not knowing, but I will tell you this: you were a good kid. You loved your sisters a lot, and they loved you, too. You were never monsters, not really."

"Then why hunt us down?"

"Because you were supposed to be."

"What do you mean by that?"

"I don't have time to explain everything now, but I promise I will eventually," I said. "Right now, my focus is getting you off this ship." As I stood up to leave, Ley grabbed the bottom of my dress, causing me to spin back around to face her.

"Wait, no," she said. "Don't leave me."

"You don't want to be released?" I asked.

"It's not that," she told me. "Of course, I want to be released. I just don't want to be left alone. I'm scared. You and Misty have been somewhat nice to me, but what if another Element comes by? What will they do to me? I doubt they'd hug me and apologize for all the attacks, and I doubt they'd listen to me vent about my problems."

She was right. There were other Elements, namely my main team, just dying for me to leave so they could torture Ley behind my back. Elahntran laws are very different from the varying laws of Earth. When it comes to torture, *anything* is allowed, physical or emotional. I couldn't let Ley get hurt, but I couldn't stand by and babysit her either. I used my powers to create a stone dagger for her.

"Use this only if you have to," I said. "Keep it hidden otherwise. If you're caught with it, things will become much worse for you. You may very well end up—"

"Thank you, Briar," Ley said, interrupting my warning.

"I'll also cover the doors to this room with stone after I leave to give you an extra barrier," I added.

I left Ley's cell, worried. I had no idea how I was going to explain things to Windy, Daisy, and Misty. Even though I was the leader of the team, I still needed their approval. If they didn't agree with me, not only would I be tried for treason against Elahntra, but Ley would have no chance of escape or survival. Still, I couldn't hide this from them; there was no way I could get Ley out by myself without being caught.

"Back so soon, Briar?" Daisy asked cheerfully. "Misty and I made a bet. Loser has to wear a clown wig and a fake mustache for a week. Misty bet that Ley would break within the first five minutes. I thought Ley would last ten or longer."

"Something happened back there, girls," I said. "We need to talk."

After Windy, Daisy, Misty, and I sat down, I began to explain the situation about Ley. None of the girls tried to interrupt me. They stayed perfectly silent the whole time with looks of shock on their faces. After I finished explaining, they stayed silent until Windy finally spoke up.

"You aren't considering letting her go, are you?" she asked. "Ley is very clearly playing you. I just can't believe you're gullible enough to fall for it."

"You're wrong!" I exclaimed. "Ley was not lying. I could tell."

"*Oh really?* I lied to you just last week when I said I didn't take your lunch from the fridge."

"I knew it!"

"No, you didn't. You believed me when I told you it was Bayu."

"You little—"

"If Briar thinks Ley is innocent, then so do I," Misty interrupted. "I trust her judgment, and so should the rest of you. She's our team's leader for a reason."

"I agree," Daisy said. "We need to let Ley go."

"Thank you, girls," I said.

"If you want to get yourselves in trouble, fine, but I won't join you," Windy said. "If I find out that Ley has escaped, I'll report all of you to the council, and you'll be tried for treason."

She stormed off, leaving the rest of us with a major moral conflict: either we would hurt an innocent girl or we would commit treason against our planet. Deep down, we all knew what the right thing to do was, even if it would cost us dearly.

***

Early the next morning, before everybody else had gotten up, we went to Ley's cell. Ley was still asleep with her dagger safely tucked away in her jacket. I disabled the force field of her cell and gently woke her up.

"What took you so long?" she mumbled.

"We needed to make sure we wouldn't get caught," Misty said. "When we set you free, the three of us will be guilty of treason."

"Thank you," Ley said. "But I can't ask you to take a risk like that for me."

"You're not asking, we're insisting," Daisy said, "because it's the right thing to do, and it's the only way to make up for all the pain we've caused."

We escorted Ley downstairs to the elevator only to find that it had been disabled. I went to the nearest control panel and checked the settings. The elevator had been disabled automatically by the computer because the invisibility panel and the oxygen field had been damaged.

"Great, the elevator is currently unavailable," I sighed. "I bet Windy did that as an extra precaution. The only way to reactivate the elevator is to fix it, which we don't have time to do."

"We could bring Ley to the escape pods," Misty suggested.

"I don't need to use an escape pod," Ley said. "I can just fly out of here if you have a window or something you can open up."

"Okay, then," I said. "We can take you to where the launched escape pods were and open a door. You'll have about a minute to fly out before you and the rest of us get sucked out. I'll close the door after you're gone."

We ran to the nearest escape pods, which had been launched thanks to Elizabeth and Linda. I was about to open one of the doors when I thought of one problem: oxygen. We were high enough that Ley would likely pass out, and while it was possible she'd wake up in time to save herself, I wasn't about to take that risk.

"Won't the air be too thin for you, Ley?" I asked. "I mean, we're nowhere near space, but we're still pretty high up."

"I didn't even think of that," Ley said. "What do we do now?"

Daisy grew a large blue flower out of her hand and gave it to Ley. "This is an Elahntran breathing flower," she explained to her. "It produces more oxygen than any other plant. It's like nature's oxygen tank. If you feel like the air is getting too thin, hold this flower up to your nose and take a deep breath. It doesn't have much since it's picked, but it should be enough to get you to the ground safely."

And with that, it was time for Ley to leave. Just before I could open one of the escape pod doors, she stopped me.

"Wait, what will happen to you?" she asked.

"Ley, the punishment for treason is death," I said, "unless you're Evian's favorite water Element; then you'll get off with just a banishment."

"Huh?"

"It's a long story," I said. "The point is, we're willingly sacrificing ourselves because it's the only way to make up for what we've done."

"There must be some way to get you three to safety," Ley said. "Is there anything I can do to help you?"

"There is something," I said. "You can go back and tell your sisters what happened here. Misty, Daisy, and I could try to find our own way out of the ship. Then, we could ask Linda if she'd be willing to let us stay at the Resistance to lie low for a while. We'd be more than willing to further explain everything."

"I'll do it," Ley said. "I'm not sure if Linda will agree or not, but I'll try to convince her, I promise."

"Thank you," I said as I gave her another hug.

Ley revealed her beautiful white wings. After I opened the door, she flew off. I made sure to close it right behind her to prevent the rest of us from being sucked out of the ship.

"Right, so how are we going to escape?" Daisy asked me.

"Like this," I said.

I created a large, stone platform and gestured for Misty and Daisy to get on. I then hit the button and used my powers to carefully maneuver the platform out of the ship, making sure to hit the button again on my way out. Daisy quickly made more breathing flowers to hand out to all of us, which was helpful. Using my powers to keep a small object elevated was one thing, but using it to carry people was another, and it was beyond stressful. Still, I knew it was our best chance of reaching the ground safely.

I expected to be surrounded by curious humans when we finally reached the ground. Anytime an Element was caught using their powers, the go-to cover story was always *I'm a professional illusionist.* When I finally had a chance to look around, I realized that the park was empty and covered in patches of melting snow. Normally there would be people walking their dogs or enjoying an early morning jog. After thinking everything through, I assumed that the park had been evacuated when Linda and Elizabeth attempted to blow up the ship the previous day and that nobody dared to go back just yet.

"Where'd you park your car, Misty?" I asked as we all switched into our human forms.

Misty led us to the center of town where her blue car was parked in front of a small café. She got in the driver's seat, and I took shotgun, leaving Daisy to sit in the back. I gave Misty the coordinates to the base so she knew where to go.

"Hey, Briar, do you think Windy will try to attack the base if she finds out we're going there?" Daisy asked.

"She may," I said. "She'd probably bring backup, too. If that happens, we should be the ones to fight."

"And if she gets past us?"

"It would be difficult with all the security at the base," Misty said, "but if she succeeded, a lot of innocent Elements and humans would be slaughtered in battle. Of course, all of this is hypothetical. We don't even know if we'll be allowed in the base to begin with."

"Good point," Daisy said.

"Misty, you should probably drive around for a little while before heading to the base," I said.

"Why?"

"Because us being allowed in depends on whether or not Linda believes what Ley tells her," I said. "She may need a minute to take it all in. Our lives depend on this."

Chapter 20 (Ley)

As I flew back to the base, I noticed that the city resembled the city where I was from, making me suspect that it was the same area, just in the future. I made sure to fly high enough that nobody would notice me. My wings became tired quickly, making each beat feel like a painful jab in my back. My wound didn't help. I remembered what Linda had said about my wings not being ready for long-distance travel, but I had to push myself. The Elements were depending on me. After I had been flying for a while, the cool air helped to numb the pain. Of course, it also numbed my fingers and my face, which wasn't very convenient for me. Luckily, it wasn't too long after that when I found myself at the base of the hill where the hideout was located. I had already forgotten where the secret door was, but I knew there had to be hidden security cameras that could easily spot me. I tried to get Linda's attention.

"Hey, can somebody let me in?" I called after I landed. "Guys, it's me! I'm not dead!" There was no response. "Sheesh, what do I have to do, flail my arms around like one of those inflatable tube things?" I waited a couple of minutes before trying again. "Linda? Savannah? Elizabeth? John?" I called out desperately. "Can anybody hear me?"

The door finally opened, and Linda came out with her gun aimed at my head. At first, I was confused, but then I realized why she seemed so hostile. She thought she had seen me die and believed that I was an Element in disguise.

"Linda, I know what you're thinking, but it's me," I said as I took off my blood-stained jacket and revealed the wound on my back. "I'm not an Element." Though my back was turned, I could feel Linda's gaze piercing through me. I half expected her to shoot, and I wouldn't have blamed her if she did. "I didn't die," I continued. "I passed out."

"I want to believe you, Ley, I really do," she said, "but I need you to give me some real proof. That wound could easily be copied. You could still be an Element. I know we haven't known each other long, but there must be something you know about me that the Elements don't."

I turned back around to face my sister. Her face was incredibly pale, more so than usual. It was like she had seen a ghost. Her eyes were watery, but no tears were shed, almost like they weren't allowed to be shed until Linda knew for sure that I was who I claimed to be. She held her stance, her gun still aimed at my head, ready to fire.

I tried to think of something personal that Linda had mentioned. My mind was so scrambled that I said the first thing that popped into my head. "You had to abandon your foster parents to work here. Most people who work at the Resistance had to abandon their families as well."

"I need something more private than that, Ley," Linda said, sounding desperate. "I *want* to believe you, but you know I can't risk the safety of my agents. I need to know without a doubt that you're you."

I thought back to what John had said about Linda in section four. There was no way the Elements would've known about that. Even if Rose somehow knew, it's not like she would've had any reason to tell her contact, and I killed her before she could report to the Elements again.

"You told John how happy you were about me and Elizabeth being your sisters the same night we arrived," I said. "You talked with him right after I showed up, and came back later that night after Elizabeth and I had fallen asleep. You were excited that you found your family." I tried to think of something else to add. "Oh, and when I first arrived here, you said that you try to emotionally detach yourself from everyone because it keeps you from getting hurt. I told you that it would only hurt you more."

"And it turns out you were right," Linda said as she lowered her gun. "After we thought you were dead, all I could think about was everything I didn't know about you. I wished I had gotten to know you more."

"That's how I felt when I thought you were gone," I said.

"That thing you said about me and John in the lab, I never told you that. I'm assuming John did?"

"Yes. He told me and Elizabeth in section four when I was recovering from my abduction," I said. "And the funny thing is, after hearing your feelings about us, Elizabeth and I realized that we felt the same way about you."

Without hesitation, Linda ran up to me and hugged me as if she feared I would disappear from her arms. I could feel her tears dripping onto my bare shoulder.

"Oh, Ley," she cried, "you have no idea how much I missed you." She kissed me on the cheek before hugging me again, carefully avoiding the site of the wound.

"I've missed you, too, sis," I said.

"Ley!?" I heard Elizabeth call out. She came running out of the base and joined in on the hugging.

"As nice as this is, I need to tell you something important, girls," I said.

I explained everything right then and there. My sisters were shocked. Linda seemed skeptical at first but agreed to keep an open mind as long as she had her gun on hand. A car came into view soon after we finished talking. Linda had her hand hovering over her holster, waiting for an excuse to draw her weapon. The car parked on the grass right in front of us.

"There's no need for that, Linda," Briar said, gesturing towards Linda's gun as she stepped out of the car. "We come in peace."

"After all the agents your people have slaughtered, forgive me for not believing you without proof," Linda said with a snarky tone.

"Isn't your sister proof enough?" Briar asked. "Why would we release her fully knowing that she could've told you not to trust us?"

"It *is* a pretty moronic move," Elizabeth said, "unless you really are on our side."

"On the contrary, Elizabeth, it's not moronic at all," Linda said. "Since they released Ley, why wouldn't she believe them? This could easily be a trick, and poor Ley could be in the center of it all without realizing."

"You promised me you'd keep an open mind," I scolded, causing Linda to roll her eyes.

Reluctantly, Linda had the car parked in section three before bringing the Elements down to the interrogation room. Elizabeth and I were allowed to sit in and listen because Briar promised to explain everything about us, the Elements, and the ourathians.

"Let's start from the very beginning," Linda said. "How long have you been keeping eyes on us?"

"We knew about you three since before you were born," Briar said. "According to prophecy, a commander of an ourathian army would give birth to triplets. One of those triplets is said to be the great ourathian weapon against the humans, the key to winning the war."

"What war?"

"The planet Ourathia has been slowly dying for ages. Despite every warning, they never tried to stop it until it was too late. They've managed to slow the process, but it won't last forever, so they're seeking a new planet, Earth, and they have no intention of sharing. The Elements have been fighting them off in an attempt to protect the human race."

"Okay, but why would the ourathians choose Earth? It's heading for destruction, too. Haven't they heard of—"

"Climate change? Yeah, we did that."

"Wait, what?" I blurted.

"Yeah, the Elements made the whole thing up and even changed the weather to try to 'prove' it was real," Briar said. "Earth is far from dying, but even after all these years, the human race still thinks the end is near. Too bad the ourathians never fell for it."

"But the idea of climate change became widespread long before we were even born," Linda said.

"Long before you were born? Way to make me feel old. It took off less than a century before I was born."

"What?"

"I'm over two hundred years old."

"Two hundred?" Linda asked. "How long has this war been going on?"

"Over a millennium," Briar said. "And the prophecy concerning the weapon came about seven hundred years ago."

"Do you know which one of us is supposed to be this weapon?"

"We know that the weapon is supposed to be the youngest sibling, but we don't know which one of you is the youngest. So, we spied on all three of you, even after you were separated, because we were determined to kill whichever one of you was the weapon, or kill all of you if we needed to."

"So, you were able to open the portals?"

"Yes. That's how we followed you. Misty was undercover as a student at Ley's school, Windy spied on Elizabeth, and Daisy and I continued to spy on you. There were other Elements stationed throughout your communities as well."

"Like Marina?" Elizabeth asked.

"How did—"

"A wall of ice started to form when I was about to walk through the portal. She was the only person present besides myself, so it had to have been her."

"That was incredibly risky," Briar sighed. "Anyway, our job got a lot harder when one of our ships was detected, and you, Linda, got recruited by the government. Once you began leading your attacks, we thought maybe you were the weapon because of the tools and the army you had access to."

"You knew about our memories being erased, right?" Linda asked.

"Yes," Briar said.

"Then why did you expect us to be working for our mother?"

"We figured that your mother had been in contact with you and restored some, if not all, of your memories. We thought that our theory was proven correct after you started fighting us and after Ley and

239

Elizabeth used the portals to come back here. We thought it was all part of your plan."

"Sure, we *used* the portals, but we didn't *open* them," I said.

"So, if I'm an ourathian," Elizabeth started, "why do I have elemental powers?"

"Your mother is ourathian, and your father is an Element," Daisy said. "You're hybrids."

"How did our parents get together then?" Linda asked. "They're supposed to be enemies, right?"

"Don't expect Romeo and Juliet," Misty said. "Your parents were, and still are, enemies. Your father used to work as an Elahntran soldier. He was captured by ourathians and locked up in one of their prisons. Elahntran men were captured more than Elahntran women during those days because the prophecy specified that the triplets' father would be an Element. Your mother… well… had her way with your father until she became pregnant. Because he became the father of the prophesied triplets, he was released after your birth. He was warned that if he was ever spotted by ourathians again, he would be killed on sight. All the other male prisoners were killed as they weren't needed anymore."

"That's terrible," Elizabeth said.

"How sick," Linda added.

"Let's change the subject," Briar said. "Do you have any other questions? I think we've explained just about everything."

"Since we've both been trying to protect humanity from each other, how many innocent Elements and humans died because of a misunderstanding?" Linda asked.

"Far too many," Briar said. "I'm more than willing to forgive you and your agents if you can forgive me and my people."

"Of course," Linda said as she shook Briar's hand. "Just one last thing."

"What?"

"Could you please tell us about our past? We want to know how we lost our memories."

"Trust me, you're better off not knowing," Briar sighed.

"That's not your decision to make," Linda said, raising her voice.

"Linda," Briar said calmly, "last I checked, John's memories were never erased. I don't know if you know this yet or not, but he played a major role in your childhood. Go to him for answers."

That was news to me, though Linda didn't seem shocked. "John slipped up yesterday in section four, and I found out that he knows about my past," she said. "He won't tell me about anything that happened because he's determined to find a way to restore my memories."

"Really?" I asked. "Will he do the same for me and Elizabeth?"

"I'm sure he will."

"I can't wait!" I exclaimed. "I'm sure our childhood wasn't nearly as bad as—"

"Trust Briar when she says you're better off not knowing," Misty interrupted. "You lived a life of pain and abuse. To be honest, saying you were abused is a massive understatement. I think John was the only good thing about your childhood."

"Speaking of John, how is he?" I asked Linda. "I haven't seen him since he began recovery in section four."

"He was released from section four yesterday around lunchtime," she replied. "After Elizabeth and I got back from our last attack on the Elements, he told me that he wouldn't sleep or eat until he finds a way to restore my memories, or at least my memories of him."

"Wow, talk about loyalty," Briar said.

"So, he's in the lab right now?" I asked.

"Yes," Linda said.

"You should probably go check on him," I told her. "The poor thing has been working his butt off for you. Even if you are angry, you still care about him, right?"

"Yeah, I do," Linda sighed. "Misty, Briar, Daisy, hang out here for a minute with my sisters. I need to go check on my best friend."

After Linda left the room, I could tell Elizabeth was nervous. That was understandable after everything we'd gone through, but I could tell it was bothering Briar. I figured she was feeling guilty and was trying to come up with a way to make things right.

"So, Elizabeth," she said, "I've noticed you've been having trouble with your powers."

"Yeah," Elizabeth said. "Sometimes I lose control. Other times I can't get them to work at all."

"Well," Misty said. "Out of control or not, I can tell that your powers are already quite strong."

"Really?" Elizabeth asked.

"Of course. You were able to beat me, weren't you? And, if it means anything to you, I'm truly sorry about what I did to Ley. I'm glad that the ice wasn't deep enough to kill or paralyze her."

"Apology accepted," I said.

"So, how exactly do I learn to control my powers?" Elizabeth asked, ignoring Misty's apology.

"Well, that's going to be tricky," Briar said. "You see, all Elements are trained from the age of seven to whatever age they are when they eventually reach the tenth level of training. Unlike Earth, the content of Elahntran schools is so difficult that most students are held back at least three times. What I'm trying to say is, since you're older, you're going to have to work very hard to properly control and strengthen your powers. If you're okay with it, I'm more than willing to train you myself since proper Elahntran training may not be an option."

"Thank you, Briar, I'd like that," Elizabeth said.

With Briar and her team answering our questions so willingly, I found myself feeling oddly relaxed. It made me realize that even if the other Elements still thought of us as a threat, we were at least on the road to peace and maybe even a few new friendships.

I dragged my feet every step of the way towards the lab. I was still angry with John for not telling me that he knew about my past when we met, but I still worried about him. He hadn't slept at all, and he hadn't eaten a thing since lunch even though it was time for breakfast. When I entered the lab, I was greeted with a familiar sight. The bright lighting contrasted from the dark brown walls. There used to be a few desks, but as of a few months ago, there was only one: John's desk. There was a small door leading to the back where the chemicals and equipment were kept.

John was typing something into his laptop and mumbling to himself. Because he wasn't doing fieldwork, he was wearing his lab uniform: a blue button-up shirt, gray pants, and a white lab coat. It was obvious from his appearance that he was sleep-deprived. His hair was a mess, he looked incredibly pale, part of his collar was sticking up, and the first two buttons of his shirt were undone. He kept looking back and forth between his laptop and the three vials sitting on his desk.

"What if I added," he said quietly to himself, "or maybe if I just—"

"John," I said, causing him to look away from his laptop. He stood up and walked over to me. I could see bags under his eyes. His stomach growled loudly, causing me to worry more than I already did.

"I still haven't figured it out yet," he said. "I'm sorry, Linda."

"Forget about that for now," I said as I began to fix his shirt. "Go get some sleep."

"But I need to—"

"You're no use to anyone if you're struggling to stay awake, so go get some sleep. That's an order."

"No. I need to make things right with you, and this is the best way I can."

"I am still very angry about yesterday, but I'll be even angrier if you don't take care of yourself. If you want to make things right with me, you can start with that."

"You're only saying that because you were pressured into saying it," John said. "I can see right through you. You didn't want to come in here and see me in the first place."

"John—"

"And I don't blame you," he continued, cutting me off. "Like you said before, our friendship was built on a lie, and if we had started dating, that would've been built on a lie, too. I deserve this for letting the charade go on for so long. So, go on back to Elizabeth, or Mark, or Dillan, or whoever it was that sent you here, and tell them that you tried, but I wouldn't fall for it."

And with that, John walked back to his desk and sat down. I just stood in silence. John had every reason to feel guilty, but he had gone way too far. I walked up to him and put my arm around him, silently expressing that I still cared about him even though I was angry. He paused for a moment but then went back to his work like nothing had happened. At that point, I figured that I wouldn't be able to reason with him, not in the state he was in. As I started to walk out of the lab, I thought of one last-ditch effort to change his mind.

"I'll kiss you," I said.

John looked up from his desk, his face glowing pink. "What?" he asked.

"You heard me," I said. "If you do what I ordered you to do, I'll kiss you on the lips."

"No."

"*No?* You've been pining for me all this time. Why—?"

"Because, first of all, you wouldn't mean it. And, second of all, I don't deserve it. I don't even deserve your friendship."

"That's it!" I shouted. "Jonathan Anthony Davis, let's get some things straight. First of all, yes, I was told to come here, but I didn't *have* to come here. Nobody can pressure me into doing anything I don't want to do. Second of all, you don't get to decide what you do or don't deserve from me. Last I checked, *I* was the one who was wronged, and if I think you're going too far in punishing yourself, then you need to stop because I said so. Lastly, I gave you a direct order to get some sleep, and ignoring said order only makes me angrier. So, in conclusion, as your boss, your best friend, and possibly your girlfriend, I am ordering you to get some rest."

"Did you say, girlfriend?" John asked, blushing even more.

"Please tell me that wasn't the only thing you heard from my angry rant."

"I thought you said that you only date men you can trust. Does that mean you can still trust me?"

"I said *possibly your girlfriend,* meaning that you still haven't earned my trust back, but I'd be more than willing to give that date a try when you finally do," I said.

John gave a faint smile as he attempted to fix his hair with his hands. "I'd like that," he said. "So, about that kiss…"

"What about it?" I asked.

"Is that offer still available?"

"I'm a girl of my word, John. So, if you want it, come get it."

John grinned. He went to shut down his laptop when he suddenly froze. He began to mumble to himself again as he typed something else in.

"Uh, John?"

"One moment," he said. He poured a tiny bit of a clear liquid into each of the three vials sitting on his desk. The contents in the vials turned purple. "That looks right based on my initial hypothesis. I think I've finally done it!" John ran up to me and hugged me. "I'd have to test it first, which is why I made three, but I think I finally have something that will restore your memories."

"Is it too dangerous to test on people?" I asked.

"Well, no, it shouldn't be," John said.

"Would you let me try it?"

"I don't know about that. There's always a chance I'm wrong about it being safe. I don't want to risk you getting hurt."

"Please?" I begged. "I just survived a suicide mission, for crying out loud!"

"But I'm not supposed to—" John started.

"As your boss—"

"Oh, boy."

"—I am ordering you to let me test it."

"Of course, you are," John sighed. "Fine, you can test it, but this is going against *multiple* science department safety policies."

"Thanks," I said happily. "I'll go get Ley and Elizabeth to see if they want to try it, too."

"*Ley* and Elizabeth?"

"Oh, right, I almost forgot to tell you. Long story short: Briar, Misty, and Daisy surrendered, they're actually on our side, Ley is alive, I'm not human, my sisters aren't human, my mother raped my father, and one of us is a deadly alien weapon from a prophecy. Any questions?"

"Yeah, a ton," John said, looking incredibly confused. "I think I'd prefer the long story if you don't mind telling it."

I explained to John everything that Briar told me in the interrogation room. He was just as shocked as I was. He thought that my powers were the result of some super-human mutation, which is what I had thought, too.

"Wow, I never thought that you could be…" John's voice trailed off. "I guess it makes sense. I should've put it together before now."

"Yeah," I said. "I've been fighting aliens this whole time and didn't even realize that I am one. This won't change things between us, will it?"

"Of course not," John reassured me. "I don't care if you end up with green skin or if you grow fifteen tentacles. You'll still be my best friend, and I'll still have feelings for you."

"Okay, you may still like me if I grow tentacles, but I won't still like me." I laughed. "Let's just hope it doesn't come to that."

I found Savannah and brought her to the interrogation room to babysit the Elements just in case something happened, though I figured everything would be fine. I then went with my sisters to the lab where John had set up three metal tables. We were all excited, but also very nervous. After all, Briar had said that we would be better off not knowing about our past.

"Before we begin, I just want to say that I'm glad you're alright, Ley," John said.

"Thanks," Ley said.

John had Ley, Elizabeth, and I lie down on the metal tables. The cool metal made me feel anxious to the point of nausea. I recognized the sensation; I feared it. Something was coming back to me, but as I tried to bring it to the surface, my mind pushed it back.

"You alright?" John asked me.

"Yeah, I'm fine. It's just… something about lying down on a metal table feels familiar, and not in a good way."

"I'm sorry."

"For what?"

"I'm sorry that I couldn't protect you from that… from him." While I didn't realize what John meant at the moment, I knew that it had to be something related to what I was about to remember. "Okay," John said as he brought three needles filled with the purple liquid. "I will be injecting each of you with the memory restoration serum. Assuming this works, you'll most likely black out as all the memories come flooding back to you. You'll be able to retain all of it for a little while, but eventually, some of your earlier memories will fade away as they would've under normal circumstances." John approached me first and started cleaning my arm with a disinfecting wipe. The look on his face let me know he was nervous.

"Afraid it won't work?" I asked.

"Yeah," he said, "but I'm also afraid that it will."

"Is my past really that bad?"

John nodded before reluctantly injecting the needle into my arm. He held his thumb on the plunger but didn't push it down. His hand was shaking, and I saw beads of sweat begin to form on his forehead. I reached over, putting my hand over his.

"It's going to be okay, John," I said before pushing his thumb down on the plunger. Everything around me went dark, just like he had predicted.

(December 3rd, 2136)

My sisters and I sat at the wooden dining room table. The walls were cream colored and had dark wood that came about halfway up. A small chandelier was hanging above the table with pink and purple streamers tied to the ends. It was our fifth birthday, and we were impatiently waiting for our cake. We had been taken in by John's father, Dr. Jonathan Davis Sr., though we always saw John as a friend rather than a foster brother, and he felt the same way about us. Ley and Elizabeth's eyes lit up as Dr. Davis came into the room with the cake in hand and seven-year-old John following behind him.

"Happy birthday, girls!" John and his father exclaimed. Dr. Davis lit the candles for my sisters and I to blow out.

"Wait, don't blow it out yet!" Ley squealed as I leaned towards the cake. "I want Elizabeth to do her magic trick."

"Magic trick?" I asked.

"I did it on accident with a candle in the living room," Elizabeth admitted, "but I think I can do it again."

"Wait, what exactly did you do with the candle, Elizabeth?" Dr. Davis asked. "I thought I told you and your sisters not to touch it." Elizabeth ignored him and reached out towards the candles on the cake, her fingers rapidly growing closer to the flame. "No!" Dr. Davis shouted, but it was too late. Elizabeth had placed her hand right into the flame, causing everyone except her and Ley, who started clapping, to panic. To our surprise, Elizabeth's hand wasn't on fire. Instead, the flames from the candles hovered just over the palm of her hand. "Where did you learn this trick?" Dr. Davis asked.

"It's not a trick," Elizabeth said. "It's real magic. I found it when I was playing pirates with Ley. I had to walk the p… pank?"

"It's plank, silly!" Ley exclaimed.

"Yeah, that! So, I got on the table. Then I fell on the candle, and the fire stayed in my hand." Elizabeth stuck her hand into her cup of water, extinguishing the flame. Dr. Davis stood frozen by the table. He mumbled something to himself before cutting the cake.

As my sisters and I enjoyed our dessert, I felt a sharp pain in my back, which I loudly announced to everyone at the table. Dr. Davis gave me a heating pad to soothe the pain and had me lie down in my room. I woke up later to John's screams. I looked around but didn't see where he was. I left my room and went into Ley's. John was standing there, gawking at her. White wings had grown out of her back. John turned around to see me, but before I could ask what had happened, he screamed again. I couldn't figure out what was wrong with me until I caught a glimpse of my reflection in the mirror. I had wings, too, but black.

John's father, who was a widowed scientist, became very intrigued. He had Ley, Elizabeth, and I line up at the front door. There, he gagged us, chained us, and threw us into the back of his work van. He no longer saw us as people; we were his new test subjects. This came as a shock since we had practically known Dr. Davis our whole lives. He and John had found us abandoned in the middle of the park one night with the only trace of our mother being a handwritten note with our names on it; we were only one-year-olds.

That night, it all began: being forced into the van, screaming for help until our throats went dry, and then coming back home to be beaten and verbally abused. The only light during that dark time was John.

When we were brought back home the next morning, I told John what happened. He hugged me before taking me to his room so we could talk more. Nerdy sci-fi posters plastered his light blue walls.

"I'm sorry I screamed," John said. "I was just startled. I think your wings are pretty."

"Thanks."

"I'm going to find a way to get you out of here. I promise."

(June 25th, 2137)

The thunder roared outside. Each flash of lightning made me more alert and awake. Despite that, I still rolled over and tried to fall asleep. After another loud crash of thunder, I heard footsteps heading towards my door, causing me to become tense and anxious. My door slowly opened. I pretended to be asleep, hoping that Dr. Davis would leave me alone; I didn't want to be beaten again.

"Linda, wake up."

I opened my eyes to see Ley staring at me. She clutched her favorite stuffed dragon, "Draggie," in her arms. She squeezed him tighter each time the thunder crashed, matting his red fur. The next flash of lightning caused me to notice that the left strap of her loose nightgown was starting to fall down her bruised arm. She, like me and Elizabeth, was too thin from being underfed.

"I can't sleep," she whispered through swollen lips. "The thunder scares me. Can I stay with you tonight?"

"Sure, Ley," I said.

Ley climbed over me and got under the covers. After she curled up next to me, I played with her hair, which she liked because it relaxed her. As she and I tried to drift off to sleep, I heard more footsteps. I could feel my anxiety rising as my door opened once again.

"I can't sleep," Elizabeth whispered as she shut the door and came closer to my bed. "Can I stay in here with you?"

"Of course," I said.

Elizabeth started to climb over me but stopped when she spotted Ley. "Scoot over, Linda," she demanded. "I want you to be in the middle."

Even though my purple and black bed was made for two people, I moved over, allowing Elizabeth to squeeze in next to me. With Ley on my left and Elizabeth on my right, I wasn't exactly in the most comfortable position. Both girls tried to get as close to me as they could, and I put my arms around them. Once I realized that sleep wasn't going to be an option for me, I decided to watch the storm outside my window. I began humming a tune I had made up a while back to calm my sisters down; it was their lullaby.

Though I was the same age as my sisters, I felt and acted much older than them. I, mentally speaking, grew up in hopes that I would be able to protect their childhood innocence. Of course, no matter how hard I tried, I was still physically a kid and couldn't protect my sisters from everything. Even after I discovered my super strength, I was still too weak to fight Dr. Davis.

(December 29th, 2138)

Anytime Ley, Elizabeth, and I were taken to the lab, John was kept locked inside the house with no way to get help. There wasn't much he could've done anyway since he was only nine. The only thing he was able to do was help me make an escape plan. We usually worked after Dr. Davis had gone to sleep. While John and I talked, Ley and Elizabeth would play together until they wore out. The only issue was, if they got too loud and woke Dr. Davis up, he would beat them harder than usual for being loud and for being awake past their bedtime.

That night, while playing in my room, Ley and Elizabeth got into a fight over a doll they both wanted to play with. I warned them to be quiet, but they kept on arguing, waking Dr. Davis. He slammed the door to my room open. Apparently, Ley was the loudest of the two girls because Dr. Davis grabbed her by the hair and dragged her into the hallway. Ley screamed and begged for him to let go. Just as Dr. Davis was about to strike Ley, I jumped in front of her.

"Take me instead," I pleaded. "Ley didn't do anything wrong. I should've sent her back to bed when I had the chance. You can do whatever you want to me, just let her go."

Dr. Davis gave an ominous smirk as if he had been hoping for me to say that. He let Ley go, threw me over his shoulder, forced me into the van, and drove me to the lab where he abused me in a way I had never been abused before. Afterwards, Dr. Davis told me that John would never want me now, though I didn't understand why. I didn't even fully understand what had been done to me. I was barely able to walk when I came back. My legs and the front of my white nightgown were drenched in blood. Elizabeth and John helped me walk upstairs to my room. On the way there, I saw Ley sitting on the top step, crying. I knew she felt bad about me getting hurt in her place. She would've felt worse if she'd known what exactly happened. What was left of my childhood innocence had been taken from me.

(December 30th, 2138)

The day after that horrid incident, Ley (with Draggie), Elizabeth, John, and I managed to escape from the house. We found an abandoned home to take shelter in. The house was old and drafty, causing us to huddle for warmth. That's when we spotted a fireplace. Elizabeth wanted to start a fire to keep us warm, but I didn't think it was safe.

"Elizabeth, don't!" I warned. "You can't control your powers very well. Don't do something so risky."

"Don't worry, Linda," she said, "I've got this."

"Lizzie, please, don't," Ley begged as she shivered in my arms.

"I'm not gonna let you freeze to death."

Elizabeth lost control of her powers and ended up setting the whole place on fire. The fire spread rapidly, and our exits were blocked off before we could get out. Someone driving by must've seen the flames, because we heard sirens soon after. A fire truck arrived, and I quickly called out for help. A group of firemen came running in. One of them grabbed John, and another grabbed me and Elizabeth. Before the last one could grab Ley, who had run over to the corner where she left Draggie, a large, flaming plank of wood fell in front of her. The fireman had to use an axe to free her just before another flaming plank fell onto the spot where she was standing only seconds prior. She nearly died that night.

We were rushed to the hospital only to find Dr. Davis there waiting for us. After being examined, it was obvious why we had run off, me especially, but Dr. Davis was a wealthy man. He paid the doctors and nurses who treated us to look the other way, and I had reason to suspect that he had dirt on some of them, too. It became nearly impossible to escape the house after that because more locks and security cameras were added to the door. I tried to break it down, but I was still a kid and not nearly as strong as I would become later. Needless to say, the super-enhanced door barely dented when I hit it.

(January 5th, 2139)

I had more night terrors than usual ever since Dr. Davis took me to the lab alone. I couldn't talk to my sisters about it because they wouldn't understand; they were too innocent. So, I found myself softly knocking on John's bedroom door. After waiting for a moment, I assumed that he was asleep and started to walk off. Just as I reached my room, his door opened.

"You alright?" he asked.

"No," I said.

"Wanna talk about it?" he asked. I quietly entered his room and sat next to him on his green dinosaur bed. "Before you start, did you make sure to plant a decoy?"

Planting a decoy meant throwing stuff under the covers of my bed to make it look like I was sleeping if Dr. Davis came to check on me, which he did from time to time to prevent me and John from scheming another way of escape.

"Yeah, I planted a decoy," I said.

"So, what's keeping you up so late?" John asked.

"My nightmares have been getting worse, and I'm afraid to go back to sleep. Normally, I'd just curl up with Ley or Elizabeth, but—"

"You don't want them to ask about it."

"Yeah."

"Why don't you stay with me just for tonight?" John offered.

"Okay," I said.

John and I barely fit his twin-sized bed. Knowing how scared I was, John was determined to stay up and talk with me as long as I needed. Sadly, our talking drew some unwanted attention. We heard footsteps growing louder outside the door. John quickly reached over to turn off the lamp. He then set his glasses aside and pushed me under the covers, holding me tight to his chest in hopes that his father wouldn't know I was there.

"Try not to move," John whispered.

He shut his eyes just as the door opened. I could hear John's heart pounding rapidly through his soft, green pajamas, letting me know that he was just as afraid as I was. Though as scared as I felt, something about John's warmth and the sound of his heartbeat seemed to calm me down. I found myself feeling more relaxed than I had been in ages.

After what seemed like an eternity had passed, John's father shut the door. Fearing that he would storm back in, John held me to his chest a little longer, and I fell asleep in his arms.

(July 6th, 2139)

The longer Dr. Davis's abuse went on, the worse his lab experiments became. One of his favorite experiments nearly killed Ley and Elizabeth. It had started a month ago when he wanted to know if Ley and Elizabeth's powers gave them some sort of special identical sibling connection. Dr. Davis began a new series of weekly experiments to test his hypothesis.

He started by taking one of them away, torturing them, and then documenting how it affected the other. He quickly found out that Ley and Elizabeth *did* have a special connection. Anytime Elizabeth was taken away and tortured, Ley would scream: "No, leave her alone! Make it stop! Make it stop!" She could feel Elizabeth's pain. If Ley was taken away, Elizabeth would curl up into a ball and scream at the top of her lungs: "Leave us alone!" She could feel Ley's pain. Further experiments proved that the pain for one had to be extreme to directly affect the other. If Ley or Elizabeth had something small, like a paper cut, the other one wouldn't feel it unless they were trying to.

On those rare occasions where only one of them would be taken to the lab for something besides that experiment, the other would begin singing a lullaby as she gazed out her bedroom window, but not the one I made up. The odd thing was, it was a duet. There were many times when I heard Elizabeth singing to Ley, who had been taken to the lab. Elizabeth would pause from time to time as if she could hear Ley singing back. While I had no way to prove it, I think Ley could hear Elizabeth, and I think that she was singing back.

(August 16th, 2139)

I managed to break out of my room in the lab; my sisters and I had been held there for a whole week. I ran as fast as I could, my bare feet chilled by the tiled floor. I was hoping to find my sisters and free them before anyone realized I was gone. Unfortunately, the lights in the halls were automatic and kicked on as soon as I passed through, alerting the scientists. I kept running until a horrific sight caught my eye: Ley. She was in a tube completely naked, her body suspended by wires attached to her arms, legs, sides, and back.

"Linda, run!" she screamed, but I was too scared to move.

The scientists finally caught up to me with stun batons. After shocking me to the ground, they dragged me back to my room. I stayed silent; screaming would be useless as nobody was around to help me.

I found out later that Dr. Davis and his crew were trying to force Ley to shapeshift by injecting her with different substances. The experiment failed, and it was discovered that only Ley herself can control when she shapeshifts and what she turns into. From that point on, the tube was only used on Ley as a punishment if she was deemed "uncooperative" during other experiments.

(December 3rd, 2140)

Come our ninth birthday, my sisters and I were becoming too strong for Dr. Davis to handle all at once. Our pain tolerance had increased, making us immune to some of his lighter beatings. He started spending his nights in his personal workspace in the basement. We didn't know what he was working on, but we knew that whatever it was had to be bad.

Ley and Elizabeth got a bit loud again while playing. Dr. Davis snapped, but instead of beating them, he injected them and me with a serum. He said it would erase our memories of everything, including each other. After that, he opened up a portal, grabbed Elizabeth, and pulled her through. The portal closed behind him, but Ley and I knew he'd be back.

"Run!" I exclaimed, grabbing Ley's hand.

I could already feel my memories fading. Within seconds, I'd forgotten the name of the girl who had just been taken, but I at least remembered that she was someone important to me, and I remembered that Ley and I would be separated permanently if we were caught.

Ley and I ran into John's room and tried to explain what was happening. With my help, John managed to pull up a couple of boards from his wooden floor. I let Ley go in first, and after we both found a comfortable position, John put the boards back in place.

"I'm scared," Ley whimpered.

"I know you are, and I am, too," I admitted. "But we need to stay quiet." Ley nodded before hugging me tightly.

It wasn't long before we heard Dr. Davis frantically searching for us, and yelling for John to help him. It sounded like John took a beating when we weren't found right away. By the time Dr. Davis reached John's room, Ley and I were perfectly still and silent.

Goosebumps formed as he walked on top of where we were hiding. A loud creak came from the floorboards.

"How strange," he mumbled. "John, I don't remember your floor being so creaky."

"It's been like that for a bit," John lied.

"The floorboards feel loose."

I found myself closing my eyes, holding Ley so tight that I thought she might burst. Everything went quiet, and I worried my heartbeat would give us away. I grew curious as the silence continued. As much as I feared what I might see, I opened my eyes. I looked up in horror and saw a bright blue, glasses-covered eye looking down through a small crack between the boards.

"Hello, girls," Dr. Davis said.

Ley let out a stomach-churning scream as Dr. Davis ripped the floorboards up. He grabbed Ley out of my arms and dragged her to the living room.

"No!" I screamed as I chased after him. "I won't let you take her!"

"Why does it even matter?" Dr. Davis taunted. "As soon as she's taken away from you, you won't be able to hold on to your memories of her. You won't know what you're missing. Now, say goodbye." Dr. Davis opened another portal. As he started to walk through, I grabbed Ley's arms.

"Help me, Linda!" she screamed. "Don't let him take me!"

I started to lose my grip. I knew that there was no way I could win. I had to let my sister go, even though I feared what was waiting for her on the other end of that portal.

"Ley, you can't fight it anymore. You have to let go!" I exclaimed, fighting back tears. "I will find you. I promise I will find you."

"How will you find me if you can't remember me?"

"I'm your sister, I could never forget you," I said. "I will find a way to bring you back home. I don't care how long it takes."

"I love you, Linda."

"I love you, too, Ley," I said. "And I won't forget, I promise." As I loosened my grip, Dr. Davis finally managed to pull Ley out of my arms, causing me to fall on my back. "I'm sorry I lied, Ley," I mumbled to myself, "but you'll forget it all anyway. I hope your new life is better."

Mere seconds after Dr. Davis returned from dropping Ley off, I had already forgotten why I was crying. Though the serum was supposed to erase *all* my memories, there were still a few things I could remember, like my name, birthday, and basic skills, like how to read and write. And, occasionally, I'd feel depressed without knowing why I felt that way. I felt like I'd lost my best friend, but John was the only friend around.

(December 4th, 2141)

I stumbled into the house after getting back from the lab. I hadn't been taken for an experiment; I was taken so John wouldn't know what was being done to me. John had turned twelve in June, giving him more courage to stand up to his father, even if it meant him getting a beating.

"Linda, what happened!?" he exclaimed when he saw the blood dripping down my legs. "What did he do to you?"

John knew that his father had abused me like that before, but my memories of it were erased, forcing John to act like it was the first time. As I explained how I was abused, John helped me walk up the stairs and then led me to his room. There, he cleaned up the blood as he tried to comfort me.

"I need to get you out of here," John said. "This isn't right. None of this has been right."

"John, there's nothing you can do," I said.

"I'll find a way to get you out of here," John told me. "If I can get ahold of my father's phone, I can call the police or child protective services. The only problem is, who would believe me? This seems like the plot of a movie."

"If there's even a chance that you could contact someone, please try?" I begged. "But be careful. If you get caught, we may not be allowed to be around each other anymore. If I don't have you, I won't have a reason to keep going. You're my only friend."

"I won't let him keep me away from you," John reassured me. "And, trust me, there are at least two other reasons I can think of for you to keep going."

"Like what, John?"

"Just trust me on this. I'll do whatever it takes to help you, alright?"

"Thank you."

That night, John snuck into his father's room, something none of us had ever dared to do before. I anxiously watched him from the doorway. He found the drawer Dr. Davis kept his phone in, but it was locked with the only way in being a small hole for the charger. It seemed he had anticipated someone attempting to steal his phone. John, knowing his father well, knew that the key would be kept somewhere on his gray, queen-sized bed, making it even harder to steal the phone unnoticed. John gently pulled back the blankets but found nothing. His father began to move. John and I froze. Dr. Davis rolled over to the other side, causing me to release the breath I didn't know I was holding. John then carefully slipped his hand under his father's pillow and pulled out a key. He quickly unlocked the drawer, pulled out the phone, and ran out of the room.

John ended up calling 911 and explaining the situation to the police, sparing some of the details that were harder to believe. Dr. Davis was arrested, the lab where he worked was under investigation, and John and I were taken away by Child Protective Services. When the child protective service agents saw my abilities, things took a different turn for me. A group of government agents came by, asking to see a demonstration of my powers. Once they saw that I did have wings and super strength, they decided to erase my memories of the only seven months I could remember. At least they had the heart to tell me first.

December 31st (2141)

I stood outside of my group foster home, standing by a black car in the middle of the night. John was allowed to come say goodbye to me, but it was probably more comforting for him than it was for me as he would be the only one who could remember anything.

"I don't want to forget you," I cried as I hugged him tightly.

"You need to listen to me," John whispered in my ear, "you are not alone. This is the second time your memories are being wiped; the first time caused you to forget your sisters."

"S-sisters?"

"I'm going to find them, and then I'm going to find you. I promise. I'll find a way to remind you of who you are."

"John, I—"

"Come on, it's time to go," an agent interrupted, putting his hand on my shoulder.

The woman who ran the foster home took John's hand and led him away as the agent tried to force me into the car.

"Wait! Stop!" I yelled, fighting to get myself out of his grip.

"It's time to go!"

I ran back towards John, only to be grabbed again. "John!" I shouted, catching his attention just as he reached the door of the house. "I love you!"

"I love you, too," John called back before being brought inside.

Those words made my heart flutter, but only for a moment. Soon, everything was empty in my mind all over again. John, the lab, it was all gone. Why? Because the government wanted me to be a blank canvas that they could turn into a powerful weapon.

I ended up being fostered by a couple working for the C.I.A. Besides my constant training, life became somewhat normal for a while, until my twelfth birthday. That's when I was given my job as leader of the Resistance. I quickly realized that I hadn't been trained for self-defense like my parents claimed, I had been trained to be the perfect government soldier.

(December 13th, 2145)

I woke up on the metal table with my hair drenched in sweat. John was standing over me with an anxious look on his face. I sat up and hugged him.

"So, does this mean it worked?" he asked, gently embracing me. "Do you remember me?"

"You're Jonathan Davis Jr.," I said, "my childhood best friend, the boy who was willing to stand up to his father, and the man I've cared about ever since. And I do believe I owe you a kiss." Without hesitation, I quickly pulled John's lips to mine.

"It worked!" he exclaimed. "I've missed you so much."

"I've missed you, too."

"There's something I've been wanting to say for a while now, but I knew it wouldn't have made sense without your memories."

"And what's that?"

"You grew up gorgeous."

"Thanks," I said, blushing.

I looked over and saw Ley and Elizabeth waking up. They both sat up quickly and then slowly looked my way. The memories of losing them came back to my mind as we locked eyes. For the first time, I finally understood just what I had been missing for the past few years. I understood why I kept crying and feeling down. The three of us began to choke up as we came down from the tables.

"That dream I had before we invaded the ship," Elizabeth started, "I remember now. It wasn't just a dream. It was part of a memory. The girl was Ley, and the man was Dr. Davis."

"You had a weird memory dream, too?" Ley asked. "My dream was of Linda holding on to me when Dr. Davis tried to pull me through the portal. And that lullaby you sang to me, Elizabeth, it was the same one Linda sang to us when we were little."

"I've missed you both so much," I said. "I don't know how I made it this long without you." I held both of my sisters tight. I had them back, and I wasn't going to let anybody take them away from me again.

"I love you, girls," I whispered to them.

"We love you, too, Linda," Ley said. "And, now that I have my memories back, I feel *very* weird about referring to John as 'hot.'"

"Wait, what?" John blurted.

"Ley referred to you as 'all caps, hot.'" I laughed. "So, you aren't hot, you're *HOT*. And I gave her permission to ask you out, so, uh, her move, I guess."

"Yeah, I'll pass," Ley said. "John, you're a great guy, and you look *amazing*, but I've always viewed you and Linda as a thing, which makes you an unofficial brother-in-law, so… yeah. No offense, but I could never ask you out."

"None taken," John said. "I only see you as a friend, so I would've politely turned you down. But I am flattered that you think I'm hot."

"Not 'hot,' *HOT,*" I corrected with a smile.

Ley, Elizabeth, and I helped John put the tables away. I kept replaying the memories in my head, still shocked by how much I'd forgotten. Things felt so chaotic that I'd almost forgotten about the Elements. I went back to the interrogation room to check up on them.

"Well, that only took you twenty-thousand years," Briar exaggerated.

"Sorry," I said. "We were just—" A loud boom interrupted me and caused the whole base to shake. The look on Briar's face became one of fear. "What was that?" I asked.

"Windy said that if she found out that Ley was released, she would turn us in to the Elemental Council so that we could be tried for treason," Briar said. "She must've known we were coming here, or maybe she followed us. Either way, it seems like we're under attack."

Chapter 22 (Elizabeth)

"So, remember what you were saying the other day about seeing Linda as more than a friend?" Ley asked John after Linda had left the room.

"Yeah, why?" he asked.

"Well, now that I've got my memories back, I can't help but think you've had a crush on her since we were kids."

"She was my first and only crush, not counting crushes on fictional characters. I realized I liked her when I was about nine years old. That's when she and I started having deeper conversations, and I helped her deal with her night terrors. I mean, I liked her long before that, but only as a friend."

"Does she know about your feelings? Because, I think she likes you, too."

"Clearly you missed what happened after Linda woke up."

"What? What did I miss?"

"A lot."

"Yeah," I butted in. "For starters, Linda and John are going on a date."

"Really!?" Ley squealed. "That's great! I hope it works out."

"Me, too," John said, blushing.

"So, what else did I miss?" Ley asked. I also didn't know what John was alluding to, so I was greatly disappointed with his response.

"If Linda wants to tell you, that's fine, but I'm not saying a word," he said. "Besides, I wouldn't want to upset you since you think I'm hot."

"You're going to keep picking on me for that, aren't you?" Ley asked.

"Yep."

Ley let out a very annoyed (and very loud) groan, making all of us laugh.

***

A loud rumble sounded and caused the whole base to shake. John, Ley, and I ran to the interrogation room to see if Linda was alright. I feared that maybe the Elements were up to something after all, that maybe they had turned on Linda and attacked. To my relief, Linda was on her way out of the room as we arrived. Her face had become incredibly pale, like she was sick.

"John," she said weakly, "we need to initiate emergency protocol six."

"Need I remind you that emergency protocol six is a *full* lockdown of the base?" John asked. "Are you sure it needs to be activated? I mean, maybe—"

"I'm positive, John. Lock the base down."

"Okay, then," John said as his face turned whiter than Linda's. "I'll get right on that."

Soon after John left, the lights turned red, everybody came running into section two, and a secret panel lifted, revealing a large variety of weapons that looked much more powerful than what the field agents used. Without thinking, I grabbed Ley's hand. When we were kids, Ley and I always stayed close, especially when we were scared. Ley, knowing I was afraid, gently squeezed my hand.

"It's okay, Lizzie," she whispered to me. "I meant Elizabeth. Sorry. I forgot that you don't like nicknames."

"Call me whatever you want, Ley," I said. "Elizabeth, Liz, Lizzie. I don't care as long as it isn't something stupid, like fartface."

"Guess who just got her new nickname?" Linda laughed, clearly trying to distract herself. "From here on out, I'm calling you fartface."

"You better not," I warned, "I can always—"

The base shook again after another loud boom, ending the banter. It became clear that someone was trying to get inside. Linda had both entrances reinforced and locked down. We were safe for the moment, but we all knew that it was only a matter of time before the base would be infiltrated, as the doors could only take so much.

Briar, Daisy, and Misty came out from the interrogation room. I couldn't tell if they looked more determined or nervous.

"It's our fault Windy's here," Briar said. "So, it should be our fight."

"You don't have to do that, Briar," Linda said.

"Yes, we do. This is a matter for the Elements, not the Resistance."

"Then I should go, too," I offered.

"Elizabeth, no!" Ley jumped. "I lost you once, and I am not losing you again!"

"We could've escaped Dr. Davis and the lab for good, but I just *had* to use my powers on that fireplace," I said. "*I* was the one who screwed it all up. *I'm* the reason we ended up stuck in that house until Dr. Davis finally decided to separate us. *I'm* the reason we spent five years trying to figure out what we had lost, what we had forgotten. *I'm* the reason we lost each other. So, now I'm going to make it up to you and Linda by protecting you both."

"Elizabeth," Linda said, "you were just a kid; you didn't know any better. I'm not going to let you leave."

"And how do you plan to stop me?"

"I could use my powers to hold you down."

"But you wouldn't do that, would you? You would never use your powers on me."

"I would if it meant keeping you safe!"

"I went on that suicide mission with you. What makes this any different?"

"This time, I remember who you are, unlike before when I didn't know you at all."

"That shouldn't change anything. You still don't know me, not like you used to. We haven't seen each other in five years. A lot has changed in both our lives."

"Elizabeth, I am ordering you to stand down."

"I don't work here, Linda," I said sternly. "You can't keep me from doing this by ordering me around. Now, get out of my way."

Linda stared straight into my eyes for about a minute before lowering her head and stepping aside. I looked over to Ley, who slowly shook her head, holding my hand even tighter than before. I had to fight to escape her grip. Without saying a word, I went with Briar, Misty, and Daisy to the exit in section one.

When we stepped outside, Windy was standing out front with more Elements behind her and a small, low-flying ship hovering just over them. Whoever was on the ship had been shooting at the base, which was what caused the noise and shaking. Luckily for us, emergency protocol six had caused a force field to form over the base.

It had been disabled only so that Daisy, Misty, Briar, and I could leave. Once we cleared the doorway, it was immediately reenabled.

"Well, look at who came to greet us, guys." Windy laughed. "It's the traitors and Elizabeth."

"Windy, you don't have to do this," Briar said. "The triplets want peace. If we have them on our side, the ourathians have no chance of winning the war. The prophesied weapon was their only hope."

"Ninety percent of the ourathian prophecies have come true, despite our peaceful efforts to stop them," Windy said. "What makes you think this will end up any different? We may try to make peace, but whoever the youngest sister is will become corrupt, and the others won't have the heart to stop her. Peace was never an option for dealing with the ourathians, and it never will be."

"You don't know that this prophecy will come true," Misty said. "Why not give these girls the benefit of the doubt? We've watched them for years. They're good people."

"You don't understand, do you?" Windy asked. "Sure, they're fine *now*, but what will they become a few years from now? It's only a matter of time before they take their places by their mother's side and become the ourathian-Element hybrid monsters we were warned about."

"Windy, please," Daisy pleaded, "don't do this."

"Look, girls, I've worked with you for such a long time now. You're like family to me; we're practically sisters. So, if you join me now and turn the triplets in, I might just forget to mention your betrayal in my report to the council. I'll say you were captured or threatened instead of willingly committing acts of treason."

"We won't let you murder these innocent girls," Briar said.

"So, you've made your decision, then?" Windy asked. "Fine. I'll have the three of you arrested." I could feel my blood begin to boil. "Then, I'll slit the triplets' throats, starting with Linda's, and ending with Ley's," she continued. My face grew hotter. "And finally, I'll blow this entire freaking base to dust!"

"You leave my family alone!" I screamed as a red blast launched out of my body.

By accident, I had turned Misty, Daisy, Windy's backup, and even the ship to stone. Briar managed to stop herself from turning just in time and quickly created a stone pillar to support the ship, keeping it from crashing to the ground.

"Nice job, Elizabeth," she said.

"I-I wasn't even trying to do that," I said. "I meant to blast Windy."

"And yet you hit everything except for your target." Briar laughed. "That's okay, though. I can undo it all after we finally reach Windy."

"Yeah, that's not going to happen," Windy said. "I am prepared to do whatever it takes to protect the humans from the ourathian weapon."

The clouds above me and Briar began to spiral. Before we realized what was happening, a tornado formed above us and carried us away from the door of the base. My hair whipped around me, and my stomach felt like it had jumped into my throat. I tried to close my eyes, but it only made the sensation worse.

"I've seen her do this attack before," Briar shouted to me, her voice sounding like a whisper compared to the wind. "She's going to lift us as high as she can and then drop us. So, if you have any last thoughts to get out, I suggest you do it now."

As hopeless as I felt in the moment, giving up wasn't an option. I had to find some way to escape. I needed to use my powers. I thought back to the last attack on the Elements' ship when Daisy was attacking me and Linda:

"Isn't there something you can do with your powers?"

"I don't know. They never work right for me, remember? The only time I managed to do something grand is when I got really angry."

"And why did you get really angry?"

"Because Misty was hurting Ley."

If I didn't escape, then Windy would most certainly kill Ley and Linda. She would also go to great lengths to destroy the entire Resistance. Her words echoed in my mind:

"I'll have the three of you arrested. Then, I'll slit the triplets' throats, starting with Linda's, and ending with Ley's. And finally, I'll blow this entire freaking base to dust!"

I focused my thoughts on my anger towards Windy. I didn't let my situation distract me. My hands began to grow warm. Chains of stone formed around them and attached to the ground, preventing me from being lifted any higher. At first, I tried just shortening the chains to bring myself to the ground, but being pulled in two different directions so harshly made me feel like I was about to be split at the waist. I needed to find a way to lower myself slowly. I fought to wrap my arms around the chains to pull myself down. Briar, upon seeing my plan, mimicked what I was doing after creating chains of her own.

"I don't see this working out for us," she yelled over the crashing sounds of the tornado. "It's getting harder and harder to pull ourselves down the lower we get."

"We can't give up!" I yelled back. "My sisters and your friends are in danger. We need to save them."

The wind's pull on us was strong, making us fight harder each time we got closer to the ground. My arms and hands were so tightly wrapped with chains that they began to hurt. I tried thinking of my sisters as I endured the pain. After a while, my hands went numb, letting me know that my circulation had been cut off. That made it harder for me to pull myself down, but I wasn't about to let it stop me. I looked over and saw Briar struggling with her hands, too. When we finally reached the ground, the tornado was still lifting our legs, though we weren't carried any higher than that. So, when Windy made the tornado go away, Briar and I fell only a short distance to the ground. Briar used her powers to make the stone chains disappear, relieving my numb hands, which had started to throb.

"Do you know how powerful that tornado was?" Windy asked, baffled by our survival.

"Not powerful enough," I retorted as Briar and I stood up.

"How exactly did you manage to—"

"I wasn't going to let you hurt my sisters," I interrupted as I successfully blasted Windy in the chest.

She flew back, hitting the ground hard. Briar trapped Windy's legs in a large block of stone to prevent her from getting back up. As she fought to free herself, I took a deep breath and tried to think about what I wanted to say. Briar put her hand on my shoulder, giving me a reassuring smile.

"Windy, hear me out," I said. "Let me and my sisters contact your council to discuss peace. Then we can set up proper terms and precautions. I want to protect the human race just as much as you do. We can work together to guard this planet."

Windy paused for a moment to think it through. She looked incredibly conflicted, which I understood. "You really want to defend this planet and its people?" she asked me.

"Yes, I do," I said.

"And you'll do whatever it takes, even if it means hurting one of your sisters to stop the prophecy?"

"Yes, but I'd try to reach her peacefully first," I said.

"Alright then, Elizabeth," Windy said, "I'll tell my backup to stand down on one condition."

"And what would that be?" I asked.

"Either you or one of your sisters has to come to Elahntra to talk with the council *in person*."

"That sounds fair to me. We have a deal. Will you give the order to stand down, now?"

"Gladly, but I think you'll need to turn everybody back to normal, first," Windy said. "I can't order stone statues to stand down."

"Oh, right, sorry about that," I said. "Briar, could you please fix that for me?"

"Sure thing," she said. Briar undid the accidental, but useful, mess I had made. Everybody seemed to be in a daze, but none were surprised when Briar, Windy, and I explained what happened.

"So that was real?" Daisy asked.

"I'm afraid I can't give you an answer if I don't understand the question," I said.

"When an Element turns somebody to stone, wood, or ice, that person goes into a coma-like state," Briar explained. "They may not be able to communicate with us, but they are aware of what's going on around them. The thing is, though, some people will start dreaming. When that happens, they become confused about what was real versus what was a dream when they wake up."

"I'm going to assume that Elizabeth flying on a bullet-dodging pegasus was part of a dream," Misty said.

"Oh, no, that was real." I laughed.

After everyone had finally settled down, Windy was brought into the base to have a proper discussion with Linda concerning our deal. I could tell that Linda wanted nothing more than to sock her in the jaw, but after looking over to Ley, Briar, Misty, Daisy, and myself, her expression softened.

"I'll gladly go to Elahntra to discuss peace with your council," Linda said, "but I'd like to take a couple of my agents with me, if you don't mind."

"Of course," Windy said, "though you shouldn't need to worry about your safety while you're there. As long as you don't try anything funny, you'll be perfectly fine."

"Good to know."

Chapter 23 (Linda)

"Wait, so you got stuck eating Elahntran food?" I asked as we all sat down to eat breakfast.

Of all the things I could've asked Ley about, I chose the subject of food because it didn't seem like it would be too traumatic. It was obvious when Ley was telling her story that she skipped plenty of details, ones that she probably didn't want to remember. While I hoped that she would eventually come to me to talk about it, I also didn't want to push it. It was nice to see her happy again, and it was comforting to recognize her face.

It felt weird after I got my memories back. It was like the old me was there the whole time, longing for her sisters. She was just out of reach in my mind. Of course, I always knew something was missing, I just didn't know what.

"Yes, I got stuck eating breakfast *and* lunch on the Elements' ship," Ley said. "Lunch was decent, but what the nurse brought for breakfast was the most disgusting food I've ever eaten. It was this thick, pink oatmeal that tasted like cake and cough syrup. I have no idea how the Elements can stomach that crap. I nearly threw up."

"That 'pink oatmeal' must've been made wrong," Daisy said, "because it has always been one of my favorite breakfast foods. We call it intergalactic garbage. Not because it tastes like garbage, but because it's a mix of breakfast foods from different planets. It's amazing if it's made correctly."

"Nah, your taste buds must be off, Daisy." Windy laughed. "Intergalactic garbage *is* garbage. My favorite breakfast foods come from Earth. I've been addicted to bacon since the first time I ate it."

"Yeah, haven't we all," I said.

We continued eating our late breakfast while debating which foods were or weren't good. The Elements then told us more about the kind of things they liked to eat on their planet vs. the stuff they liked to eat on Earth. According to them, "Earth donuts are second to none."

The table grew silent for a bit, mostly because we were all scarfing down our food, but also because we were still trying to process everything that had happened. I'd never suspected that I could be an alien because I didn't look like an alien. Besides my wings, I looked normal. *Why was that?* My curiosity only grew as we neared the end of our meal.

"So, Briar," I said after we finally finished our breakfast, "since I'm not human, and since my sisters aren't human, why do we look human?"

"That isn't how you naturally look," she said. "You're just in your human form."

"What do you mean, our *human form*?" Elizabeth asked.

"You should know, Elizabeth. You were in your true form on the ship, after all."

"I was wearing body paint on the ship."

"Oh," Briar said. "In that case, I think it would be easier to show you than to explain it."

Ley, Elizabeth, Briar, and I went into the ladies' restroom. Misty came in a few minutes later with three syringes she had taken from John's lab and a greenish serum she grabbed from Windy's ship.

"We use these to help younger Elements who have a hard time switching between their true form and their human form," she said. "So, hopefully, it'll do the trick for you, too."

"The fact that you have been maintaining your human form without trying to means that you must've been given an injection from your mother before she sent you to Earth," Briar said. "When we undo the effects of that injection, you'll look like your true selves. It may be frightening at first since you're used to looking human, but you'll get used to it. And don't worry, we'll teach you how to maintain your human form on your own so you can still keep yourselves disguised when you need to."

"Okay," Ley said nervously.

"So, are you ready to see what you look like in your true forms?" Misty asked cheerfully as she sucked the serum into each syringe.

Before we could answer, she gave each of us the injection. Ley's skin became ultramarine. Her eyes turned pitch black, even beyond her irises. I looked in the mirror and realized that I looked the same as her. The skin didn't bother me that much, but the eyes disturbed me. They looked empty and soulless. Because there was no clear pupil, nobody could tell just where I was looking. Elizabeth was the luckiest out of the three of us. She looked like a fire Element. Her skin was orange, and her hair turned bright red. Her eyes turned red, too, perfectly matching Briar's.

"How come Lizzie and I look different?" Ley asked.

"Your powers make you look different, despite your matching DNA," Briar said. "However, it's your matching DNA that causes your human form to be the same. So, you are identical, but only when you're in your human form."

"That's cool, but also kind of weird," Ley said.

"Okay, Briar," I said. "You've shown us what we really look like, now please show us how to look human again."

We spent the next couple of hours working on maintaining our human forms. Much like our powers, the main key was concentration. Once we finally managed to change back into our human forms, it didn't take much for us to keep it up. The problem was, keeping it up long-term could take a toll on our bodies.

"I suggest sleeping in your true form," Briar said. "That way, your body can rest properly."

"Since we're discussing powers and keeping them hidden," I started, "can any of you Elements explain to us how Ley and Elizabeth didn't discover their powers sooner after their memories were erased?"

"Because we were there to cover it up," Misty said. "From Marina's reports and my time with Ley, I know both of your sisters used their powers without realizing. It was minor stuff, for the most part, but we always took care of it to keep everyone around them safe."

"Speaking of Marina's reports," Briar said, "we can reopen the portals to send Elizabeth and Ley back to where they were."

"Really?" Elizabeth asked, her tone unreadable.

"You know what's funny?" Ley asked. "I had forgotten about the portals. I guess I already felt at home here."

***

We went back up to section one. There, Briar pressed a few buttons on her communication cuff, and a bright green portal opened up.

"This is Elizabeth's portal," she said.

Elizabeth looked torn as she walked towards the portal. She reached out to touch it, but quickly pulled her hand back and turned to me. "I-I don't know if I want to go back," she said. "I know I've spent the last five years there, but this is my true home. If I go back... I don't see myself living a life I'd enjoy. If it's alright with you, I think I'd like to stay here."

"You want to stay with me?" I asked. I was thrilled, but tried to hide my excitement as Elizabeth nodded her head. "Of course, you can stay. You'll probably need one of these, though." I handed Elizabeth a purple phone.

"But Linda, isn't this phone yours?"

"It's a spare. I use it on missions so my main one doesn't get damaged. My number is already programmed into it."

"Thanks." Elizabeth smiled. "Oh, and I still have Ley's phone." Elizabeth handed Ley her phone, and the girls began exchanging numbers.

"Okay," Briar said. "Since Elizabeth won't be using her portal, I'll go ahead and open up Ley's."

The portal to the orphanage disappeared and a new one took its place. Ley seemed just as reluctant as Elizabeth did as she walked up to her portal.

"What is it?" I asked. "Don't you want to go home?"

Ley broke down crying before walking back over to me. "Please don't send me back," she begged. "I don't want to go back there. There's nothing waiting for me."

"What about your foster parents?"

"They're gone all the time for work, and they don't want to retire any time soon. I barely know them. Could I just stay here with you? Please? I'll do anything."

"You really want to stay with me? Even after all you've been through these past few days?"

"Yeah, if it's okay with you. But if you don't want me to stay—"

"Of course, I want you to stay," I said. "I can get you and Elizabeth your own rooms, and you two can help me with missions. You could become official Resistance agents if you wanted to."

"I'd like that," Ley said with a grin.

"Is there any of your stuff you want to bring back here?" I asked. "I bet Briar can keep the portal open long enough for you to grab some clothes or something. And she could do the same for you, Elizabeth."

"I don't really have a lot of stuff, and none of it is worth bringing back here," Elizabeth said. "Well, besides Marina. Could she stay here, too?"

"She returned to this time shortly after you did," Briar said. "So, what about you, Ley? Have anything you want to bring back?"

"I do have a few things I'd like, but you have to come with me, Linda," Ley insisted.

"Why?"

"Because I don't want you to have Briar close the portal after I go through."

"I wouldn't—"

"Please, just come with me?"

I realized as I looked into Ley's eyes that she truly feared I'd leave her behind. Of course, I wasn't going to abandon her, so there really was no point in me going, but I didn't want to do something that would upset her or make her anxious; she'd been through enough.

"Okay," I said. "I'll go with you."

I followed Ley through the portal and was not ready for the stomach-churning experience that followed. While said experience was short-lived, I was still surprised that neither Ley nor Elizabeth had thrown up when they arrived at the base. After a few moments, I found myself in the kitchen of Ley's home. Her phone immediately went off as a flood of texts came in.

"You'd think being in the future would've made those texts come in already," I joked, though Ley didn't laugh; she looked worried. "You okay?"

"My friend-slash-bully, Jaime, sent a whole bunch of texts while I was away. She's furious with me."

"So?"

"You have no idea how bad she makes me feel."

"And you don't have to face her ever again," I said. "So, go on and pack your stuff. The faster we leave, the faster you get away from Jaime."

Ley ran upstairs to her room, and I went up after her. She grabbed clothes, extra shoes, her toothbrush, her hairbrush, her electronic devices, and a few of her collectible items. She ended up filling three suitcases. We went back down to the kitchen where Ley left a note to her foster parents explaining as best she could where she was going, sparing the whole "alien from the future" thing.

"Hey, I think I recognize this house," I said as Ley finished the note.

"Really?" she asked.

"Yeah," I said, looking out the window. "It seems you and I have been living in the same city, just in different time periods. I think this house was recently listed for rent."

"I'm surprised it's still standing."

"You know, if you want, you could always rent the house," I said. "I could pull some strings so that your age doesn't cause any issues."

"I would love that, but I don't have any money."

"Your Resistance paycheck would probably cover most, if not all, of the rent. I'd be more than willing to pay anything extra. We could also work overtime to get some money to cover the cost of furniture."

"You don't have to do all that."

"I *want* to. The Resistance provides all my necessities, so my paycheck is usually just spent on a bunch of crap I don't need. Let me do something good with that money for once."

"Okay," Ley said.

The doorbell rang, startling us. Ley answered the door and was almost instantly berated by the girl standing on the porch.

"Ley, where the heck have you been!?" she yelled. "If you were sick, the least you could've done was text me so I wouldn't come here to pick you up for school this past week."

"Jaime..." Ley said, thinking carefully about her next words. "I'm sorry I didn't give you a heads up. I wasn't sick."

"You were ditching? I find that hard to believe."

"I had that dream again."

"Ley, just shut up! There is no black-haired chick trying to find you!"

I walked up to the door and put my arm around Ley. Jaime looked like she had seen a ghost. "Y-you're r-r-real?" she asked.

"I said I'd find her, and I'm a girl of my word," I said.

"Jaime, meet my sister, Linda," Ley said with a smirk.

"So, Ley, is this the 'friend' who keeps picking on you?"

"Yes."

Jaime looked like she was on the verge of peeing herself. I dragged her inside and pinned her to the wall.

"Let's get something straight," I said, "you are never to pick on Ley or speak ill of her again. I'm taking her home, but rest assured, I will find out if you say something behind her back, and I will come for you. Understand?"

"Y-yes," Jaime said, breaking out into a nervous sweat. "I-I'm sorry I picked on you, Ley."

"Apology accepted," Ley said. "Now, get out of my house."

Jaime started to leave but froze as she spotted the portal. "What's that?" she asked.

"It's how I'm taking Ley home," I said. "It's a portal to the future, but you probably shouldn't tell anyone about it unless you want to be thrown into the psych ward."

Thoroughly freaked out, Jaime charged out the door and down the street.

"Thanks, sis," Ley said, closing the door. "Let's go home."

And with that, Ley and I went through the portal.

***

The following day, I went to John's house for our tutoring session. Upon arriving, I realized that the house was larger than I remembered it, though I figured part of that came from me being used to a tiny room in the base. The walls remained cream colored, but the wood at the bottom of the walls had been removed. After Dr. Davis was taken away, everything he owned went to John. Though he had been taken by child protective services when he was twelve, he was recruited by the Resistance shortly after he was put into a foster home. With the help of the government, he ended up going back to his old house, where he used some of his father's money to fix it up to his liking. Most of the inside of the house looked the same as it did when I was a child, causing me to shudder.

"You don't have to be afraid," John reassured me. "Nobody is gonna hurt you. This place is perfectly safe now."

"Oh, I'm not afraid," I lied. "I'm not even nervous."

"Don't lie to me," he said. "You were trembling from the time you stepped into the hall."

There was an open doorway to my right leading to the kitchen. The living and dining rooms were to my left. Directly in front of me was the staircase to the second floor, where the bedrooms were. The main bathroom was behind the staircase, and the door to the basement was directly connected to the back of the staircase. John led me into the living room and sat down next to me on the black leather couch.

"Before we get started, do you want anything to eat?" he asked.

"No," I said. "I'm not hungry."

"This house is giving you flashbacks, isn't it?"

"It's fine, John. I'll be alright."

"We can go back to the base, if you want to."

"I'll feel better once we get started," I said. "It'll be enough to distract me."

John gave me a concerned look before pulling out a textbook for algebra. He gave me a spiral notebook and a pencil to take notes with. He went through everything that had been confusing me in class and took his time when demonstrating how to solve some of the homework problems I had.

"Thanks for helping me out," I said when we finished.

"You're welcome," he said. The room went silent for a moment as we awkwardly stared at each other.

"Uh, John," I said, breaking the silence, "I just thought you should know that you have regained my trust one hundred percent."

"Does that mean you'll go out with me now?" he asked.

"Yes," I said, "if you still *want* to go on that date with me."

"Why don't I take you out to dinner the night before you leave for Elahntra?" John asked. "That way, if it goes horribly wrong, we'll both have plenty of time to forget about it."

"Sure," I said.

***

Six days later, things had already gone back to normal at the base. Ley, Elizabeth, and I went to school with the team and the Elements, who also started helping us with missions. Things started to get better in my life.

John took me out to dinner that night. We ended up going to a nice Italian restaurant. The lighting was dim, gently illuminating the off-white tablecloths and black seats. The olive-green walls were covered with black-and-white photos of the restaurant and some of the food. John wore a black suit, and I wore a black dress with a fake diamond necklace. It was pretty awkward at first since I didn't know how to talk to John in that kind of setting. The most formality we had before that was when I first got my job. I'd referred to him as "Davis" or "agent Davis," but even that didn't last long.

"You're being awfully quiet," John said. "Did I mess things up already?"

"No," I said. "It's just… how do we talk here? I've never been on a date this fancy before, and I don't want to embarrass you."

"You couldn't embarrass me," he said. "Just talk to me like you normally would. Even though we're on a date, you're still my best friend."

"Okay," I said. "How's your recovery from the imposter incident going?"

"I'm feeling a lot better now," John said. "My follow-up with the doctor is next week."

"That's good," I said. "Speaking of follow-ups, can we revisit a conversation from a while back?"

"Sure."

"You said I'd still be your best friend, and you'd still have feelings for me even if I had green skin and fifteen tentacles."

"And I meant what I said."

"What about blue skin and pitch-black eyes?"

"Doesn't make a difference to me. You're still you, right?"

"Well, yeah, but I look like a freak," I said.

"I doubt that."

"No, really. If you saw me—"

"You'll just have to show me after dinner," John said. "But I doubt you could scare me away so easily."

The rest of the date went wonderfully. We enjoyed our meal and spent a long time just talking after. It made me realize that John was right when he said nothing could ruin our friendship. At least, I hoped he was right, because I knew I wanted to go on another date.

Once we got into the car to go home, John turned to me. "So, are you gonna show me what you really look like?" he asked.

I took a deep breath before relaxing myself and allowing my body to change into its true form. John looked shocked for a moment, but his look of shock then turned into a warm smile. His expression seemed genuine, but part of me still feared that he was just trying to comfort me.

"S-so," I said, "what do you think?"

John leaned in and kissed my forehead. "I think you're beautiful," he said.

"Would you like to go see a movie with me when I get back from Elahntra?"

"Do you mean as friends, or are you asking me out on a second date?"

"I'm asking you out on a second date," I said. "I enjoyed our date tonight, and I'd love nothing more than to do it again. I guess I owe you an apology for rejecting you before."

"Nah," John said. "Having dinner with you was worth the wait. And, yes, I'd love to see a movie with you."

When we got back to the base, I kissed John on the cheek before unbuckling my seatbelt. As I went to open my door, I froze.

"Something wrong?" John asked.

"There's something I haven't been able to get out of my head since you restored my memories," I said.

"And what's that?"

"I said *I love you* before I had my memories erased by the government."

"Yeah, and I said I love you, too."

"So, do we count that or not?"

"What do you mean?"

"Well, we were just kids, and I was scared, and we hadn't even gone on a proper date, so I wasn't sure if we should—"

John gestured for me to stop before saying, "The way I see it, we weren't romantically involved, so there's no reason to take that 'I love you' romantically. There are different types of love, you know."

"Alright then," I said before heading back to my room in section one.

Ley and Elizabeth were sitting on the bed, waiting for me. They had been staying at the base with me since Ley didn't have any furniture in her house yet. We were sharing a room as I still hadn't gotten them one of their own (not that I had been trying all that hard). To be honest, I didn't mind sharing a room with my sisters, especially after I got my memories restored. Nightmares of the lab haunted me almost every night, and they always managed to comfort me.

"Honey, I'm home," I joked as I walked in and sat between the two of them.

"So, how did your date with John go?" Ley asked, making kissing sounds.

"It went wonderfully," I said. "We ended up talking for another hour after we had dessert. I think the waitress was worried that we wouldn't leave."

"Who paid the bill?" Elizabeth asked.

"John paid for everything. We agreed that whoever gives the invite covers the bill. That way, we aren't stuck feeling like we have to do something we can't afford."

"And will there be another date for you two?"

"I'm going to take him to a movie after I get back from Elahntra," I said. "Speaking of which, will you two be going with me?"

"On your movie date or to Elahntra?" Ley asked. "I don't wanna be a third wheel to you and John."

"I'm inviting you to come with me to Elahntra." I laughed. "But I'd gladly take you to a movie sometime, just not on the same night John and I are going."

"You want us to come with you to Elahntra? Like, for real?" Ley asked.

"*Yes,* Ley. Of course, I want you and Liz to come. You're my sisters. Why wouldn't I bring you? Besides, you've both proven yourselves. Elizabeth stopped Windy, and you saved the team from the Elements when they were trying to rescue me."

"Yeah, but that was on a mission that neither of us were supposed to be on."

"Exactly. If I don't take you, you'll find a way to come anyway."

"She has a point." Elizabeth laughed.

"Okay, you got me on that one," Ley admitted. "I've always wanted to see another planet like the ones I've seen in movies. It's funny how I've been obsessed with movies about aliens for years, but I never figured out on my own that I am one."

"Yeah, I'm still getting used to that, too," I said. "I thought I was some superhuman."

"Same, well, after I discovered my powers," Ley said. "Does John mind that you're an alien?"

"Obviously not. I mean, I can make myself *look* human anytime I want, if appearances become an issue, not that I think they will. John seemed to like me in my natural form."

"That's good," Elizabeth said.

"Yeah, I guess."

"What's wrong?" Ley asked.

"Ley, have you seen how creepy our eyes are?" I asked. "I'm glad John sees beauty in them, but it still doesn't change the fact that *I* hate them. I never had any issues with how I look until I saw my true self. I'm more comfortable with myself when I look human."

"I understand," Ley said. "I'm not comfortable with my true form either. But it is good to know that John likes it. Because imagine if in the future you got married to him—"

"Married?"

"And you had a whole bunch of kids together—"

"Kids? Oh, Ley, I don't even know if I—"

"Would they end up with powers? Would they be blue with black eyes? Would they look like Elements? It's good to know that John would be okay with that."

"Look," I said, blushing, "John and I just got back from our first date. We are *far* from marriage and kids. I'm not even sure if I want any kids. If I do choose to have any, my job could put them in danger."

"You don't see yourself retiring one day?"

"By the time I decide to retire, I'll be too old to have children."

"You could always adopt."

"Okay, Ley," I joked. "When I retire, I'll adopt fifteen kids just for you."

"I'm serious, Linda. We used to fantasize about our future weddings and families when we were kids. Don't you remember?"

"Yeah, I do," I said. "But we can talk about my non-existent, half-human children later. We need to get ready for bed. We're going to be doing a lot of packing tomorrow."

Chapter 24 (Ley)

"Ley, wake up," Linda softly whispered to me. I opened my eyes to see her holding a plate of French toast. I checked my phone and realized that I had slept in, meaning that the cafeteria had just closed.

"Thanks, sis," I said as I sat up and started eating.

"I already packed a couple of bags for you while you were asleep," she told me.

"Well, now I feel bad," I said. "You didn't need to do that for me."

"I wanted to," Linda said. "You had a hard time sleeping last night, so I thought I'd let you sleep a little longer than usual."

"How did you know that I had trouble sleeping?"

"You woke me and Liz up with your tossing and turning. You mumbled a bit, too."

"I'm sorry."

"It's alright," she said. "I was having nightmares anyway. Now, pack the rest of your bags. We're supposed to meet the Elements in section three this evening at five-thirty."

After I packed my bags, which mostly consisted of clothes, I joined Linda and Elizabeth in the lounge. We had plenty of time before we had to leave, so we ended up playing video games with John and Dillan.

"Hey," Dillan said. "I know we haven't had a chance to speak since the Elements brought you back from their ship, but I just wanted to say, again, that I'm sorry."

"We're good," I told him. "I understand now why you did what you did. Not to mention, Linda's back home safe, and I'm not petty enough to hold a grudge. If anyone should be sorry, it's me."

"No, Ley, you had every right to be angry. You did nothing wrong."

"Yes, I did. I went too far in what I said to you and John."

"You were grieving. I probably would've said similar things in your position. So, please, don't beat yourself up over it."

I smiled before giving Dillan a hug, almost missing the ticked look on Linda's face. "Thank you for being so understanding," I said.

"By any chance, w-would you like to hang out sometime?" Dillan asked, his face turning pink.

"I'd like that," I said. "I kind of need to make some friends around here."

"Dillan, stop flirting with Ley," Linda ordered as she leaned over on John.

"I'm not flirting with her. I just—" Dillan panicked, causing Linda to laugh.

"I'm just messing with you, Dillan," she said. "You're my… coworker. I know that you'd never even *consider* dating my sister."

After playing a few racing games, Liz and I told stories about our lives before having our memories restored. I was happy to finally have a group of friends to hang out with. I felt more at home than I did when I was stuck in 2017.

"So, are you excited for your trip?" John asked.

"Yeah, I can't wait to visit another planet," I said. "I'm a bit nervous, too, but I know I'll be fine."

"Same," Elizabeth said. "The thought of leaving Earth is beyond nerve-racking, but I'm excited to be around other fire Elements."

"You'll both be perfectly fine," Linda said. "I'll be looking out for you every step of the way."

"And by *looking out for you*, she means she'll be keeping all those Element boys away," Dillan said. "She'll go into protective sister mode."

"Nuh-uh!" Linda exclaimed.

"I don't need her help driving any boys away." I laughed. "I'm so awkward and dorky that they'll be instantly repelled by me."

"Don't say that," Dillan said. "I think you're sweet and pretty."

"Really?"

"I thought you said you weren't trying to flirt," Linda said as she glared at Dillan.

"I'm not," he insisted. "Just because I tell someone they look pretty doesn't mean I'm trying to flirt."

"Sure," Linda said flatly as she gave the "I'm watching you" gesture.

"He's just being friendly," I said, causing her to roll her eyes.

***

When the time finally came for us to leave, Linda, Elizabeth, and I met up with Savannah and the Elements in section three. A small, purple ship was waiting for us by the exit. The walls of the inside of the ship were covered with pale, violet padding. The floors were a bright, neon blue. Briar was the one flying the ship with Misty sitting next to her as the copilot. Linda and I sat with Windy in the middle row, and Savannah sat with Elizabeth and Daisy in the back. I worried that flying to Elahntra from Earth would take at least a week, depending on how good the Elements' technology was, but Briar informed us that the trip would only take two hours due to the incredible speeds the Elahntran ships could reach. She also informed us that Elahntra is very close to Earth, but the Elements messed with human space technology to keep their location secret.

"You have no idea how many scientists are out there looking for you," I said. "Most people believe that aliens don't exist since none have tried to make contact."

"It's best that we work in the shadows," Briar said.

"Why?" Elizabeth asked.

"You of all people should know. Humans fear what they can't explain. They try to mask that fear with random scientific theories, most of which are disproven or coincidentally proven. If we were to reveal ourselves, that mask would be shattered. The humans would become fearful and curious, and they'd do *anything* for answers. We'd all end up as test subjects in labs, poked and prodded daily. Why? Because they will fear us the way they fear everything else that is even slightly out of the ordinary."

"Then why do you defend Earth?" Linda asked. "Why do you protect the human race?"

"Because it's the right thing to do," Briar said. "It's what we've always done. And, to some degree, we understand their fear. Humans are one of the few species in our galaxy without powers, which would make us even more intimidating. I know humans can be arrogant sometimes, and they can be quite cruel to each other, but a lot of species are that way, including the Elements. The Earth is worth defending for all the innocent lives on it."

We arrived in a city made of quartz. We were told that it was the capital city, the only neutral place on Elahntra. The rest of the planet was divided into water, fire, wind, and earth territories. The Elemental Council met in a tall quartz tower in the center of the city. We were brought to the three-hundredth floor where the council met. There was a blue, translucent bridge that led to the end of the room. Four chairs hovered above the end of the bridge: one made of ice, one made of stone, one made of clouds, and one made of wood and vines. The Elemental clan leaders, Evian (water), Azar (fire), Zephyr (wind), and Venus (earth) sat there. The left side of the room was divided into two sections: water and fire. The right side of the room was also divided into two sections: wind and earth.

Evian wore a long-sleeved top with an open-front skirt and leggings. She also wore boots. Her clothes were light blue and very shiny, almost as if they were made of ice. Her blue hair was tied into a tight bun. Azar wore a long-sleeved crimson shirt and pants with dress shoes. His bright red hair was cut short in the back and on the sides, but his bangs were kept long. Zephyr wore a purple kimono-inspired outfit with sandals. His hair was long, going past his shoulders. He also had a mustache and a short beard, unlike Azar who was clean-shaven. Venus wore a brown top with vines as straps. Her green skirt went down to her ankles but had two slits going up to her thighs. A few vines were loosely wrapped around her neck. More were wrapped around her legs, leading to her heels. Her hair was pulled back into a high ponytail, like Daisy's. I noticed that Evian's skin and hair were lighter than Misty's and Venus's skin and hair were darker than Daisy's.

Linda, Elizabeth, Savannah, and I slowly walked down the bridge with Elahntran guards beside us. I spotted Misty, who gave me an encouraging thumbs-up, sitting in the water section. I felt sweat dripping down my forehead. None of the Elemental clan leaders smiled. They looked disgusted by our very presence. I began to worry about what would happen if things turned sour, if we weren't able to work something out. If that happened, we'd be stuck on an enemy planet filled with Elements wanting to kill us.

"We have held this council meeting to discuss peace with the prophesied triplets and their human army called the Resistance," Evian said. "Linda Smith, you may begin by pleading your case."

"Thank you, Evian," Linda said. "My sisters and I grew up believing we were humans. Not *normal* humans, but still humans nonetheless. We all made human friends, and we had human families. We never tried to use our powers for evil. Ley and Elizabeth didn't even remember they had powers until they came here, and the first thing they did when they rediscovered their powers was use them to protect each other and me."

"Now that you girls have your memories back, hasn't your perspective changed?" Venus asked as she tucked a loose strand of her vine-like hair behind her ear. "The three of you were abused by a scientist, and you, Linda, were used by the government for your powers. Don't you hate the human race for that?"

"That's a good question," Linda continued, "but the answer is no. I may be angry with specific people, but not the human race as a whole. And, yes, I had been pushed into working at the Resistance, but I have also grown to love my job. I only ever fought your people because I thought I was defending the planet; I believed that the Elements were trying to annihilate humanity."

"We never sought to destroy Earth or the human race," Evian said. "Our job is to defend them and to change the seasons."

"I know now that you are no threat to Earth, and I plan to help you from now on," Linda said. "Not with changing the seasons, of course, but with defending the human race."

"You would defend a species that has hurt you time after time?" Zephyr asked.

"Yes, I would. Not every human is good, but that doesn't make them all evil. I'm sure there are bad Elements, right? It's not like your species is perfect."

"You have a point," Azar said. "We've had plenty of rogue Elements that we've had to stop. So, you're willing to make peace with us and help us to protect the human race *no matter what*?"

"Yes."

"But what if the prophecy starts to come true?" Evian asked. "What if one of your sisters becomes the ourathian weapon? What would you do then?"

"I can't say for sure how I'll react," Linda said, "because it hasn't happened, and it may not ever happen."

"What do you think the right thing to do would be if it *did* happen?" Azar asked.

"I think that, if my sister couldn't be reached by any peaceful means, I'd have to use physical force, even if that led to me taking her life," Linda said.

"One final question," Venus said. "What exactly is the Resistance? We know it's an army, but not much beyond that. If we're going to work with you, we'd like to know more about your agency first."

"The Resistance is a top-secret government project," Linda explained. "While we occasionally deal with regular criminal activity, our main specialty is the extraterrestrial. We were created after one of your ships was detected. Our goal is to keep Earth safe from alien lifeforms. All of our agents are quite young. Most were recruited around the age of thirteen. There are multiple reasons for that. The younger agents can work longer, they tend to be more open-minded, and they have better covers. It's true that most of them abandon their families, but the general public is unaware of that. We've paid some families off, changed the identities of some of our agents, and had to transfer others to different Resistance locations just to keep everything a secret."

"That's very intriguing," Azar said.

"Yes, it is," Evian said. "The council will now speak privately to come up with a decision."

We were brought into a small, green waiting room with flowers growing out of the walls. Linda looked just as nervous as I felt. We both knew that the stakes were high.

"You did good, sis," I reassured her.

"You think so?" she asked.

"I know so. Who else would've had the courage to go up to the council and give a defense without slipping up even once?"

"If this fails, will you be disappointed in me?"

"No. Why would I be disappointed in you? If anything, I'd be disappointed in the Elements for not keeping an open mind. They could use a kick-butt soldier like you on their side."

"Yeah, right. We both know that they're more powerful than me."

"If that's the case, why did they have to try so hard to kill us before? Even better, why did they fail to get information out of you?"

"Ley's right, you know," Elizabeth said. "If this goes south, the only ones who should be afraid are the Elements."

Linda just gave a faint smile before lowering her head. I put my arm around her and she leaned on my shoulder. It was the only thing I could do to help her since, clearly, my words weren't enough.

"Boss," Savannah said, "I've worked with you for a while now, and if there's one thing I've learned, it's that you are a fighter. You always do whatever it takes to do what's right. I'm sure that the Elements could see that. They'd be stupid not to."

"Thanks," Linda said, "all of you."

Misty stepped into the room and escorted us back to where the council met. Her face was unreadable, causing me to panic a little. I reached for Linda's hand as we stepped through the doorway, but she didn't notice. She seemed distracted. I looked ahead and noticed that Evian wasn't in her chair. Instead, she was standing at the end of the bridge with something in her hand. I started to fear that maybe the council decided not to trust us, that maybe they were about to execute us right then and there.

"The council has come to a decision," Evian said, sounding a bit monotone. "We are pleased to announce that we are officially forging an alliance with the prophesied triplets and the Resistance army."

"Thank you, Evian," Linda said.

"Please, accept this gift as the beginning of our peaceful alliance." Evian handed Elizabeth one of the Elemental crest necklaces. Instead of being colorful, like the other ones we had seen, it was completely white. She continued, "When you put it on, it will become colorful based on your powers. This isn't just some ordinary necklace. Wearing this makes you, and by extension your sisters, truly one of us."

Evian nodded, encouraging Elizabeth to put the necklace on. As soon as she did, it glowed until it became colorful, the top part becoming red to represent fire.

"T-thank you," Elizabeth said. "I'll wear this with pride."

Evian moved towards Linda and extended her hand to shake. "I look forward to working with your organization."

"Might I make one request?" Linda asked.

"Sure."

"Misty, Briar, Windy, and Daisy have been at my base for the past week to ensure that this meeting would happen. During that week, they've become quite close with me and my fellow agents. So, I was wondering if you would let them be stationed at my base as an official part of my team."

"I think they'd like that," Evian said.

"I'd like to be stationed at the base, too!" a voice called out.

We turned to the water section and saw a girl in a hoodie standing up. As soon as she removed the hood, Elizabeth smiled. "Marina!" she exclaimed.

Evian seemed frustrated at the interruption, but after a quiet grunt, said, "If there's room, you may go, too."

"She's a friend of Elizabeth's," Linda said, "I'll make room."

***

Linda, Elizabeth, Savannah, and I enjoyed our time on Elahntra. We were shown each of the territories. The water territory was coated in snow and the buildings were made of ice. There were large glaciers that led to a long, winding river that flowed into the earth territory. The earth territory had tall, overgrown grass and incredibly large trees. The buildings there were made of trees and vines that had been twisted together. The fire territory was covered in stone; the buildings were made of stone, too. There were many lava lakes surrounding a volcano. The ground of the wind territory was

303

covered in grass, but no trees. The wind Elements had tornados circling the area. Their buildings were in the clouds.

A banquet was held to celebrate our new alliance. Both Elahntran and Earth foods were available. I was especially intrigued by a red pastry with purple filling. It smelled like clay, in my opinion, but it tasted so sweet and amazing. I couldn't pinpoint the exact flavor, but the filling vaguely reminded me of passion fruit. Linda said it reminded her of pomegranate. We had never felt so welcomed. To make things better, the rooms we stayed in were incredibly comfortable. The bedsheets were silky and the pillows were the softest I'd ever felt.

On the second day of our trip, the day before we were set to leave, Daisy took my sisters and I down to the population labs at the capitol as part of the tour. The room was made up of various platforms stretching up and down farther than we could see. An entire wall was made up of young Elements frozen in tubes. We learned that Elahntra had a controlled population. The surplus Elements were raised to the age of seven and then cryogenically frozen until there was room for them on the planet. Because of that, the Elements didn't have last names. Instead, they each had a unique name that became available to another Element in the event of their death. The only Elements that had last names were the ones that went to Earth undercover.

"Your planet has a limited population?" I asked. "That must be so sad. Imagine having your child taken away from you for years and years. If I were a parent, I'd be incredibly depressed, not to mention worried."

"Oh, most Elements aren't made in the *natural* way," Daisy said. "Most of us were created and born artificially in this lab. It's been that way for centuries. It's actually the reason we can make ourselves look human; we were genetically engineered to disguise ourselves ages ago."

"What happens when a couple ends up with an unexpected surprise?" I asked.

"Elahntran females can control when they do or don't release ovum, so we never have to deal with surprises."

"Not gonna lie, I'm kind of jealous of Elahntran females right now," Linda joked.

Daisy showed us the nursery where Elements younger than seven were raised. The walls were colorful to reflect the four elements. Rainbows, butterflies, and flowers were painted all over. The Element children were gray, which confused me since the other Elements were colorful based on their powers.

"Why are the children gray?" I asked.

"They don't have their powers yet," Daisy said.

"Huh?"

"Elements born naturally, like Elizabeth, have their powers from birth," she explained. "Because these Elements were born artificially, they don't have powers."

"How do they get their powers if they're not born with them?" Elizabeth asked.

"Our powers originate from the four elemental stones. We use those stones in a special ceremony where a young Element's powers are chosen."

"So, you chose to be an earth Element?" I asked. "I would've chosen water."

"You misunderstand," Daisy said. "The stones make the decision, not the Element child or the Elemental Council. I didn't choose earth; earth chose me."

"That's so cool," I said.

"It's why some Elements have names that don't match their powers. There are ways to predict what powers an Element will end up with, which is how the names are chosen, but it's not always perfect. Take Briar, for example. Her name would better suit an earth Element, but she's a fire Element."

"So, because I'm only half Element, am I weaker than a fully trained fire Element?" Elizabeth asked.

"Well, you are *now*, but you wouldn't be if you were trained," Daisy said. "If you were less than half Element, however, then no amount of training could make you that powerful. You see, people who are less than half Element can't have full elemental powers; they only control half of their element. For example, maybe someone can only control water in its liquid form, or maybe it's the opposite, and they can only control water in its solid form. Because they can only control half of their element, we call these Elements halflings."

"Does that mean any of us could one day have children who are halflings?" I asked.

"Yes, and that isn't necessarily a good thing," Daisy said. "Halflings also tend to lose control of their powers. If they become too much of a danger to society, we step in and terminate them."

"Why can't you just train them?" I asked.

"Because halflings tend to be very unstable. If they can't learn to control their powers on their own, we can't help them. They become beyond our control, and the only thing to do then is stop them from killing the people around them. That means termination."

"Have you had to terminate a halfling before, Daisy?" Linda asked.

"I'd rather not talk about it," Daisy said, her eyes filling with tears, "but yes."

"That's so sad," I said.

"Yes, it is, which is why most Elements are advised to refrain from romantic relationships with humans or any other species. It doesn't matter if the Element can keep their powers a secret, or if the human accepts the Element for who they are, it always ends in tragedy. At least, that's what the council says. I disagree. I think that relationships with non-Elements can turn out just fine so long as caution is exercised."

"What does that mean for us?" Linda asked. "What if one of us has children with a human?"

"I thought you said you didn't want kids," I said.

"I could change my mind," she said.

"Look," Daisy said, "in the end, it's up to you. If you have children, they could end up as halflings, they could end up with ourathian powers, or, if you have children with a human, they could have no powers. The same goes for your grandchildren, your great-grandchildren, and so on. I understand why you would be afraid, but not every halfling reaches the point of termination. Centuries ago, we had a case of a water Element halfling who completely lost control of her powers and nearly killed her sister. She managed to regain control before reaching the point of termination. Every halfling is different."

***

When it came time for us to leave, we met Misty, Daisy, Windy, Marina, and Briar back at the ship. They seemed happy to be stationed with us. After we returned to the base, Linda worked to clear out rooms for the Elements, which caused me and Elizabeth to have to continue sharing a room with her. We didn't mind, though. We had some interesting conversations on nights when none of us could sleep. Not to mention, we started to suspect that Linda wanted us to continue staying with her. She had frequent nightmares, worse than ours. She'd sometimes wake up screaming or crying, and we were able to calm her down. She would do the same for us on the rare occasions when our nightmares caused us to yell or scream.

After the trip to Elahntra, the Resistance agents and the Elements became closer than ever. As for me and my sisters, we were happy. We found what we had all been looking for during our separation: family.

Chapter 25 (Savannah, December 5ᵗʰ, 2145)

After Ley, Elizabeth, and Linda went down to the cafeteria on their first night together, I went into my room to contact Commander Skye, their mother.

"Savannah, what a pleasant surprise," she said.

"I don't understand the use of that phrase, considering you opened the portals," I said. "I just called to let you know that all three of your girls are back together."

"What's the status of their memories?"

"Still gone for all three of them. I had to stop Linda from killing Ley. I knew she wouldn't believe she's her sister without a blood test, and it took a while to get the results."

"What about that human boy they were friends with? Does he still have his memories?"

"Yes," I said, "his memories are intact. He's been working on a memory restoration serum since he started working here."

"That could be useful," Skye said. "We think we've figured out how to make one of our own, but we can't distribute it. My girls aren't ready to meet me yet. I want you to hide the formula somewhere where the human will find it. Make it look like it's his work."

"What if he doesn't go for it?" I asked. "What if he tries to make something new?"

"If he doesn't figure it out on his own, find some way to get involved."

"Yes, ma'am."

"And one last thing, Savannah," Skye said. "Do everything in your power to keep my youngest daughter safe until it is time for her to become our great weapon. The others, while they may still be of use to me, are expendable."

"The girls are wanting me to open the portals to get them home," I said. "What do I do about that?"

"Stall," she said. "After they get their memories restored, check in with me, but do not let them go back beforehand."

"Understood, Commander."

***

A little over a week later, when the triplets went to the lab to get their memories restored, I was left in the interrogation room to watch the Elements. At first, the room stayed silent, but as I noticed the girls staring at me, Briar finally spoke.

"We know what you are," she said. "Does Linda know? She is your boss after all."

"I don't know what you're talking about," I lied.

"Don't play dumb with us," Misty said. "We know you're the android the ourathians sent to protect Linda."

"This whole peace discussion must tick you off," Daisy taunted.

"No, actually, it doesn't," I said.

"But making peace with us goes against your programming, right?" she asked.

"I was initially programmed to keep the triplets hidden from the Elements," I explained, "but I never got to act on that since they were taken in by the Davis family. Once they were separated, and

310

Linda got out, I was told to protect her. Things have changed now that Elizabeth and Ley are here, too. My orders now are to protect the youngest sibling from the Elements. The other two are a secondary priority. Preventing peace between you isn't in my programming. And since I know you'll go back to attacking the triplets if they don't cooperate, why would I get in the way? Allowing peace is what's best for the triplets' safety."

"What will Commander Skye do to you if she finds out?" Briar asked.

"She'll probably disable me and use my parts for another machine. Though, I doubt she'll find out right away."

"What makes you so sure of that?"

"I cut off communications with Commander Skye a while ago," I said. "Last she heard: Linda was kidnapped and Ley and Elizabeth found a way to be part of the rescue mission. I did not tell her the result of said mission. As I said before, to follow my programming, the most logical thing to do is allow the triplets to make peace with your people. If the Commander finds out, she'll try to stop it, which could put the triplets in danger. So, by cutting off communications with her, I delay that issue."

"But, if you didn't tell her that Ley and Linda came back from the ship," Briar started, "that means you cut off communications with Skye before you even knew we were making peace."

"Correct."

"May I ask why you chose to cut things off then?"

"Because I didn't want to cause Skye unnecessary worry by telling her Linda was rescued and Ley 'died,'" I said. "She has quite a temper. I was waiting to see how the revenge plan would go before breaking the news."

"Sounds convenient."

"If you are implying that I had another motive, then you're wrong."

Briar just stared at me with a cocky grin. She seemed to think she understood me; everyone who knew the truth about me thought they did, too. They all thought I could make real connections and friendships, but they were wrong. When I was being developed, my creator thought he had developed a friendship with me. He thought I cared about him. I guess that goes to show how well he programmed me. I could play the part well enough to fool just about anyone into thinking I was a real girl with real feelings.

"Savannah, can you be reprogrammed?" Daisy asked.

"Yes," I said.

"To avoid future issues between you, the Commander, and us, would you allow us to reprogram you? It would be the most logical thing to do if you want to protect the triplets, right?"

"If you have access to a robotics lab, then yes, I would allow you to reprogram me. I am technically programmed against allowing such things, but my orders concerning the triplets override that."

"We've got a robotics lab on Elahntra," Misty said. "If we're able to make peace, we can come up with a reason to take you there."

"Savannah?" Briar asked. "You have artificial emotions, correct?"

"Yes, and don't think I don't know where you're going with this."

"Could those emotions have evolved into something real?" she asked. "Is it possible that you're doing all of this because you see Linda as a friend?"

"Of course not," I said. "Sure, I can laugh, cry, or get angry, but none of it is real. My emotions are based on what I see around me. For example, if someone is called stupid, they tend to become angry. So, if I'm called stupid, I react the same way. I have fake feelings that can get hurt. I can become sad over the loss of a teammate, and I can become aggressive or sassy when my work is disrupted, but it isn't real. I can't feel anything."

"None of it is real? Seriously?"

"It's similar to my eating mechanism," I said. "I've got storage compartments inside of me that allow me to eat and drink. I occasionally excuse myself to the bathroom to empty those compartments. But just because it looks like I'm eating doesn't mean that I am. I have no stomach, I have no taste buds, and I have no appetite. I simply mimic what I see around me."

***

During the trip to Elahntra, Daisy took the sisters down to the population labs while Misty took me to the robotics lab. There, I was fully reprogrammed. I no longer had special orders regarding the triplets. I was simply programmed to be an ordinary Resistance agent and an ally to the Elements. That way, I could protect all of my teammates.

When we returned from Elahntra, Linda asked to speak with me in private and escorted me to the interrogation room. I figured that Briar had told her about me being an android, and I was ready to explain everything.

"Savannah, I've been meaning to ask about this for a while now," Linda said. "Why did you let Elizabeth go on that rescue mission? She had no business being there."

"I thought that her powers made her immune to fire attacks," I said.

313

Technically, it was the truth. The ourathians didn't know anything about Elements fighting each other or how their powers worked, so I thought Elizabeth's immunity hypothesis had some merit. Though the reality was, she wouldn't stand down any time I tried to reject her, and I knew that she was expendable.

"Even if she *were* immune to fire attacks, what would've protected her from other kinds of attacks?"

"You're right, and I'm sorry boss," I lied. "It seems I had a lapse in judgment. Is there anything I can do to make things right with you?"

"There's no need," Linda said. "Elizabeth's okay, and so is Ley. I just wanted to hear your reasoning behind that questionable decision."

"Well, if that's all—"

"And I also wanted to know if the reprogramming worked."

"What?"

"The Elements told me about you, Savannah," Linda said. "Not gonna lie, it took everything in me not to bust up your circuits when I found out, but I think I've come to terms with it."

"You do understand why I couldn't tell you, right?" I asked.

"Of course, I do," she said, "but it still hurts. You're my closest friend besides John."

"I can still be your friend, Linda," I said, "but you can't be mine."

"I know. If you could feel, though, do you think we'd be friends?"

"Assuming that my current persona became my real personality, then I'd say we'd most likely be friends."

"The thing that gets me is, I've seen you bleed. You were wounded right in front of me on countless missions."

"I have artificial blood pumping through my body. So, yes, I bleed. The only problem is, the blood doesn't clot. So, I normally have to use some type of sealant on the wound until I can get more artificial flesh and blood to repair myself. There's a reason I always find a way to avoid section four."

"So, do you really need those glasses you're wearing?"

"Yes, actually," I said. "Unlike other parts of the body, it's difficult to make artificial eyes that are as good as the real thing. My green eyes came from the body of a human named Savannah Grace Wilson, whose name I took along with her eyes. I could've chosen eyes that weren't defective, but I figured that my dependence on glasses would only help my cover since fake glasses are so easy to spot these days. If something happens to my eyes or my glasses, I do have sensors to help me navigate."

"That's clever," Linda said.

"Thanks," I said. "And to answer your question about the reprogramming, yes, it worked."

"That's good. Oh, and I didn't tell any of the other agents about you being an android, not even Ley, Elizabeth, or John. The Elements are also keeping it a secret. They only told me about it because I'm in charge. So, your secret is safe with me, that is, if you still want it to be a secret."

"I have no problem with people knowing, but I figure it would make missions more difficult. My teammates may not feel comfortable working with an android who they once believed was human."

"I get that," Linda said. "I'll keep it a secret unless it becomes absolutely necessary to tell the others about it."

"Thank you, boss," I said. As Linda started to leave, I stopped her. "Wait."

"What now?"

"The reason I gave for letting Elizabeth go on the mission was true, but there was more to it than what I said."

"My mother sees Elizabeth as expendable, doesn't she?"

"Yes. She wanted me to keep her safe if I could, but if she got in the way… well, at that point your mother wouldn't care about what happens to her. She only cared about keeping her youngest daughter, her weapon, safe."

"I won't tell Elizabeth about that," Linda said. "So that would mean that either I'm the youngest, or Ley is the youngest, right?"

"Yes."

"Do me a favor; don't tell me which one of us is it. I don't wanna know unless I have to know."

"I understand, boss."

Epilogue

Commander Skye Eustryla of Starship Ourathia walked towards the communications section of her ship. The deep blue walls of the ship seemed to tremble at her very presence. The black, metal floor rattled, almost nervously, under each step of her feet. Commander Skye's crimson hair was tied into a tight bun. Her pitch-black eyes were narrowed. This wasn't an unusual sight, as Skye was always angry about something, but it always struck fear in the hearts of her coworkers. Anytime Skye came for one of her "visits," anyone who could escape the room would. She was known for her violent tendencies, as most ourathian Commanders were, but there was something about Skye that made her different. She had the rarest and most powerful ability an ourathian could have, the ability everyone wanted to have: telekinesis. Because she had telekinesis, Skye used her powers to injure those who failed her. So, when she approached the desk of Azura Starlytta, a young girl who was relatively new at her job, Azura cowered down.

"Azura!" Skye yelled. "Why haven't I received an update on our android's status?"

"I'm sorry, ma'am," Azura mumbled as she tried to squeeze herself underneath her blue metal desk. "W-we've l-l-lost contact."

"You've what!?"

Azura pushed herself against the wall of the ship, trying to avoid the gaze of the Commander, but Skye wasn't about to let her off that easily. Skye used her powers to pull Azura out from under her desk and put her back in her seat. She then grabbed Azura's face and lifted it up until she was making eye contact. Skye had to fight back a smile as she saw sweat forming on Azura's forehead, wetting part of her bright yellow hair.

"Repeat what you said, Azura," Skye said firmly. "But this time, don't stutter."

"We lost contact about a week and a half ago. I think the android shut off communications with us, Commander."

"I sent that android to Earth the same day I sent my daughters there," Sky said. "It gave us weekly reports about my girls. Why would it cut off communications with us now? It's not like its identity was discovered. Our android blended in perfectly."

Skye turned her back on Azura as she tried to figure out what could've happened with Savannah. Once again, Azura tried to crawl under her desk in hopes that it would somehow protect her from Skye's wrath.

"What do *you* think happened with our android, Azura?" Skye asked, sounding a little calmer.

"I'm not quite sure, Commander," Azura said. "Maybe it decided to betray us."

"No!" Skye yelled as she spun back around and forced Azura back into her seat. "It knows better than to do that. It knows that I'll destroy it if it turns on us."

Skye had to hide her fear as she began thinking about her precious daughters. She knew that losing contact with Savannah meant that maybe the triplets were in grave danger. The last update she received was a text to inform her that Ley and Elizabeth had gotten themselves involved in the mission to rescue Linda. She never got confirmation that any of the triplets were okay. Not getting another report meant that either Savannah was destroyed, Azura screwed something up, or Azura's theory was correct. No matter what the situation was, it couldn't be good.

"Andromeda…" was all Commander Skye could say as her fear turned to rage.

Skye paused for a moment as she decided just how to take out her wrath. She could break Azura's neck, or maybe crack all of her ribs. No, none of those options were good enough, not when the safety of her great weapon was at stake. But no matter what the punishment was, Azura had to live. She was still needed since she was one of the best communications graduates from the Ourathian Starship Academy. Skye needed to harm Azura enough to take out her frustration, but not enough to kill her. She used her powers to slowly lift Azura into the air.

"Commander, please, don't hurt me," Azura pleaded. "It's not my fault."

"The android knows better than to turn on us. This *has* to be your fault." And with that, Skye snapped both of Azura's legs, dropped her, and then left her lying on the floor, screaming.

Skye stomped out of the room and headed for the bridge of the ship. She knew what she had to do. The life of her greatest achievement, her great weapon, was at stake.

"Commander Skye, what are you—?" Captain Ylroid started to ask.

"Captain, set our course for Earth," Skye interrupted. "We've lost contact with our android, and my weapon is in danger. I'm hoping that the issue has resolved itself, but just in case it hasn't, we need to go to Earth. We can't let the Elements destroy our weapon of prophecy; we can't let them hurt Andromeda."

"Understood, Commander," Ylroid said. "Just give me her coordinates, and we'll set our course for Earth right now."

Skye accessed the ship's database to search for the Resistance coordinates given to her by Savannah. To her surprise, the coordinates weren't there. They had been deleted.

"Azura was right," Skye mumbled.

"What was that, Commander?" Ylroid asked.

"The android that had been sending me updates on my daughters, it turned on us," Skye said. "Not only has it cut off all communication with me, but it has also hacked into our ship's database and deleted all of our files concerning my daughters' locations."

"What do we do now?"

"We try to find Savannah. If we find it, we'll find my daughters."

"What makes you think Savannah hasn't self-destructed by now?"

"That would seem like the smart thing to do, but I figure it's looking to be reprogrammed."

"Why?"

"Because it was programmed to do what's best for the safety of my daughters. The fact that it found a loophole doesn't mean that it wouldn't still seek to keep my daughters safe. It can't keep them safe if it self-destructs. The next logical thing is reprogramming to mask itself from us."

"So, we need to find Savannah's location even though we won't be able to trace its signal anymore?"

"Yes."

"Do you know how many androids are on Earth?" Ylroid asked. "Do you know how many satellites and computer signals could throw us off? Finding Savannah could take years."

"Then I suggest you start now, Ylroid," Skye said. "We need to find my daughters, especially my weapon. She's the key to our victory against the Elements."

"But—"

"Start searching, *now*!" Skye yelled. "I won't ask again. Do I make myself clear?"

"Yes, Commander."

The Resistance will return